ALSO BY JENNIFER ST. GILES

The Mistress of Trevelyan

HIS DARK
DESIRES

JENNIFER ST. GILES

POCKET BOOKS

New York   London   Toronto   Sydney

This book is a work of fiction. Names, characters, places and incidents are products of the author's imagination or are used fictitiously. Any resemblance to actual events or locales or persons, living or dead, is entirely coincidental.

An *Original* Publication of POCKET BOOKS

POCKET BOOKS, a division of Simon & Schuster, Inc.
1230 Avenue of the Americas, New York, NY 10020

ISBN-13: 978-0-7434-8626-2
ISBN-10:   0-7434-8626-9

This Pocket Books paperback edition November 2005

10 9 8 7 6 5 4 3 2 1

POCKET and colophon are registered trademarks of
Simon & Schuster, Inc.

Cover illustration by Franco Accornero

Manufactured in the United States of America

For information regarding special discounts for bulk purchases,
please contact Simon & Schuster Special Sales at 1-800-456-6798
or business@simonandschuster.com.

I dedicate this book to The Music of the Night
and to all those who fill my life with
love, laughter, and inspiration.

❧ *Acknowledgments* ❧

As I fill this page, I again find myself with so much to say. There are many people who help make my books reality, and many people who add to my life, helping me make my dreams come true. Every year that goes by, more unique and wonderful people enter my life. So if I inadvertently leave a name out, forgive me and know that you are cherished.

To my agent, Deidre Knight, my eternal thanks for always being there, and for your tireless work, brilliance, and unfailing kindness and support no matter what chips fall or how the wind blows. To my editor, Micki Nuding, thank you for your honesty, your keen eye, and your belief in me. To Maggie Crawford, for your publishing vision and great success.

To Jacquie D'Alessandro and Wendy Etherington, thank you forever for the loving friendship, the brains, the Godivas, and the champagne. To Sandra Chastain, Wendy Wax, Karen White, Rita Herron, Pam Mantovani, and Debby Giusti, thanks for your invaluable feedback and encouragment with this book and my career.

To Georgia Romance Writers, Romance Writers of America, and KOD and all the pubbed and prepubbed members and sister chapters. Never give up on your dreams.

To the ladies and gentlemen at the University of Tulane's main library, the Howard-Tilton Memorial Library, for their help and research in my many questions about New Orleans after the Civil War. And to the many other area libraries and librarians who were so helpful in my quest for answers via the phone and Internet.

To Katherine Falk, the *Romantic Times BOOKclub Magazine*, its warrior volunteers, and the whole network of authors, readers, reviewers, booksellers, and cover models who make gathering together and networking so much fun! To Rosemary from Down Under, to Annette, Jax, Kathy, Sophia, and the RT party animals. And to the RT Lance, for loving *The Mistress of Trevelyan*. Thanks for a tremendous conference.

To my very much-loved family, thank you for filling my heart and for making every book that is written possible. My husband, Charles; daughter, Ashleigh; sons, Jake and Shane; my parents, Ron and Diane; my grandparents, Maggie, Len, and Jan; my sister and fam, Tracy, Jeff, Tye, Shannon and Kacie (and Tracy's writing pal, Jennifer); my brother and fam, Ron, Susan, and Tory. And the many other aunts, uncles, and cousins who are the best cheering section any writer could want.

To the many friends whose support is so very much appreciated: Colleen, Luke, Alec and Jordan. Nila, Eric, Emily, Aiden, Pam and J.B., Nancy, Ruth, Lindy, Rolland, Chantel, Josh, Amanda, Lee, Minna, Yari, and Katie at OD who is a promo whiz, and Jennifer, her helper.

To the Tarts and Fans and Filippino Tarts who adore Gerard Butler: Believe, achieve, imagine, and inspire forever!

And finally, to the many fans and reviewers who went the extra mile to tell me how much they loved *The Mistress of Trevelyan*. You do me a very great honor.

Thank you.

My soul is full of whispered song;
My blindness is my sight;
The shadows that I feared so long
Are all alive with light.

—Alice Cary

HIS DARK
DESIRES

New Orleans, Louisiana
June 1874

As a child, whenever winter came to our grand home, *La Belle du Temps,* I'd slip away to the attic and stare at the black water of the Mississippi, just visible through the ghostly Spanish moss and live oaks. I'd huddle in the cold, watching the river rise, sure its greedy swells would some day steal all that I held dear. It was a childish fear, but one that set a precedent for shadows in my life.

Shadows that would never recede, I thought as I curled my hand around the warning telegram in my pocket, sent to me by Mr. Goodson, the investigator from Baton Rouge I'd secretly hired. "Mrs. Boucheron, You are in danger. Trust no one."

Though the river had never touched my family home, other ills had flooded my life, and *La Belle* had stood strong through them all. She gave breath to my fondest memories and held my deepest sorrows with gentle arms. She'd been the one constant in my life, stalwart during the occupation of Federal troops, solid throughout the war; and now she was the means by which I, my son, Andre, and my sisters Ginette and Mignon survived.

I could not lose her and I would never sell her—something Mr. Latour had yet to understand.

"Ahem. I don't know how much clearer I can be, Mrs. Boucheron," Mr. Latour said for the third time. "With the tax increase this year and maintenance costs on the rise, I do not think you realize how difficult things will be. Your hardships will be greatly reduced with a smaller property, and by moving closer into town, you would have a steadier income from boarders year round."

The man's pompous manner had a way of making *La Belle*'s double parlor, with its high ceilings and wide windows, seem as small as a hatbox. Though he was a former friend of my husband, I could listen no more. I'd been polite beyond the point of duty these past two months.

"I don't know how *I* can be much clearer, Monsieur Latour. *La Belle du Temps* is not for sale."

He glanced at my sisters for support.

"Juliet speaks for all of us," Ginette assured him firmly.

"*Pardon,* monsieur, but we cannot sell our home. It would not be right." Mignon's expression implored the man to understand; she hated to disappoint anyone.

"You're making a mistake, Mrs. Boucheron." Mr. Latour's spectacles magnified his displeasure. "This is the last offer Packert Investment Company will make. And I must say this new offer is very generous."

"Exceedingly generous, which makes me wonder why."

"Concern for your family. The company does not wish to take advantage of your reduced circumstances."

The bald lie irritated me even more than his persistence. His family, along with the Hayeses, had led New Orleans's beau monde in shunning me and my sisters after my husband's supposed crime. Their social and financial reprisals had been crushing. And since the war's end, most businesses had had little regard for any family's hardship. They'd been vultures circling a battlefield, raking the South with greedy talons.

My patience was at an end. "Whatever Packert Investment's reasoning, it is of no consequence to us. Our answer is final, Monsieur Latour. Now, if you don't mind—"

"What about Jean Claude?"

My spine stiffened. "What did you say?"

"Ahem. You give me no choice but to bring up this delicate matter. I'm sure you have heard the rumors that he is in Europe."

"Those are old rumors. No one has ever seen him, and they won't, because he is dead. He wouldn't have abandoned his family."

"A desperate man will do anything, and he was desperate. I am sure he took the gold and escaped. You need to realize that nothing can stop him from taking control of your boarding house enterprise, should he return." He lowered his voice to a conspiring tone. "I can change that. Sell to me, and I'll help you and your sisters buy a property to which Jean Claude has no legal claim."

I dug my nails into the velvet upholstery and fought to keep a calm mask on my face. My husband, Mr. Latour, and the Hayeses had played a dangerous game during the war. Though New Orleans was occupied by Federal troops, they'd pooled gold and bought supplies for the Confederate Army. No one knew what had happened on their last venture, and the mystery haunted me. Officially I considered myself a widow, and in nine years no one in New Orleans had intimated otherwise. So why did Mr. Latour now insist that Jean Claude was alive? From Mignon and Ginette's expressions, I could tell they were equally upset. "What exactly do you mean, monsieur?"

"Surely your father's attorney explained this to you?"

"I can't say that Monsieur Maison did. Why don't you tell me what you mean?" Grief over my father's death had blurred any business matters at that time.

"I suggest you see your attorney. Louisiana's inheritance laws permit women to own property, but a husband has the right to oversee his wife's property. She can only manage it if he allows it."

"The courts could not be so unkind." Mignon's voice shook. She and Ginette sat on the rose brocade settee, their faces as pale as their faded damask gowns.

I squared my shoulders. "Even if what you say is true, Monsieur Latour, and Jean Claude should return alive after all this time, I am sure there are other options available besides selling *La Belle*." I stood, and moved decisively to open the doors. "Monsieur, our answer is final."

"My apologies for bringing up an unpleasant subject, but you really should let me direct you in these matters."

"I am more than capable of deciding what I need to do," I replied.

His cheeks reddened, and he cleared his throat again. "The offer to buy at this price will stand for two weeks." He straightened his spectacles and hefted his ample girth from the brocade armchair. Then he stepped uncomfortably close to me and lowered his voice to a forceful whisper. "You won't get a better offer, Mrs. Boucheron, so be careful whom you insult. There are other ways to get what I want."

The threat sent a shiver of fear through my irritation. "Not here, I can assure you of that."

"Is there a problem, Miz Julie?" Papa John, outfitted in his best "butlering" suit, appeared in the doorway and stepped imposingly next to me. Though gray-haired and worn with age, his tall stature could still make a man pause.

"Monsieur Latour was just leaving."

Mr. Latour nodded tightly, plopped on his hat, and left.

"Good riddance," I said, finally feeling as if I could breathe.

"It's more like bad riddance iffen you ask me, Miz Julie," Papa John replied. "Something about that man don't sit right with me."

"Next time he calls, please tell him we are indisposed."

Mignon glanced anxiously at the door. "I fear we have already offended the gentleman."

"With good reason, Nonnie." Ginette patted Mignon's shoulder. "He was not being very gentlemanly himself." She met my gaze, reading the worry I'd unsuccessfully tried to hide. "What are we going to do, Juliet?"

"The first thing we are going to do is to stay calm. Mr. Goodson is investigating the rumors about Jean Claude, and I'll speak to Monsieur Maison about protecting our inheritance when I meet with him today."

"You'll be seeing Monsieur Davis, then," Mignon said, biting her lip.

Mr. Davis was Mr. Maison's new assistant and had recently been calling on Mignon.

"Most likely," I said. "Why?"

"He mentioned last night that he is lonely, being so far from home and knowing so few people. I wondered if we should invite him to dinner."

I winced at having to face his garrulous nature two evenings in a row. "Do you want to see him again so soon?"

No special smile lit her eyes as she spoke. "I just hate for anyone to be sad."

"You cannot save the world from every scraped elbow," I said gently.

She sighed. "I know."

"Besides, we've enough problems of our own." Ginette rubbed her temples as if another of her recent headaches plagued her. Her pale, heart-shaped face contrasted starkly with her shadowed eyes.

I set my chin at a determined angle. "My biggest question is, why now? Why, after all these years, is Monsieur Latour so insistent on buying *La Belle*?"

Mignon's eyes danced. "Perhaps we have a pirate like Jean Laffite in our family, who left a map to buried treasure hidden here. Just think, if we find it, we could go abroad and see the DePerri castle and meet handsome princes and—"

"And fold the laundry," I said, before Ginette could add more. The pair of them could spin a tale faster than the devil could lie. "We've no more time to waste today. One of you needs to help Mama Louisa in the kitchen and the other must get Andre to assist with the laundry."

Both Ginette and Mignon groaned. Getting my son to help with domestic chores was the hardest task of all.

Papa John cleared his throat—not a sound I associated with good news.

"Please tell me Andre is still at his lessons?" I asked.

"That boy is as wily as a hunted fox," Papa John said, shaking his salt and pepper head. "He must have high-tailed down the magnolia tree outside his window, because he ain't nowhere to be found."

"He knew he had chores. Ginette, I don't suppose you would go look for Andre and—"

"I am sure Mama Louisa is awaiting me in the kitchen, *non*?" She ducked out of the room and ran.

"Mignon, could you—"

"The laundry, *oui*? I must hurry, for it is very late." She dashed from the room.

I looked at Papa John. He shrugged. "A boy's gotta run a little wildness out of him every now and then."

Lately, it seemed there had been a whole lot of wildness that needed running off.

Usually I savored the long walk to town, enjoying the cool breath of air off the Mississippi, the languid warmth of the sun, and the bustle of life in New Orleans. But today not even the shade from the lush magnolia trees relieved the heat. As I reached Blindman's Curve, a swampy area where the foliage grew so thick and the road turned so sharply that no one could see more than a dozen feet ahead, I realized something was wrong. The crickets, usually silent this time of day, suddenly throbbed with a deafening sound. I came to an abrupt stop and gripped my parasol, alarmed at the noise. A dark shadow fell over me, bringing a deep chill. Suddenly I couldn't breathe, speak, or even move my feet, as if an unseen force pressed against me, keeping me from moving forward or crying for help.

Then, equally swiftly, the shadow and the cold disappeared and the crickets fell quiet. I stood there stunned and frightened for a moment, then I ran. It wasn't until I reached the outskirts of the city and saw people going about their normal business that I slowed to a gasping halt. Bright sunshine filled the sky and whispers of clouds brushed the horizon.

At Rue Royale, in the heart of the Vieux Carré, I paused outside Madame Boussard's Dress Shop to compose myself as I brushed the dust off my pleated skirts; disquiet clung to me as uncomfortably as the worn silk of my cinnamon dress stuck to my skin. The shop door opened and I turned with a start, finding myself face-to-face with a woman I had counted as my best friend until my husband's disappearance.

"Letitia," I said before thinking.

Letitia Hayes wasn't alone. Two other ladies, dressed just as stylishly as Letitia, stood behind her. Letitia didn't even look at me, but commented to the other ladies on how insolent the help was these days.

Though fire burned my cheeks, I held my shoulders straight and smiled. "Didn't you wear that gown to my wedding? My, how the years have flown. Good day, ladies."

Ignoring Letitia's gasp, I marched down the street to Mr. Maison's law office, opening the door more forcefully than I meant to.

"Good heavens, Mrs. Boucheron, you gave me a fright! I thought the door was locked," Mr. Davis said.

"*Bon jour,*" I said, forcing a cheerful note. Mr. Davis stood on a ladder and appeared to be cleaning the upper shelf of a bookcase; stacks of gold-embossed books were pushed out of place. Setting the book he held on the shelf, he quickly climbed down, brushed off his shirtsleeves, and straightened his tie. Then he peered through his round spectacles. "Surely you are not alone?"

An odd question. "Is there a problem?"

"Did you not hear?" He looked nervously about, shut the door to the street, and lowered his voice. "A man was stabbed in the back right here on our doorstep in broad daylight yesterday. It was terrible."

A strange tingling pricked my scalp, making my mouth go dry. "*Mon Dieu.* Who?"

"A gent visiting on business, I was told." Mr. Davis shook his head. "Imagine, dying like that in a strange city."

My mouth dried as I pictured such a fate.

"Forgive me, Mrs. Boucheron, I quite forgot myself. What can I do for you?"

"Monsieur Maison asked to see me. I told him I'd stop by before my suffrage meeting this afternoon."

"I'm sorry. I don't have you on the schedule; otherwise I would have sent you a note. Mr. Maison left for Washington early yesterday to attend to a sudden problem. He will not be back until the end of the month. Perhaps I can be of assistance."

"I haven't a clue why he wanted to see me." I drew a breath and gathered my thoughts, deciding not to speak about my husband and my inheritance. "If you would, please tell Monsieur Maison that I stopped by."

"Certainly."

"*Merci.*" Shifting my parasol, I turned to leave, then swung back. "Will you be in correspondence with Monsieur Maison during his absence?" The idea of waiting a month knotted my stomach.

"I expect to be, as soon as he is settled."

"Then I will check with you later," I said, moving to the door.

"Wait, Mrs. Boucheron, a woman alone, after yesterday's murder . . ." He shivered. "You must allow me to escort you to your meeting." He moved toward me, worry creasing his brow.

The knot inside me tightened. "It's only a few blocks over to Chartres."

"Nevertheless, it may not be safe and I'd never forgive myself if something happened."

I swallowed my refusal. "If you wish. But I must warn you, the heat is grueling."

"Like the devil has made himself at home."

His words so aptly described the feeling settling around me that I studied him more closely as he slid on his brown frock coat and square-crowned bowler. He didn't give the impression of being extraordinarily perceptive behind the thick lenses of his spectacles, and he didn't act as if he'd said anything of note.

Yet it seemed to me as if something sinister had entered my life. "You are in danger, trust no one."

"Accompanying you will be a pleasure. You and your sisters are too alone in the world." He opened the door and followed me out, locking the door behind him. "It shakes me up, thinking of that man being stabbed in broad daylight."

The recesses of the old buildings seemed deeper, the shadows darker, as if the place I had lived all of my life had changed. "The man was here to see Monsieur Maison, then?"

"I cannot say for sure. I did not know anything had happened until I heard people shouting for help. The man was begging to be taken to a doctor and for someone to find his friend. As badly as he was bleeding, I hope that friend was not far."

"Then he was alive after being attacked? Why didn't you go with him to the doctor?" *Mon Dieu,* were a man to be attacked on my doorstep, I wouldn't leave his side.

Mr. Davis slowed his step and blushed. "The sight of blood has an adverse effect upon my nerves; I'd have only been a detriment. The merchant next door accompanied him instead. I learned later the man lived for a bit, but passed on before the doctor could save him. Forgive me, I should not be burdening your sensibilities with this."

"I assure you, I am not so delicate, nor are most women that I know. The war left little room for such nonsense."

"Yes, I quite admire your and your sisters' fortitude. And I have been meaning to speak to you about Mignon. She is such a lovely and amenable young woman."

I barely kept from frowning. Surely he wasn't about to ask for Mignon's hand so soon?

The Carr House, where the National Woman Suffrage Association held their meetings, was just ahead, and I smiled. "*Merci* for the company, monsieur. I am already running late for my meeting, so we'll have to speak of Mignon later. Perhaps you can come for dinner soon?"

"Could I possibly come ton—"

"Friday? With our duties to our boarders, weekends are best for social calls. Shall I tell Mignon to expect you Friday evening then?"

He looked flustered. "Yes, but Friday there will be a carnival in Jackson Square and I would like to bring—"

"What fun! We would love to come. Shall we meet you there at seven in front of the cathedral?"

"I guess—"

"Wonderful. We'll see you then. *Bon jour,* Monsieur Davis." I walked away waving, feeling as if I'd just stepped all over the man; but wanting to take my sister out for an evening, even chaperoned, was a much more serious step toward courting her than calling at our house. A step I was fairly certain Mignon wouldn't want to take but could easily be led into just to keep Mr. Davis from being lonely. And heavens . . . lovely and amenable? I'd learned during my brief years of marriage that being lovely and amenable was woefully impractical.

The meeting on women's voting rights ran so long that by the time I left, evening shadows had erased the day. I spared a few coins on a carriage to take me to the telegraph office so I could send a message to Mr. Goodson in Baton Rouge before going home. It had been two days since his telegram had arrived, more than enough time for him to have contacted me with an explanation of the mysterious danger.

Through the carriage window on my return home I studied Blindman's Curve, searching for an explanation to the chill and the shadow, but I saw nothing out of the ordinary. Still, the incident troubled me, made me restless, and I decided to walk the short distance to *La Belle* once we reached my street, to calm myself.

Rue Jardin and its grand park of aged, moss-strewn

live oaks and blooming wisteria were as much home to me as *La Belle*. With tall columns across her four-storied front and a dozen dormers on her gabled roof, *La Belle* had been the toast of New Orleans during her prime, and traces of her glory still clung to her. In the evening shadows I could almost pretend her white paint had not faded and cracked, that disrepair did not sully her inner courtyard, and that rust did not mar the iron railings wrapping her galleries like overworn lacy garters.

A light breeze swayed through the trees and brushed a cooling hand to my cheeks as I paused to take in the sweet smell of jasmine mingled with the mouthwatering aroma of Mama Louisa's creamy red beans, andouille, and fresh bread. Mama Louisa's cooking could warm the soul of the devil.

" 'Half light, half shade, She stood, a sight to make an old man young.'"

"Mon Dieu!" Startled, I spun around to see who had spoken.

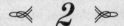

2

A tall man stood beneath the shadows of a twisted live oak just behind me. The deep voice was unfamiliar, cultured, and sensual. I backed away several steps, chastising myself for being so lost in my thoughts that I'd been unaware of his presence and the hint of tobacco in the air.

He tossed his cigar to the ground, extinguishing it with his heel, and courteously stepped further away from me into the fading light, easing my apprehension. "Forgive me for frightening you. But those words were made for you."

"Monsieur, the evening shadows have misled you. There is no comparison between me and Lord Tennyson's extraordinary verse," I replied, drawing back another step, this time from his dark appeal. His hair cut a rakish line across his brow, with a few errant strands that beckoned for order. I clenched my hand and moved my gaze on, absorbing the sensual curve of

In his eyes, I saw a haunting sadness that matched his voice. It struck a note of kinship inside me. "I hope you weren't misinformed about my boarding house. It does not possess the grandeur of the hotels in the Vieux Carré."

"I value quiet and privacy more than ostentation, Mrs. Boucheron."

I slipped his card into my pocket. "Then let us see about a room for you, *oui*?"

He fell into step beside me. "Thank you. On my journey down the Mississippi, I'd heard New Orleans is unlike any other place, and already I am intrigued by the city and its . . . people." His voice deepened to a caress.

I kept my gaze on the path, refusing to respond to his flirtation. Surely the pace of our walk was what made me slightly breathless. "*Oui*, no other city has the history we do, monsieur, but I think we are different because we are more stubbornly set in our ways."

"It's more than your culture. There's a forgiveness here that doesn't exist other places."

"Forgiveness?" It was an odd remark, coming from a stranger. Halting, I faced him. "What do you mean?"

He shrugged. "I sense an acceptance of man's humanity here, rather than an abhorrence of it."

I hadn't experienced acceptance or forgiveness here, since the war; even my husband's relatives blamed me for the loss of the Boucheron Plantation, and had broken all ties with me. "Don't be fooled," I told him.

"New Orleans is famous for its masks. What you think you see here is not always real."

Leaving the intimacy of the twilight behind, I hurried up the stairs to *La Belle's* brightly lit entrance and winced at the uproar inside. My son's screeching violin was loud enough to wake the dead, and Mama Louisa was shouting about devils from the North in the dining room. It was a wonder Mr. Trevelyan didn't march right back out of the house.

"Welcome to my home, monsieur. If you'll please set your luggage by the stairs, Papa John will take it up for you. I have a quiet room available at the far side of the house, but there are several matters requiring my immediate attention. If you wish, you may wait with the other boarders in the parlor, *oui?* You will find brandy, sherry, and other spirits available."

He set down his bags, and I pointed him toward where the boarders were having a loud discussion. Tonight it sounded as if Mark Twain's *The Innocents Abroad* was the focus of their criticism. Any author other than Shakespeare ranked low in their opinion.

I dashed into the dining room to handle Mama Louisa's disaster before dealing with my son.

"That man is back, I tell you. Spoons Butler has stolen our silver ladle," Mama Louisa cried.

"Shh," I admonished gently. The hated Federal general had ransacked New Orleans, and it was only because we'd had the foresight to hide what little silver we had left that we had any now. Troops still occupied the city even though the war had ended nine years ago. "General Butler is in Washington, Mama Louisa."

"Those Northern devils are still here though," she said, shaking her head. "General Butler's got men working for him. You mark Mama Louisa's words, now. The shooting ain't over. No, ma'am. And if he ain't got men working for him, then he's got ghosts. I heard them last night."

I tapped my finger on my lips. "You will scare the boarders. The noise last night was only the heat making the rafters groan."

Mama Louisa's dark eyes widened. "I sure am sorry, Miss Julie. I don't want to scare anybody, but that ladle just ain't nowhere to be found and those noises weren't groaning rafters. It's gotta be a ghost."

"Did you check in the pie safe for the ladle? I caught Andre dipping into the apple pie with it late last night." I'd heard the noises, too, and had found nothing to explain them in my midnight search, but I wasn't about to consider any reason but the most practical.

Mama Louisa pulled an apple-pie-crusted ladle from the pantry. "Well, I'll be."

Having solved that problem, I went to find my son. I had no doubt he'd be barefoot and muddy in the grand music room. Though Andre could play the violin like a master when he chose, he presently screeched his bow across the violin strings with discordant abandon, a tactic he used whenever he didn't want to practice. His philosophy was the louder and less harmoniously he played, the sooner he'd be told to stop.

I nearly bumped into Mr. Trevelyan, who stood in the doorway. In the light, his eyes were like blue fire, burning and intense, and just as disruptive as his aroma of spice and sandalwood, which curled around me like warm silk. I wanted to lean closer and savor his scent.

"Goodness," I murmured.

His brow angled. "Surely I did not frighten you."

"No." Frightening didn't describe him. Dangerous did. There was an edge to him that sharpened my senses, as if something primal lay beneath the surface of his charm, something that drew me to him. "Was the parlor not to your liking?"

He shrugged. "You are much more interesting than a literary discussion."

I didn't know whether to smile or to call a halt to his flattery. Thankfully, Mignon dashed past us, her face crinkled with worry, her hair askew from its bun, and her arms heaped with fresh towels. She was partway up the stairs before she noticed me. "Oh, Juliet, you have returned. Ginette fainted. The kitchen and this heat were too much for her. Andre returned a mess and refused to help with the laundry because I told him he had to bathe first. Mama Louisa says the silver soup ladle is missing and—" Her gaze settled on Mr. Trevelyan and she blushed.

"Monsieur Trevelyan. Please meet my youngest sister, Mademoiselle Mignon DePerri. Mignon, Monsieur Trevelyan is a writer and will be staying with us."

"*Bienvenu* to New Orleans and our home, monsieur." Mignon smiled radiantly and curtsied slightly.

"Thank you for the warm welcome. I'm finding the South a rather remarkable place. Beauty and graciousness abound."

"Much like your charm, it would seem," I replied dryly. Mr. Trevelyan's smile had Mignon completely mesmerized. "Mignon, hurry and place the fresh towels in the rooms. I will speak to Andre and see to Ginette after I settle Monsieur Trevelyan into his quarters."

Still looking dazed, she nodded and ran up the stairs.

Apparently having heard my voice, Andre changed the sound of his violin in midscreech to the melodious tones of Bach's *Invention in B flat*. The music became progressively louder in the entry hall until he entered the room with an angelic expression on his face.

"You are back, *Mère*," he said, feigning surprise as he lowered the violin from his chin. Mud splattered his bare feet, and dotted his clothes, and his dark hair hung in an unruly mess. Curbing my need to brush the locks from his face, I stared at him a moment, realizing where he might have gotten so muddy.

"Andre, have you been to the river?" The adventurous call of the Mississippi had lured many a boy to an early death.

"*Non, Mère.* We didn't go in the river. We were just playing near it."

I warred between irritation and the need to pull him into my arms and understand his recent penchant for trouble. "Where by the river, Andre?"

"Phillipe Doucet and I went with his cousin, Will Hayes, to a camp in the woods by Will's house."

Dieu. I wondered if Letitia knew her son was playing with mine.

"Why didn't you tell me about the camp?" he demanded. "Will's father used it to spy on the Federal Army during the war. He said that my grandfather and my father helped build it right under the Federal Army's nose and stayed there often during the war before they were killed. Why did you never mention it?" He sounded hurt, as if I had withheld something vital from him on purpose.

"I did not know about the camp," I said softly.

"A real camp, is it?" Mr. Trevelyan asked genially, as if trying to ease the tension that had been building between me and my son. "I have two nephews who would be green with envy. When I left, they were trying to convince their father to build them a fort in the woods, like one they'd recently read about."

"Andre, this is Monsieur Trevelyan. He is a writer who will be boarding with us. Monsieur, my son, Andre."

Mr. Trevelyan held out his hand. "A pleasure to meet you, sir."

Andre, looking surprised at being treated as an adult, shook Mr. Trevelyan's hand. Even my eyes widened; I didn't think of my son as being grown.

"Thank you, Monsieur Trevelyan," my son said. "Is it a fort from the war that they want to build?"

Mr. Trevelyan smiled. "No, this fort is much more interesting. They recently read a book about a shipwrecked family who built a mansion in the trees, and now they want to build one."

"A house in the trees?" Andre asked, clearly fascinated. "What book is it?"

Had my son just asked about a book? I envied how easily Mr. Trevelyan had sparked my son's interest.

"*The Swiss Family Robinson*," Mr. Trevelyan said. "The book is full of ingenious inventions. They even build their own bridge."

"How, monsieur?"

I spoke then. "*Pardon.* Andre, I am afraid we will have to save bridge building for another day. Dinner will be ready soon and I need to settle Monsieur Trevelyan into his room. I suggest you go scrub yourself from head to foot, *oui*? I will have Papa John bring your dinner to you, then later tonight we have a number of things to discuss about your behavior today. Do you understand?"

"*Oui, Mère*," Andre said, keeping his gaze directed at his feet. Mud flaked off his toes onto the carpet as he wiggled them, and I closed my eyes so I wouldn't have to see. Perhaps muddy toes were like runny noses and just needed a loving hand. Yet I feared that my son needed more than that now.

He properly excused himself, then scrambled quickly up the stairs, making sure he stepped heavily on the one that creaked. Turning, I saw that Mr. Trevelyan had collected his bags.

"You are fortunate," he said. "You have a lively boy."

"Lively is an understatement, but you are right. I am blessed." I had to keep reminding myself of that as Mr. Trevelyan and I followed the trail of mud on the polished wooden stairs.

"All of the boarders' rooms are on the second floor. The door directly at the end of the corridor is the bath and water closet. Everything for your personal needs should be in there. The third floor is reserved for family, and the fourth is an attic for storage. You will find we have an excellent library, a full music room, and a double parlor should you wish to entertain guests. Three meals a day are provided for you. Mama Louisa keeps the food on the sideboard piping hot. A private tea can be served to you in the parlor if requested in advance. I ask that all boarders conduct themselves with the utmost level of decorum and respect."

His chamber mirrored mine in furnishings but differed in the colors threaded through the cream wallpaper and upholstery. Dark greens dominated his decor, whereas burgundy gave mine its feminine touch. The mahogany writing desk, armoire, and mosquito-netted bed stood in sharp contrast to the light summer drapes. Moving to the desk, I lit the oil lamp, turning up the wick to let soft light flood the room. When I glanced in his direction, I found that Mr. Trevelyan still stood by the door, satchels in hand. He'd made no attempt to make himself at home.

"Do you find the accommodations unacceptable, Monsieur Trevelyan?" I asked.

"Not at all, Mrs. Boucheron. They exceed my expectations, as a matter of fact." He kept his gaze centered on me, making me wonder if he spoke of the room at all.

An odd sense of expectancy and heat settled in my stomach as I stared back at him. The sensations were as disturbing as Mr. Goodson's warning to trust no one, which included my darkly handsome new boarder. He barely stepped aside as I reached the doorway, making me even more aware him. "I will see you at dinner, monsieur."

"Mrs. Boucheron?" he called softly.

I couldn't have ignored his voice even if I had tried. The timbre of it grabbed at me, urging me to pause next to him. "*Oui?*"

"I offer my condolences. From what your son said, I gather you and your family paid a heavy price in the war—both a husband and a father."

"It cost us more than you could imagine, but *merci* for your kind words." I could tell by his manner that he knew grief, yet I didn't ask how. His appeal was too temptingly strong for me to linger. Better to save my questions for another time.

His intense gaze followed me down the corridor, making me feel things I hadn't felt in a long time, things that no stranger should make me feel.

3

"Ginette?" I called, knocking lightly. She opened the door with an apron in her hand.

"*Pardon,* Juliet. I will be down in a minute to help with dinner." She was as pale as the white lace trimming the soft pink satin of her bed hangings and drapes.

"What is wrong? Nonnie said you had a fainting spell."

"I am not sure. After you left, I worked with Mama Louisa in the kitchens. By the time we had the meal on the stove, I had a mild headache. So I went to the sitting room and worked on my tapestry for a little, then a sharp pain lashed through my head and I must have fainted. Nonnie found me on the floor and fetched the smelling salts."

I pressed my palm to her forehead. Summer in New Orleans always came with the fear that a fever would sweep through the city and steal loved ones away.

"Your skin feels cool, but you should have a cup of sassafras tea anyway. And we'll call for Dr. Lanau to come see you in the morning."

"Tea would ease my nausea. But there is no need to call the doctor. I'm sure it was just the heat."

Taking the apron from her hand, I shooed her back into her bed. "Then you rest. Dinner is almost ready, and Nonnie and I can handle the cleaning up. I'll have Mama Louisa bring you some soup and put a pinch of lemon verbena in your tea to help you rest until morning. How does that sound?"

She sighed. "*Bon*. But first you must tell me what Monsieur Maison had to say about Jean Claude and *La Belle*."

I delayed my response by helping her slip off her worn boots and settle her in the bed. Sometimes it seemed as if just yesterday we were buying party dresses, with nothing more on our minds than how pretty we could make ourselves. Then there were times like now, when I felt as if parties and dresses and dreams had never been a part of our lives.

"You have stalled long enough," she said, staying my hand from fussing with the covers. "You know you avoid sharing burdens as strongly as Andre objects to housework."

"Surely not."

She arched an eyebrow. "The increase in taxes, for example. How long have you known and didn't tell us?"

"Since January," I admitted.

"Even if it is bad news, Juliet, you must tell me. How else can I help?" She gently squeezed my hand.

"Monsieur Maison was unexpectedly called to Washington until the end of the month. So we will have to wait a bit for our answers."

"I can't help but feel there is more you aren't telling us. You were tense and distracted even before Mr. Latour's visit today."

Guilt flushed my cheeks. I had not told anyone about the telegram. I started to, then bit my lip. Until I knew more about Mr. Goodson's warning, it would only be a needless burden for Ginette. Instead, I voiced another concern that weighed heavy on my heart. "Why does Andre keep getting into trouble? It's as if he has lost all sense of responsibility."

"Andre is just being *un jeune petit*." She smiled. "Surely you haven't forgotten how we used to send Mother to her swooning couch with the vapors? Mama Louisa was forever fishing our shoes out of the fountain, or darning the stockings we tore climbing trees. Ladies were *never* to do those things, and Mother was convinced we were destined for ruin."

My lips twitched. "We were more than a handful."

She squeezed my hand. "He's going to make a fine gentleman. Just give him time." She then drew a troubled breath. "Do you believe Jean Claude is alive?"

"In my heart, no, and hopefully Mr. Goodson's investigation will prove the rumors false." Rising, I paced across the room to the window and peered out at the darkened shadows. "But in my mind, sometimes I question. What if Jean Claude really did steal the gold and is alive? I've led Andre to believe his father died a noble death, and I'm not sure he will forgive me if I'm wrong."

"What could you have done differently?"

"I don't know." I stiffened my shoulders, pushing away the doubt. "I do know that I'll do whatever is necessary to stop Mr. Latour from taking advantage of us."

"If he'd said another word today, I fear you would have tossed him on his ear."

"I think Papa John would have booted him out before I could have."

A blush tinged Ginette's cheeks as a half smile curved her lips. "*Oui*. Just like he did when Captain Jennison stumbled into the house, smelling like a brewery. Papa John tossed him out before the captain could explain that he'd just had a bullet taken from his shoulder, with only whiskey to kill the pain."

Memories of the war always hurt, for I wondered what joys our lives might have held had it not been for the bloodshed. I didn't understand how Ginette could look back at Captain Jennison and the Federal occupation of our home fondly. That time was dark and painful for me.

Shaking off the past, I leaned down and hugged

Ginette. "Get some rest. Tomorrow we'll bake your favorite nut bread."

"We had better save that treat for your birthday. What are we going to do about the increased taxes this year?"

"We've a new border, which will help. You'll meet him in the morning. Otherwise, we'll do exactly what we have done every year since the war ended. The very best that we can, even if we have to sell nut bread at the market."

"But what if—"

I pressed my finger to her lips. "We will be fine." We *had* to be; I wouldn't consider anything else.

Ginette caught my hand as I stood to leave. "Have you noticed anything strange recently?"

"What do you mean?"

"I am not sure. It is just something I feel. Something isn't right."

A chill hit me, not unlike the one that had swept over me on Blindman's Curve. I glanced around the room, looking for the shadow I'd seen before, then shook my head at my imagination.

"It is most likely the heat. June has never been this sweltering," I said, even though I was chilled. A bump in the hall caused us both to turn toward the door.

Andre stood in the doorway, looking puzzled. "Was that man outside Ginette's door a new doctor?"

"Who, Andre?" I asked.

"I don't know. I waved to him and he hurried down the stairs."

"Stay here with Ginette." Forcing a deep breath, I

ordered myself to ignore the anxious feeling inside me as I ran to peer over the railing. The curving staircase was empty, and no footsteps sounded above the echo of voices from below. I dashed down the stairs and met Mignon on the second-floor landing, coming up. Mama Louisa rang the dinner bell.

"Juliet, you're as white as a ghost. What is it?"

"Did someone just come by?" I asked, leaning over the rail, finding the entry hall empty.

"No one passed by me." Mignon shook her head, her brow creasing with concern. "Why? What is—"

A door behind us opened, and I whirled around to see Mr. Trevelyan, dressed in a different black suit, exit his room at the far end of the corridor. Although I didn't think it possible for him to have been outside Ginette's room and make it back to his own room without me seeing him and with time to change his suit, I still stared as he approached. Perhaps it was his eerie timing that unnerved me.

"Was that the dinner bell?" he asked.

"*Oui,*" I said, gathering my wits. "You are right on time. Mignon will escort you to the dining room and introduce you to the other boarders."

He made a point of meeting my eyes as he passed. "Will you be joining us as well?"

"I'll be down in a few moments," I said, my cheeks warming from the heat of his gaze.

"It is wonderful to have you here, Monsieur Trevelyan." Mignon's winning smile broadened.

"The pleasure is all mine," he said, offering his arm to her.

They left, and I forced my mind back on the man Andre had seen. Either he had disappeared into thin air or no one had been there. Just to be sure, I quickly looked into each of the rooms on the second floor. It wasn't until I opened Mr. Trevelyan's door that I felt as if I'd intruded on the boarder's privacy. His traveling suit lay on the bed in such disarray that I went inside and straightened it before questioning my action. When I pulled the folds of the material even, three cigars fell from the pocket of his coat. I put them back and drew a deep breath of the sandalwood and spice aroma in the room, letting my fingers linger on the rich material longer than necessary.

His suitcases stood open, and the urge to peek at what he carried with him was so strong, I had to stuff my hands into my pockets and hurry from the room. I shut the door as if the devil himself been there. Andre and Ginette waited for me at the top of the stairs, their expressions wary.

I forced a smile at my son. "Can you describe who you saw? Perhaps it was one of the boarders?"

He frowned. "The shadows in the corridor were too dark for me to tell. I know he had dark hair and wore a gray suit. And that he was tall and thin."

"Well, I'm sure there is a simple explanation that we'll learn of soon enough. Perhaps one of the boarders came to the family's floor by mistake. Meanwhile,

Andre, you get a bath, and Ginette, you go back to bed."

Ginette waited for Andre to leave before speaking. "You don't think it was one of the boarders, do you?"

"It has to have been," I reassured her, even though the chill I'd felt earlier told me differently.

Outside the dining room, I paused to collect myself. Low-toned voices and the smells from Mama Louisa's cooking eased a sense of normalcy over me until I heard Mr. Trevelyan's deep voice. Then, as if I were finger-testing water for a hot bath, I peeked cautiously into the room before I entered.

Mignon and the two women from the Shakespearean troupe, Mrs. Edmund Gallier and Miss Charlotte Vengle, were more interested in Mr. Trevelyan than their conversation about the weather. Mr. Edmund Gallier and Mr. Horatio Fitz, lead actors in the troupe, each had one eye on the women watching Mr. Trevelyan and one eye on Mr. Trevelyan himself. Their expressions mirrored my own disquiet. None of the men wore a gray suit, though Mr. Gallier did have on blue that could be mistaken for gray. But Mr. Gallier's hair was decidedly silver, not dark.

Mr. Trevelyan emanated subtle power and sophistication despite his relaxed stance against the mantel. His waist and hips were slimmer and his shoulders broader, more imposing than the other men, as if the expensive, tailored cloth of his suit could barely contain what lay beneath. He immediately turned my way, sensing my arrival before the others.

Smiling, I entered the room. "My apologies for keeping you all waiting. Mignon, has everyone been introduced?"

"Yes. In fact, Monsieur Trevelyan is trying to recall if he has seen Monsieur Gallier's troupe perform before."

"And have you, Monsieur Trevelyan?" I asked, curious. His card had cited San Francisco as his home; Mr. Gallier and Mr. Fitz were from the East.

"Not that we have ascertained as of yet, though we've frequented the same establishments. I spent time studying theater and attending a number of performances from Boston to New York the year before last. Shakespeare's plays are a particular favorite of mine," Mr. Trevelyan replied.

"Well, then we all have a great deal in common, it seems." Though I had generalized my remark, the look Mr. Trevelyan brushed over me made it seem as if I'd spoken only to him. He had a way of smoothly walking through barriers with a simple word or look. "Mignon, would you say the blessing after everyone is seated?"

Unless we were having special guests, I kept the dining arrangements informal, allowing the boarders to choose each night where they wished to sit. I was always at the head of the table, and Ginette and Mignon sat in the middle on opposite sides to mingle with the guests. Mr. Trevelyan chose the seat to my right, making me wish I'd assigned seats.

Soon bowls of savory red beans, plates of rice with slices of spicy andouille, and buttered bread filled the table. As I ate, I remembered when invitations to *La Belle du Temps* had been sought after by the most celebrated members of the beau monde. In the gilded mirror above the mantel, I could almost see an elegant dinner party in progress and taste the old times on the tip of my tongue. The flavorful meals had passed from one course to the next with delicacies that only New Orleans could offer the genteel palate. China, sparkling crystal, silver, and delicate white lace had graced the tabletop, while the chandelier above had glowed warmly, casting a rich sheen on the expensive silks and satins below.

Now the china was chipped, the silver sparse, the crystal aged, and the guests paid for the meal, which the hostess helped prepare with her own hands. Many of *La Belle*'s treasures had been stolen or sold, and repairs had been neglected for lack of funds. But traces of her beauty still lay evident in her marble mantels and ornate moldings—a grand dame whose faded wall coverings and tattered draperies exposed her age and now needed candlelight to mask realities too harsh to face.

I noticed Mr. Trevelyan watching me in the mirror, his expression dark and searching until he met my gaze and smiled. I should have averted my gaze, but some part of me chose to meet the challenge I saw sparking in his eyes. I studied him in return, and his smile deepened.

The richness of his suit, the silver of his vest, and the gold of his ring and cuff links sparkled like the patrons and guests who used to grace the table, and I wondered if that was why he didn't seem the stranger that he should.

"Miles to travel before you sleep?" he asked softly, shifting his gaze from the mirror to me. "You looked lost in thought."

I sipped my wine to wet my dry mouth. Meeting his gaze in the mirror was infinitely easier than a direct encounter with his piercing blue eyes. "I was thinking about *La Belle* and the way things used to be for my family."

"*La Belle*? An unusual name. Have I missed meeting more of your family?"

"Only my sister Ginette. She is unwell this evening but should be fine by tomorrow. *La Belle du Temps* is the name of our home. My DePerri ancestors never settled for the ordinary. Everything had to be special."

He studied the detail around him. "They were wise. The results are beautiful." The last remark was said as he looked at me. Even though I thought his flattery overdone, a blush still warmed my cheeks.

"And what about you, Monsieur Trevelyan? Were your ancestors wise as well?"

"I am afraid the answer to that is a matter of opinion. Most will say Trevelyan Manor has no equal to her beauty within a hundred miles, yet the Trevelyan men are not exactly viewed as wise or . . . trustworthy. Some deserve the criticism, but others, like my brother, do not."

Not trustworthy? The man was shockingly direct. Before I could decide in which category he put himself, Mrs. Gallier spoke.

"I hear you went to town today, Mrs. Boucheron. Tell me, was Madame Boussard's Dress Shop open? I spent some time there yesterday while Mr. Gallier and Mr. Fitz attended to business, and I was quite taken by her wares. She had several gowns that were imported directly from Paris this year. Of course they were exorbitantly expensive, but—"

"Now, Mrs. Gallier. You've no need for more dresses," Mr. Gallier directed.

"Of course not, Mr. Gallier," Mrs. Gallier said meekly, the sweet smile on her face faltering slightly. Though I could tell she often felt differently, she always agreed with her husband, reminding me of a pastel-hued painting I'd seen. It gave the impression of a woman, but when I looked closely there were no details—just brush strokes that her husband seemed to be constantly orchestrating. I decided I would leave some of my suffrage articles on the parlor table near the chair she frequently used.

Mr. Gallier was obsessed with finery, making up for his wife's lack. From watch fob to frock coat, he spent his every waking moment impersonating an English dandy.

Sitting on Mr. Trevelyan's left, Miss Vengle leaned surprisingly close to him and whispered something that I couldn't hear. From the irritation pulling on Mr. Fitz's handlebar mustache, he thought the action overly familiar, too.

"The dress shop was open today," I said, making a point of answering Mrs. Gallier's question. "So you and Monsieur Fitz were in town yesterday, Monsieur Gallier?"

"Yes, with excellent results," Mr. Fitz said. "We now have a theater at our disposal, and as soon as we agree on which play to perform, we can begin advertising."

Mr. Trevelyan narrowed his eyes. "From our earlier conversation, I thought your Shakespearean troupe was well established and contracted to prominent theaters for performances in advance, not that you were just forming a troupe."

Mr. Gallier cleared his throat. "We customarily do. But we canceled our plans for New York this summer because Mrs. Gallier"—he patted his wife's shoulder—"had a horrific bout of arthritis this winter, and the doctor suggested a warmer climate. Though I am not sure he meant New Orleans. This heat is murderous."

"It *is* murderous, which proves my earlier point, Edmund. *Macbeth* is a poor choice for our play," Mr. Fitz commented. "Ask anyone here if I am not right."

Sitting straighter in his chair, Mr. Gallier bristled. "I have no doubt *Macbeth* will be well received, and Miss Vengle plays Lady Macbeth so well. The public will love us."

"Murder is always welcomed under the guise of entertainment. We are a bloodthirsty breed." Mr. Fitz slashed his eyebrows together and wiggled his mustache. "Your abilities as an actor are not in question here, my friend, but rather the health of the audience is at stake."

"In what way?" Mr. Trevelyan asked Mr. Fitz.

"Simple, sir. Once you have been here a day or two, you will sense what I do. Tensions are rising, especially in this infernal heat. And human nature being as it is, tempers rise also. I have seen it before. Senseless murders are apt to follow unless intercessory measures are taken."

"Like yesterday," I said. "There was a murder on the steps outside of Monsieur Maison's law office. Monsieur Gallier, did either you or Monsieur Fitz hear of it? Madame Boussard's is on the same street."

Mr. Trevelyan dropped his spoon, making everyone jump when it clattered into his bowl. He was staring at me as if I had committed the deed myself. Had he heard of the murder? Was his surprise due to the fact that I spoke of it during dinner? I'm sure *Godey's Lady's Book* would not consider murder a proper dinner conversation.

"Juliet, how horrible." Mignon's cheeks faded from

pink to white. "You could have been in danger. Why did you not tell us immediately?"

"A murder in broad daylight?" Miss Vengle asked. "How awful! Was the man robbed?"

I hadn't said the victim was a man, but it was an assumption anyone might easily make. "Monsieur Davis did not mention it if he was."

"And Mr. Davis would be?" Mr. Trevelyan asked.

"The assistant to my attorney, Monsieur Maison." I answered.

"Perfectly dreadful," Mrs. Gallier said. "And to think that I had been in town myself. When did you say this happened?"

"Midday, I believe."

Mrs. Gallier paled. "That's exactly when we were there."

"Thankfully, we missed the horrible event," Mr. Fitz cut in, then returned to his earlier subject. "So you see, Edmund. I am right. Tempers are too volatile under this heat. I suggest Miss Vengle and I do a comedy." He dipped into his soup with his spoon. "*The Taming of the Shrew* would be preferable to *Macbeth*."

"A play cannot affect an entire community, Horatio," Mr. Gallier said.

"Words have determined the fate of nations." Mr. Fitz glowered back at him.

"Theater does change lives," said Miss Vengle. "Why, just look at poor little ol' me. I would likely have starved to death if you all had not come to my town."

Her thick southern drawl reminded me of old molasses in the winter—oversweet and excruciatingly slow—and didn't match the dramatic flare of her dark hair and eyes.

"Do not upset yourself, Miss Vengle. Edmund and I will settle this." Mr. Fitz patted her hand from his place next to her. "High emotion during meals leads to bilious attacks."

I found his advice amusing, since he and Mr. Gallier were generating a fair amount of tension themselves. In fact, now that I took a moment to discern it, the tension in the room had grown tenfold since I spoke of the murder in town, as if they were forcing themselves to act normal.

"Well, gentlemen," Mr. Trevelyan said, breaking into the tension. "Were I given the choice, I would much rather be entertained by the wiles of a woman, such as Petruchio's Kate, than by the dark intrigues of murder and betrayal. What is your opinion in the matter, Mrs. Boucheron?"

The way Mr. Trevelyan emphasized "wiles of a woman" with his blue gaze centered on me was entirely too . . . enticing. "As I see it, *Macbeth* is the lesser of two evils."

Six pairs of shocked eyes met my gaze. Mignon spoke first. "Why ever would you say that, Juliet? Lady Macbeth pushes her husband to kill their king."

"Macbeth and Lady Macbeth were at least masters of their own destiny. They had a choice. Kate, in *The*

Taming of the Shrew, was a pawn. She had no choice."

"Preposterous," Mr. Gallier said, his side whiskers seeming to bristle with outrage.

Mr. Fitz cleared his throat. "Hush, Edmund. I, too, am curious as to why our hostess would choose murder and betrayal over love."

"Yes," Mr. Trevelyan added. "Are you saying you condone murder as a means of directing your fate?"

His conclusion startled me. "You both misunderstand me, gentlemen. I only meant to say that I prefer choosing one's own fate as opposed to having it chosen. But we have strayed from the subject at hand. Were I to choose a play, I would pick *Much Ado About Nothing.*"

"Beatrice's sharp wit equals her man's," Mr. Trevelyan said, studying me. "And though they are tricked into confessing their hearts, the hero and the heroine choose their own fates."

"Exactly so, Monsieur Trevelyan." His perception was disquieting.

It didn't escape my notice that Mr. Fitz had diverted the conversation away from the murder in town, and that all of the men had refrained from commenting on the crime. I had the distinct feeling they knew of it and had chosen to remain silent.

"There's nothing more appealing than a woman who knows her own mind," Mr. Trevelyan said.

His low-spoken words were a caress that made me tingle inside.

Mr. Gallier choked on his wine, Mignon winked at me, and Mr. Fitz coughed.

"A man after my own heart," Miss Vengle said, batting her lashes as she leaned toward him.

"A cheer for the ladies, then." Mr. Trevelyan sounded as if he thoroughly enjoyed disrupting the men and captivating the women. He picked up his water goblet and toasted the room. As he did so, light sparkled off the gold ring he wore on his little finger. The face, a flattened disk, held an unusual design of interwoven circles. I could have sworn that I'd seen that design before, but I couldn't recall where, which bothered me.

But I knew one thing: I'd never met a man like him before.

She looked above a straight line abolish near her, while it Mouse or fire and furniture that had not known April cleaner, the voice which was have told us about the survival in town.

When Mr. Robert Mama's over there, Mama loved

"When do you think I'm playing for the outside?"

Mama shook her head, "shut off will say with

You believe it to us, Okla mask built a thing we know it will pursue a

Un moment a White

4

"We finished early tonight," I said to Mama Louisa as she placed the last of the cleaned pots on the shelf. Wiping a final crumb from the kitchen table, I folded the dishcloth. It felt good to see the tasks for the day coming to an end.

"Done early means there's more work the Lord must have for us to do, and we just don't know about it yet," Mama Louisa said.

"Let's hope not. I am going to check the house to make sure it is properly locked, though."

"I already had Papa John do that. There's a strange feelin' in the air, Miz Juliet, and it isn't a good one. I'm going to check with him about it right now."

"Thank you," I said as she headed up the stairs leading to her and Papa John's quarters. Many times over the years, I wondered what we would have done without their love and loyalty.

Mignon marched into the kitchen just as I turned to

leave. She looked almost angry, a surprising emotion from her. "Juliet, if Monsieur Fitz and Monsieur Gallier had not brought up the subject, when would you have told us about the murder in town?"

"Soon."

"When? My guess is you wouldn't have mentioned it. You treat Ginette and me as if we were children."

My eyes widened. "How can you say that?"

"You do not trust us. You do not tell us things we should know, like the increase in the taxes."

"I did not want you to worry."

Mignon sighed. "I know, but it has been ten years since Father died. I am not a child anymore. When you were seventeen, you were already engaged and putting together your trousseau."

"Which is exactly what you should be doing, instead of scrubbing your hands to perdition."

"What I *should* be doing is helping. Now, I want you to tell me how much we lack in being able to pay the taxes."

"If Monsieur Trevelyan stays as long as he plans, that will cover a good portion of it. But once the acting troupe moves on, we'll need to fill their rooms."

"Then perhaps we should put another advertisement for boarders in the *Picayune*. How long did you say he would be staying with us?"

"At least six months."

Mignon broadened her smile. "Plenty of time for *you* to get to know him, is it not?"

Warning signals rang in my mind. "Nonnie, Monsieur Trevelyan is a man of sophistication and means who will be returning to San Francisco once he has concluded his business here. He is far above our station in life."

Mignon did not seem to be the least daunted by my words. "Don't you think he is handsome?"

"Very."

"And wonderfully charming."

I tried to lie, but couldn't. "Yes. But the Lord put all manner of beasts upon the earth, and some of those are meant to be seen and not touched."

She blew out an exasperated breath. "Why do you not like him?"

"I did not say that. I do not even know Monsieur Trevelyan, but there are some things you can tell just by looking. You know fire is going to burn before you touch it, *oui*?"

"Did you love Jean Claude?"

I shut my eyes, then I met Mignon's questioning gaze with honesty. "Papa arranged the marriage and Jean Claude was much older, but I believe over time we might have made a happy life together. If I could go back and relive my life, though, I wouldn't marry for any other reason than love, and I wouldn't marry a man who was so many miles down life's road that he never saw the same roses I did." I patted Mignon's shoulder. "Now, no more talk of me or Monsieur Trevelyan. There is something you need to know.

After calling you lovely and *amenable,* Monsieur Davis gave me the impression he's getting serious about you. Has he mentioned what his feelings for you are?"

Mignon blanched, biting her lip with concern. "*Dieu,* he asked if I enjoyed his company, and of course I had to say yes, but the truth is that he talks so much, I find myself wishing for my embroidery just to keep myself awake."

I laughed. Mignon hated embroidery. "Well, we will have to find a way to let him know you do not return his affections. He wanted to take you to the carnival Friday, and I managed to insert our whole family into his plans. We're to meet him at the cathedral at seven o'clock."

Mignon laughed. "At least he won't be lonely. What exactly do you think he meant by amenable?" she asked, her brows arching to a puzzled look.

"I think it means being like Madame Gallier with Monsieur Gallier."

"Wherever did he get that notion from? Were I Madame Gallier, I would be sore pressed to keep a civil tongue. Monsieur Gallier makes it seem that his wife's only purpose in life is to be the pedestal for his big head."

Surprise widened my eyes. "It heartens me to hear you've made such an observation. I am sure that if you expressed your thoughts on occasion, Monsieur Davis would not think you so amenable and wouldn't wish to court you. Now I had best go see to Andre and Ginette."

"I'll see to Ginette. I'll sleep on the divan in her room in case she should wake and need anything. She gave me such a fright this afternoon, seeing her on the floor pale as death itself. She did not come around until I used the smelling salts. Even then she was disoriented and did not know who I was for a moment or two."

"I had not realized it was that bad. She seemed fatigued but well when I spoke to her earlier. I will send a note to Dr. Lanau in the morning, asking him to stop by tomorrow. If Ginette—"

"Has any problems that I cannot handle, I will call for you, I promise." She hugged me, patting my back almost as if she were the elder and I the younger. I returned her embrace, realizing she was right. She had grown up, and I'd been too busy to notice.

The three of us were graced with the DePerri heart-shaped face, dark eyes, and hair as black as the Mississippi on a moonless night, but Ginette's ethereal delicacy set her apart, as if she were an angel temporarily sent to live among mortals.

I found my son in bed, though not asleep yet. He'd scrubbed his face shiny, but still had mud caked between his toes and on his bed sheets, which would now have to be laundered again.

"Andre, why didn't you take a bath?" I sat on the bed beside him, at a complete loss.

He sleepily rubbed his eyes. "I'll only get dirty again when I meet Phillipe and Will in the morning at the camp."

"I've told you many times that what a man does determines who he is. There are more important things for you to do than to spend every day off with your friends. Tomorrow you are to stay home and do the things you were supposed to do today, plus do whatever laundry needs doing by yourself. That includes the sheets you've now muddied."

He sat up as shock dropped his mouth open. "M-m-myself?"

"*Oui.*"

"But I must go. I promised Phillipe and Will that—"

"You made a promise to *me* today."

He lowered his gaze. "You just don't want me to go back to the camp."

"That's not true." I brushed a curl back from his forehead, noting he had spread across his pillow the soft blue coverlet my mother had made him before he was born. After all these years, he still liked to feel the worn material against his cheek. "I expect you to be a man of your word. Do you understand?"

"Yes, but you don't understand about the camp. It is important."

"We'll talk more about it tomorrow. And just so you know, Friday we'll go to the carnival that's in town. Won't that be fun?"

He shrugged. "Going with Phillipe and Will to the camp my father helped build is fun."

I sighed and kissed him good night, then arranged the netting about his bed. "I'll see you in the morning."

He nodded and shut his eyes. As I left his room, I felt unsettled that he'd shown no excitement about the carnival. His interest in the army camp was understandable, in some ways I'd underestimated his need to connect to his father. I hoped Mr. Goodson's report proved what I believed in my heart to be true about Jean Claude.

I took a long bath, letting the steam ease my tension, thankful that my father had had the foresight to have modern amenities installed. My mind kept wandering to Mr. Trevelyan, and my reaction to him, and I had to force myself to concentrate on more practical matters.

I donned my nightdress, robe, and slippers, and as I left the bath, I searched the pockets of my dress for the telegram. They were empty except for Mr. Trevelyan's card. My stomach sank when I dug into the pockets of my robe and found them empty, too.

I must have dropped the note somewhere in the house. Grabbing a lantern, I retraced my steps on the third floor. After finding nothing in the corridor or in Andre's room, I hurried down two flights of stairs. A quick scan of the kitchen and the butler's pantry turned up nothing, but the tinkling of glass from the parlor brought me to a halt in the center hall. I swung around, my pulse leaping as I realized I was not alone downstairs. The parlor seemed dark and unwelcoming for the first time in my life. I snuffed out the light and tiptoed to the doorway.

Given Mr. Trevelyan's habit of being where I least expected, I shouldn't have been surprised to see his unmistakable form standing at the window. Oddly, he had a drinking glass held up to the moonlight and appeared to be staring at it. After a long moment, he slowly took a sip, swore harshly, then dumped the rest of the glass's contents in a nearby potted plant.

I winced that he'd found our spirits so unpalatable, even as the thought of pickled geraniums irked me. "I daresay Mama Louisa has already watered the flowers today."

He swung around and I smiled, pleased that I'd caught him off guard.

"Did I wake you?" His voice grated harshly, as if he wrestled with things greater than the night.

"I'm looking for a paper I've lost."

I moved to the nearest lamp and lit it, casting the shadows from the room, but not the intimacy of being alone at night with him. He turned from the light, moving to the mantel where he set his glass.

"A telegram, perhaps?" he asked, with his back to me.

"You found it?"

He faced me then, his expression shadowed. "After dinner, on the floor of my room."

I swallowed the hard lump in my throat, my relief short lived. "I must have dropped it when showing you to your room."

"And I must have missed seeing it before dinner," he said softly as he crossed the room. The look in his eyes told me he didn't believe a word of what we'd just said. He stopped only inches away from me, so close that I could feel the warmth of his body as well as the heat of his raking gaze. The thin cotton of my nightdress and the silk of my robe were little protection from the force of his interest. I tugged the lacy edges of my robe closer together, and he smiled slowly, lifting his gaze back to mine. A dark desire smoldered in his eyes.

"The telegram, monsieur?" I held out my hand.

He reached into his coat pocket, pulling out the telegram. Instead of putting it into my open hand, he brushed my cheek with the edge of the paper and trailed it down to the neck of my gown. My pulse pounded so loudly in my ears that I knew he had to have heard it, too. Bolts of heat shot through me, curling in my center, awakening sensations I'd never known before.

My lips parted in surprise, and his gaze dipped lower for a long moment.

"I suggest you be more careful," he murmured. When he slid the paper a fraction below the neckline of my gown, I caught my breath and grabbed the telegram from him.

"You have a way of making me forget things that I

shouldn't," he said softly, then turned to leave. "Good night, Mrs. Boucheron."

He had a way of making us both forget things that we shouldn't.

Somehow, I gathered my thoughts enough to douse the parlor light and dash to my room, firmly shutting the door. I crawled into bed, unable to face what I knew had to be lingering in my own eyes—a yearning response to the desire in his eyes. I didn't know him, he was a stranger, but he attracted me as no one had before—and that frightened me more than the warning telegram or the murder in town.

Early the next morning, the sound of my son's disgruntled muttering, punctuated by the thud of a heavy stick hitting the side of an iron cauldron, filtered through the kitchen window where Mignon and I worked preparing breakfast. I'd set Andre to washing his sheets first thing, and he wasn't happy. The day had not started off well in other matters, either. Jean Claude's letters weren't in the blue box in which I had left them, or anywhere in the study that I could see. Neither Andre nor Mignon had seen them.

Ginette entered the kitchen, her cheeks flushed. She grabbed an apron. "Why didn't you wake me?"

"You needed the extra rest, and by the looks of you, we were right," I replied. "Mama Louisa's tea must have helped."

"And from what I heard the boarders talking about

in the parlor this morning, I was right: something was wrong last night. I asked you, and did you tell me the truth? No. A man murdered in broad daylight and you didn't say a word."

"I'm sorry. I didn't want you to worry." She nodded, but the irritation in her eyes remained. "What did the boarders say?" I asked.

"Only that they had to be very careful about what they did, especially when in town."

"Who said that?"

"Mr. Fitz did. Whatever is Andre doing outside?"

"The laundry," I said, wondering exactly what the boarders thought they had to be careful about.

Ginette's eyes widened with surprise. "By himself? No wonder he is unhappy."

"I feel as if this is my fault." Mignon paced across the kitchen floor.

"How can it possibly be your fault, Nonnie? You have too soft a heart." I finished kneading the biscuit dough, then leveled a look at her.

"Well," she said, frowning. "Maybe I shouldn't have demanded that he bathe before helping me. I know how he hates to do that."

"So you would rather have had muddy streaks on the boarders' bed sheets and cost us all another day's hard work instead? Andre must learn. At twelve, he is old enough that his very future could be at stake." I winced as a particularly loud bang sounded from the courtyard. His resentment at having to do "women's chores" could probably be heard at the state line.

"It sounds as if he is upset with more than just doing his chores," Ginette said.

I told them about the camp. "I think he needs to know more about Jean Claude. Which reminds me, do you have Jean Claude's letters, Ginette?"

She crinkled her brow. "Why ever would I have them? Aren't they on the shelf in the study?"

"They're missing," I said, shaking my head. "The box is there, but no letters."

"That's strange."

"You think there will be any cotton left on those sheets by the time you finish?" Mr. Trevelyan's unmistakable voice interrupted the clanging outside, and I froze with a half-shaped biscuit in my hand.

"Who's that?" Ginette whispered.

"Our new boarder," Mignon answered, moving to the window.

"Dudn't matter," grumbled Andre. "It will serve her right for making me do laundry. All the boys would laugh at me if they saw me. I bet *you* have never had to do a maid's work, either."

"He's a pirate prince," Mignon whispered.

"*Dieu*, Juliet. You neglected to tell me how . . . handsome our new boarder is," Ginette added, fanning her face.

Unable to resist, I joined my sisters at the window, trying to decide if I had a punishment stern enough for my son. Andre had stepped over the line by speaking so. *Serve me right for making him do laundry!* Thoughts of punishment flew as my gaze settled on Mr. Trevelyan. His black hair, still damp from a bath, glistened in the morning sun. Dressed in form-fitting black pants, an unbuttoned linen shirt, and no shoes, he reminded me of a musketeer I'd seen illustrated in Alexandre Dumas's adventurous story. Hot embarrassment crept up my cheeks at the thought of facing him today. Ever since lying to him last night, I knew I had to apologize and explain why I'd been in his room.

"I have been in your shoes a few times," Mr. Trevelyan said. "It's not a fun place to be."

"You've done laundry?"

"No, but I've been angry and resentful enough that I didn't care if what I did was right or wrong," Mr. Trevelyan replied. "Your feelings are more important than anything else, right?"

Andre stopped beating the cauldron. "I didn't say that."

Mr. Trevelyan squatted down to be eye level with Andre. He didn't sound irritated as he spoke. "You didn't have to say the words, because your muttering and banging are saying them for you. But it's all right to feel that way."

I saw Andre's mouth drop open. It was about the same moment that my teeth clenched. Whatever did the man think he was about?"

"*Bon,* monsieur? But that's . . ."

"Not right?" Mr. Trevelyan said. "Does that stop you

from feeling angry? Is it going to stop you from feeling embarrassed or resentful?"

Andre shook his head.

Mr. Trevelyan shrugged. "It didn't stop me from feeling those things and worse. Everyone has a dark side and feels things that aren't exactly right, but most people are afraid to admit it. What is important is what you do with those feelings. That's what determines if you are a man or a boy."

"What do you mean, monsieur?"

"A man does what is right regardless of how he feels, even if he thinks others will laugh, even if it doesn't make him happy. Even if it causes him pain or embarrassment. A boy just does what he wants when he wants, and doesn't care if he hurts others who count on him. It seems that your mother and aunts work very hard and could use a man's help around the house. My advice is for you to figure if you are strong enough to be a man now. If you wait until you're all grown up to do it, it's not only much harder, but bad things can happen."

There was a long silence. Andre stared at his sheets in the pot, his shoulders tense as he weighed Mr. Trevelyan's words. "Like what bad things . . . monsieur?"

Mr. Trevelyan stood and drew a deep breath. "For me, it cost lives. People died." His voice rasped like jagged glass. "Don't make the mistake I did." He briefly touched Andre's shoulder as in comfort or warning and then left the courtyard, climbing the gallery stairs to his room and disappearing inside.

Nobody said a word. Nobody moved. We were all shocked, especially Andre. He stared at the door to Mr. Trevelyan's room for a long time. Then he began washing again, quietly.

Nothing I said seemed to reach my son, but in moments this stranger had gone right to Andre's heart. Mr. Trevelyan had entered my home, disturbing everything, and though his dangerous air grew darker, somehow he'd touched my heart as well.

Mr. Trevelyan didn't appear for breakfast or dinner, and his absence weighed more heavily than his presence. I couldn't stop thinking about him or his conversation with my son. Tensions that had taken root last night seemed to have grown during the day. Mr. Fitz and Mr. Gallier continued their discussion about plays, but on a less amiable note. I began to wonder if they were truly arguing over which play to perform or if the point was which of them would star opposite Miss Vengle, as both of them seemed to be vying for her attention.

After dinner, I decided to take a tray to Mr. Trevelyan's room and apologize. I stood before his door, gathering the courage to knock, which was ridiculous—never before had butterflies plagued me over so simple a task. I'd knocked on men's doors countless times without a thought to the intimacy that now filled my mind. Frustration made my rap on the door louder and more insistent than I meant.

Mr. Trevelyan opened his door quickly, appearing much the same way he had in the courtyard with Andre. Only this time his shirt was buttoned halfway up.

"You've missed the meals today. I thought you might be hungry."

He studied my face for an uncomfortable moment before taking the tray. "Thank you."

"You're welcome. Are you ill?"

"No. Just . . . just writing."

"I disturbed you, then. I'll speak to you another time," I said, stepping back.

"No, now is fine. I need a respite." He moved and my gaze scanned the room, but I saw no evidence that he'd been busy writing. His desk was clear, no papers were about, and the only thing mussed was his bed. I snatched my gaze away only to meet his querying one.

"What did you want to speak to me about?" He'd set the tray on his desk, then crossed his arms and leaned back against his bedpost, comfortably watching me examine his room. His shirt gaped, revealing the hard planes of his chest and a glimpse of dark hair.

I swallowed hard. "About the telegram." I could hear Mr. Fitz and Miss Vengle coming up the stairs, and I didn't want to be caught in Mr. Trevelyan's doorway. Taking a step into his room, I pulled the door closed.

Mr. Trevelyan raised his brows, but didn't move from his stance by the bed, which almost seemed like a dark invitation. My mouth went dry.

"This is difficult to say, but last evening, just before you left your room for dinner, Andre said he saw a man in the corridor on the family's floor, eavesdropping on my conversation with Ginette. Rushing down the stairs to investigate, I met Mignon coming up the stairs. Then you exited your room. After you left with Mignon, I peeked in all of the boarders' rooms to see if anyone else was about. I found no one. But when I opened your door, I saw your suit lying rumpled. Though I shouldn't have, I moved inside to straighten it, then realized I was intruding and left. I must have dropped the telegram then."

Mr. Trevelyan walked toward me; his piercing gaze now sparked fire. "Did your son say he saw me?"

I backed up a step and hit the door, my palms damp, my pulse racing. His eyes widened when I did and he stopped, holding his hands up. "I didn't mean to frighten you, but I know without a doubt your son could not have seen me. I was in my room."

"The hall shadows were too dark. He couldn't identify who it was, but he thought the man had dark hair and wore a gray suit."

His hands fisted, and he stepped closer. "You don't believe me, do you?"

"I don't have an answer. You wouldn't have had time to make it to your room, change suits, then meet

Mignon and me on the landing. So I don't necessarily think it was you, but everyone else was downstairs."

"And nobody had on a gray suit. Could it have been someone else? Someone you didn't know was in your home?"

I shivered at the thought. "It's possible."

"Mrs. Boucheron, I suggest you make a habit of locking your doors."

"We do every night."

He caught my hand in his, his touch gentle but firm, and far too welcome. A hot tingle raced up my arm as the warmth and the strength of him seeped into me. "Not just at night. Lock them during the day as well. The telegram I read said you were in danger. What did it mean? Who was it from?"

"I don't know any details yet," I said, pulling my fingers from his grasp. "But I do know it said to trust no one." I opened the door to leave, but he planted his hand on it, closing it, trapping me. For a long moment, I stood looking into his eyes, my heart beating as if I were running.

"You can trust me," he said, his voice low, and as deeply hypnotic as his gaze.

"You're a stranger," I whispered.

"Am I? Somehow, since the moment we met that word hasn't fit between us, Mrs. Boucheron. I think you feel the same attraction that I do." He leaned in closer, and I drew an expectant breath.

He smiled slowly, then surprisingly stepped away.

"Thank you for the dinner and for the apology. They are both appreciated."

"You're . . . welcome," I said, managing to quit the room, though the very foundations of my life seemed to be shaken.

Mr. Trevelyan was right. I didn't think of him as a stranger. I should. I had to.

≺ *5* ≻

"Jean Claude's letters have to be somewhere," I told Mignon and Ginette as we opened the dormer windows. Sunshine streamed into the attic, revealing an entire floor filled with baggage, from useless antiquities taking up space to precious treasures, like the old six-legged rocking chair I'd placed by the window yesterday to sit in while searching through boxes.

The Swedish-made chair had been my mother's favorite, and my father had stored it up here after her death. Perhaps it was time to bring it back downstairs and let other memories fill the worn seat.

I still had not heard from Mr. Goodson—no responding telegraph to my demand on Monday for more information about the danger I might be in, no letters in the post. Short of making a trip to Baton Rouge, there was little that I could do. At this point, I thought it prudent to stay close to home and keep a wary eye on my boarders.

Four days had passed, and I felt as if I was still against the door in Mr. Trevelyan's room with him leaning toward me, despite my careful maneuvering to avoid any intimate conversations or situations with him. I kept trying to act as if he was a stranger, and he wasn't cooperating. Whenever I turned around, I found him watching me, smiling with a knowing look in his eyes, as if he expected me to act on the attraction his gaze kept inflamed.

"Are you sure the letters are in a blue box?" Ginette asked.

"Positive, but just in case I'm wrong, we'll check all of the boxes."

"All?" Ginette groaned as she turned in a circle. She seemed to grow more fatigued as the week passed. "Why, we haven't cleaned up here since—"

"It was over two years ago." Mignon plopped a feathery hat on her head, then sneezed at the dust that showered down. "And I wore this hat the whole time. It was just before I turned fifteen, and I was sure we'd find a trunk full of forgotten treasure. All of our money woes would have been solved and I could then have the biggest birthday ball ever."

I bit my lip, wincing. "Nonnie, I wish that we could have—"

"Oh, foo, Juliet. I have long since realized other things in life are more important to me. Enough about the past." She pointed to a stack of trunks near the window. "However are we to search those?"

I frowned. "I don't remember the trunks being stacked like that yesterday. Has Papa John been up here cleaning?"

Mignon shrugged.

Ginette shook her head. "Well, before I become too tired, I say we get started and have Papa John move the trunks later. Where did you leave off, Juliet?"

"I only had time to search through the boxes by the door here. Nonnie and I can do this if you need to go rest a little."

"I have already rested. I spent the morning in the sitting room. I only worked a few minutes on my embroidery before I set it aside and fell asleep. At the rate I am going with my tapestry, I will be eighty before I finish it," Ginette said with a sigh.

Mignon laughed. "Sometimes it seems as if we will all be eighty before we finish all of the chores that need doing."

"If we keep talking, we will still be cleaning this attic at eighty." I picked up a large box and carried it over to the rocking chair by the window, then I heard the sounds of music coming from the courtyard. Curious, I set the box in the chair and turned to the window. Andre and Mr. Trevelyan were sitting by the fountain, sunlight gleaming off their dark heads, which were bent close together. It appeared Mr. Trevelyan was showing Andre how to play the harmonica. A smile tugged at my lips.

"What is it?" Ginette came to the window.

"It looks as if Andre is learning a new instrument." I moved over, making room for Ginette, bumping the rocker when I did. Suddenly a deep chill stabbed through me and a force pressed me against the window. I grasped the windowsill.

"Watch out!" Mignon shouted.

Whirling around, I saw the stack of trunks falling toward Ginette and me. I pushed her to the side and jerked away from the window as a heavy trunk crashed down on top of the rocking chair, splintering its wooden arms and crushing the box I had set there.

"*Mon Dieu,*" Ginette gasped.

My knees shaky, I stared at the chair, speechless, amazed by how narrowly I had escaped severe injury, if not death. I drew several deep breaths, forcing a calmness I did not feel to my voice. "Are you all right, Ginny?"

"*Oui,*" she whispered, staring at the trunk.

The thunder of feet coming up the stairs shook me from my frozen state, and Mr. Trevelyan and Andre burst into the room.

"What is it? What happened?" Mr. Trevelyan demanded, slightly breathless from running up four stories.

"A trunk fell from the stack," Mignon said.

Mr. Trevelyan bent down and studied the broken chair. After a minute he lifted the trunk off, pushing back the stack it had tumbled from with his shoulder to keep the other trunks from falling, too.

"Who piled them so dangerously high and uneven to begin with?" Fury roughened his voice. He set the first trunk down with a thud and then separated the rest of the trunks, placing them around the room. Strength and anger poured from the tense set of his straining muscles and clenched jaw, showing me a deeper side to his dangerous edge. But this was a comforting side, as was his outrage for my safety. Still my heart pounded harder as he marched toward me, for the passion in his gaze tied a knot of anticipation in my stomach.

"Well?" he demanded. He stood inches from me, close enough for me to feel the heat of his body, a heat that seemed to double in seconds. "Who?" he asked again, grasping my shoulders. His hands heated my chilled skin and his concern warmed my heart, easing my shock.

"I don't know, I don't remember seeing the trunks stacked like that yesterday." I shivered. "I was about to sit in the chair. If I hadn't heard your harmonica, I would have been sitting there when the trunk fell." *And if something hadn't pushed me toward the window, my legs would have been hit.*

His piercing gaze searched mine; then after a long and tense moment, he released me and turned away. "You need to be more careful," he said harshly. "I don't think this was an accident."

"What do you mean, Monsieur Trevelyan?" I bent down, examining the rocking chair.

"The back legs are splintered now, but look here and here." He pointed at two smooth cuts in the wood. "It was meant to collapse backward into the trunks, and they were piled to cause serious harm."

My blood turned cold, making me shiver.

"*Mère?*" Andre's voice called for reassurance.

"I am all right," I told him.

"I am *not* all right," Ginette declared, her dark eyes angry and her cheeks flushed. "There is something happening to our home, Juliet. I feel it. Something evil!"

"Ginette's right," Mignon said, her eyes tearing. "Just before the trunk fell, I saw the shadow of a man appear behind you, Juliet. I blinked, disbelieving it, and the shadow disappeared. Then the trunk fell." She backed up several steps. "It was a ghost; it had to be."

"We have a murderous ghost!" Andre turned white.

"No," Mr. Trevelyan said firmly. "Ghosts don't set traps."

"Monsieur Trevelyan is right. There are no ghosts."

"How can you be so sure?" Mignon asked, surprising me by her challenge.

I opened my mouth to assure her, but the words wouldn't come. *What about the incident at Blindman's Curve and the deep chill that had struck me?* For the first time in my life, I didn't have a practical answer.

The rest of the day resonated with tension, making me thankful for Mr. Davis's invitation to the carnival.

During an early dinner, we learned everyone planned to attend the affair, and Andre, finally showing some enthusiasm, invited Mr. Trevelyan to ride with us. Everyone strained to put on a happy face, determined to leave what had happened in the attic behind and to enjoy the carnival.

One jostle of the carriage sank my week-long efforts to think of Mr. Trevelyan as a stranger. His hard thigh pressed against mine, and the warm muscles of his arm constantly brushed my shoulder, rendering my clothing and the presence of my family little protection against his seductive spell. Right or wrong, I wanted to lean into him more to feel the things he awakened inside me. His ungloved hands rested in his lap and were more interesting than the passing scenery of magnolia trees and sprawling homes along the river. Though large and capable, his hands bespoke a man who enjoyed touching. The edge of my skirt lay against his leg and his fingers absently brushed the dark blue silk as he conversed with Andre, telling him about a traveling adventure. I felt as if he were touching me, softly, secretly.

"By stowing away on our father's ship, my brother and I got a full tour of the coast of South America before our mother got her hands on us back in port. Though she had us on our knees for a week in penance, sore knees were well worth the price."

"I would love to stow away on a real ship and see the world," Andre said with enthusiasm.

Mr. Trevelyan quickly curtailed Andre's notions. "My brother and I had special circumstances. My father not only owned the ship, but was captaining it as well, so we knew we were safe. I've heard stories of young boys being sold for slaves when caught as stowaways."

"Truly?" Andre asked, horrified.

"Adventure is like a two-edged sword. The very next year, the adventure we took was the last one we made together."

"What did you do, monsieur?" Andre pressed, completely captivated by Mr. Trevelyan's words.

"We went on a treasure hunt. Both Benedict and I were sure an island in the bay concealed buried treasure. We'd seen the lights at night from our manor's tower, our raft was ready, and not even the heavy fog could stop us. Luckily, my brother left a note of our plans with Katherine, our sister, so she wouldn't worry. I thought the note unnecessary, for I was sure we would find the treasure and return home before she awoke."

"Real pirate treasure? Like gold?" Mignon asked, thrilled.

Mr. Trevelyan nodded. "Exactly. We pushed from the shore with poles until the water became too deep. Then we used oars. The fog was so thick, Benedict and I could barely see each other across the raft. We argued. My brother wanted to turn back, and I wanted to keep going after the treasure. Suddenly a ship appeared out of the fog and smashed right through our raft. We floated until we were rescued, because my brother managed to lash us to a barrel. I ended up with a lung ailment that took months to recover from, and my brother bore the brunt of the criticism for our folly." His voice roughened. "It changed everything in our lives." Then he shook his head, as if he'd spoken too long.

"Things we experience when we are young can affect us forever," Ginette said softly, her eyes shadowed with what appeared to be pain. I wondered if she referred to the war, the years of it and how its aftermath had stolen our youth.

Andre frowned. The idea that a childhood jaunt could have long-lasting consequences did not sit well with him. Again, in just a few words, Mr. Trevelyan seemed to convey what I had been trying to get Andre to understand for years.

"My apologies. I did not mean to put a damper on the evening. Do you know I have never been to a carnival?"

"Never?" Andre sounded as surprised as I was. With Mardi Gras celebrated every year, carnivals were the flavorful spice of New Orleans's charm. A life without that taste seemed unimaginable.

"Then you are in for a treat," I said.

"I hope so," he murmured, his voice vibrating over my senses and heating my cheeks.

"You must let us show you all of the fun things to

do, right, *Mère*?" Andre said, dispelling my hopes of escaping from Mr. Trevelyan's seductive presence.

Still, I tried to save myself. "I'm sure Mr. Trevelyan would—"

"Like nothing better than to have your company for the evening."

"Perfect," Mignon said. "Ginette can chaperone me with Monsieur Davis, and Andre can accompany you and Monsieur Trevelyan."

I shot Mignon an admonishing look. She knew very well Andre would likely run from one attraction to another so quickly that Mr. Trevelyan and I would often be alone. But there was little that I could say to change the arrangements without seeming contrary.

The music coming from Jackson Square reached us before the sights and smells did. We exited the carriage near St. Louis Cathedral. Mignon's dress caught on the carriage door, and Mr. Trevelyan helped free her.

I gazed over the square, waiting for them. The cool breeze off the Mississippi softly brushed my face as the passion of the celebration captured my blood. Musicians belted out a lively tune, garish clowns mingled with the crowd, and men and women shouted for the revelers to sample their wares or play their games.

"I was beginning to think you'd forgotten," Mr. Davis said, quickly approaching. He interjected himself between Mignon and Mr. Trevelyan, who'd just joined the rest of us. "I am so pleased that you came," Mr. Davis said, taking Mignon's hand.

She slipped her hand from his, but smiled. "It was a wonderful idea."

I introduced Mr. Davis and Mr. Trevelyan.

"Where did you say you were from, and your business?" Mr. Davis asked Mr. Trevelyan.

"I didn't," Mr. Trevelyan replied. "Nice evening, isn't it?"

Mr. Davis sighed, inching his spectacles further down his nose. "A hot evening, but nice. And nicer still now that the DePerri beauties are here."

I hid a smile. Mr. Trevelyan had politely curbed Mr. Davis's nosiness in one exchange, whereas Mignon, Ginette, and I hadn't been able to in two months. I wondered how effective Mr. Trevelyan would be in curtailing Mr. Latour's persistence in trying to buy *La Belle*.

"On that we can agree," Mr. Trevelyan said.

"*Mère*, I must try and win that bag of candy," Andre said, pointing to a nearby booth for tossing rings.

"Excellent idea," Mr. Davis said. "Meanwhile, I'll show Miss DePerri some jewelry. The necklaces are so colorful. Several would go well with your cream gown." He held his arm out to Mignon.

"We'd love to see them," Ginette said, taking Mignon's hand in hers.

After a moment's hesitation, Mr. Davis apparently resigned himself to having a chaperone and offered my sisters each an arm. "It will be an honor to escort two lovely ladies tonight. There's a green necklace that will match your dress perfectly," he told Ginette.

Breathing a sigh of relief, I turned to find Andre had already dashed to the booth. Mr. Trevelyan narrowed his eyes at Mr. Davis's back. "A rather rude gentleman."

"Other than talking too much, he usually isn't. I think you made him jealous when you helped Mignon from the carriage. He's been calling on her."

"Does she return his interest?"

"No." I narrowed my gaze. "Why do you ask?"

"He doesn't seem to be the right sort of man for either of your sisters. Marriage to the wrong person can destroy lives."

He spoke with such conviction that I took a step back.

"You speak as if you've had a personal experience. Are you married?"

A muscle jerked in his jaw. "No. And I have never been, but I saw my brother's life ravaged by an arranged marriage."

I forced a smile, unable to hold his gaze as a pain hit my heart. "We had better catch up with my son."

Mr. Trevelyan caught my elbow. "Look at me, Mrs. Boucheron," he said softly.

I glanced up, and he slid his thumb under my chin to keep my gaze on him. "Your marriage was arranged, wasn't it?"

My stomach clenched, and my pulse sped. "*Oui.* His death in the war was tragic, but our marriage was fine. Being older, Jean Claude was patient and kind."

"How much older?"

I pulled back from him and started toward the booth where Andre stood clapping and happily shouting. Mr. Trevelyan edged too close to raw emotions I didn't want exposed.

He caught up to me. "I'm sorry," he said. "I had no right to probe into your personal life."

I sighed. Given the attraction between us, questions were inevitable. "It's not that," I said. "It's just that it doesn't really matter. My marriage gave me Andre, and I'll never regret that. Jean Claude was fifty."

I thought I heard Mr. Trevelyan curse under his breath, but I chose to ignore it, for I looked up to see Mrs. Gallier and Mr. Fitz approaching us.

"Excellent carnival, isn't it?" Mr. Fitz held up a fried confection. "I have never tasted food as good as the fare in New Orleans, and that includes your wonderful meals, Mrs. Boucheron."

"Thank you, Mr. Fitz."

Mrs. Gallier, who'd been scanning the crowd, turned and smiled. "We're just looking for Miss Vengle and Mr. Gallier. We seemed to have lost them in the crowd."

"We haven't seen them," Mr. Trevelyan said, setting his warm hand to my back. "We've just arrived."

"Then don't let us keep you. You know, Mr. Fitz, they may have stopped back there. A woman had some wonderful shawls for sale."

Nodding their good-byes, Mr. Fitz led Mrs. Gallier away.

Mr. Trevelyan's arm stiffened, and he turned me firmly toward the booth where my son stood. "Wait with Andre. I'll be back in a moment," he said, and left before I could question him.

I continued on to my son, but glanced back to see Mr. Trevelyan disappear behind a booth. The incident unsettled me. Reaching Andre, I found he wasn't alone. Phillipe Doucet and Will Hayes stood with him, and not far away was Letitia Hayes. I kept back from the boys, letting Andre have a few minutes with his friends.

Letitia, elegantly turned out in a rich black lace and burgundy dress, kept glaring at me. After a short time, she marched my way.

"Nice to see you again, Letitia," I said as she neared.

High color flagged her cheeks. "I have never been more embarrassed in my life. Don't you dare speak to me in public again! How dare you infer to Mrs. Drysdale and Mrs. Pitts my dress was as old as the ones you wear. They're presidents of the Royal Fashion Society, no less. That dress I had on was brand new, and I'll never be able to wear it out again."

Her anger over so trivial a matter surprised me. Had I ever been as caught up in fashion as she was? Every dress I owned had been bought before the war. Several people nearby turned to look at us. "You're right, Letitia. You do a good enough job embarrassing yourself."

"Mrs. Boucheron, forgive me for being delayed. The

evening was quite empty without you by my side," Mr. Trevelyan said seductively, placing his hand against my back again as he stepped close to my side.

Letitia's eyes widened as she looked at him, clearly wondering why so sophisticated and richly dressed a man would have any interest in me.

"Monsieur Trevelyan, this is Madam Hayes, an old acquaintance of mine."

"Madam Hayes." Mr. Trevelyan nodded. "I'm sure you won't mind if I steal Mrs. Boucheron away. We've had so little time together that I am greedy for every moment."

"Of course," Letitia murmured.

Mr. Trevelyan swung me around and brought me to the edge of the crowd, acting like a besotted, attentive lover.

"You're incorrigible," I said, smiling at him.

"What I am is incensed. That woman is a witch."

"She used to be my friend. We grew up together."

"There's an old saying: 'With friends like that—' "

" 'You don't need any enemies,' " I said.

He smiled. "Besides, I didn't lie. The evening was empty without you."

"Where did you go?"

He shrugged. "I thought I saw someone I knew. I was mistaken." He glanced toward Andre, who now stood alone, about to take his turn at the ring toss. "Let's go win some confections. I have a sudden craving for something sweet."

Looking up, I discovered that Mr. Trevelyan had his gaze centered on my mouth. If I'd been capable of moving, I think I would have bridged the heated gap between him and kissed him. Instead, Andre called to us, and Mr. Trevelyan led me to my son. Regaining my sanity, I put my best effort into making the evening as much fun as I could. Mr. Trevelyan showed Andre some pointers on how to toss the rings, and they both won bags of sweets. We saw bears dance, had our fortunes told, watched magic tricks, and then saw a sleek black panther leap through a circle of fire. Mr. Trevelyan bought Andre and himself fur hats with tails, which I teasingly banned, declaring that I'd have no critters in my home. We didn't encounter Mignon and Ginette with Mr. Davis, but I didn't worry. There were so many people jostling about the square that they could have been standing next to me and I wouldn't have known it.

The sun had dipped below the horizon and torches lit the square. The spires of St. Louis Cathedral cut a black silhouette against the dark blue sky. The moon, full and bright, hung low, just tempting a dreamer to reach out and grasp it. I didn't.

Andre ran to the next booth to watch a group of clowns juggling. Across the brick walkway, a trio of stringed musicians played a lilting waltz.

"It is your turn for a treat, and you must have that," Mr. Trevelyan said, snatching my attention. He pointed at a beautiful silver shawl that shimmered in the moonlight.

"No. But thank you. That is much too fancy and expensive. If you must buy me something, I'll take a hat to match Andre and yours," I said teasingly.

He caught a loose tress of my hair and sifted it between his fingers. "Midnight silk. It would be a crime to cover it up." Before I could catch my breath, he sauntered over to the woman selling the shawls and bought the silver one without even haggling over the price. Returning, he slipped it around me. The silken shawl made my plain blue dress feel like a ball gown. We were on the edge of the square, by the rush of the river, just within the flickering torchlight with few others around.

"Dare to dance with me a moment, here in the moonlight amidst the magic of the music and the night." His voice was low and seductive.

He had a way with words that could sweep a woman off her feet. I nodded and he took me in his arms and swung me gently around. He danced with assured elegance and grace, deftly moving me in a slow waltz. His black suit and embroidered vest, along with the flickering lights, made me feel as if I were once again at a masquerade ball, swirling with excitement, with life anew and happiness within my fingertips. I hadn't danced in over a decade, and as I gazed into Mr. Trevelyan's smoldering eyes, I knew I'd never known real desire before. He drew me closer to him, and a dark passion wrapped around me, making me want to touch him, to experience all those forbidden things kept hidden in the night.

"Mrs. Boucheron," he whispered, leaning toward me, his sensual mouth parting. I knew he would kiss me, that anyone strolling into the shadows would see, but I couldn't resist the lure of desire.

Just before his lips touched mine, just as his warm breath mingled with my expectant one, a scream splintered the night.

"Juliet!"

❧ *6* ❧

"That's Mignon," I cried, turning toward the river, from where the sound had come.

"Stay here," Mr. Trevelyan said, pushing me back and rushing toward the yawning black water ahead.

"No." I ran after him. To the right, in the dark shadows beneath the trees, I heard weeping and the wild thrashing of foliage.

"Mignon!" Ginette also ran toward the river. Ahead of us, she didn't see Mr. Trevelyan and me until I called to her.

"Juliet! *Mon Dieu.*" Ginette stumbled and sank to her knees.

"What happened?" I said, turning to her. Mr. Trevelyan kept going.

She pointed to where Mr. Trevelyan was headed. "Mignon and Mr. Davis were standing just there, and this man came out and attacked them. He knocked Mr. Davis down and pulled Mignon toward the river."

I helped her up. "Where's Mr. Davis?"

"He got up and raced after the man, threatening to kill him if he didn't release Mignon."

"I've got her!" Mr. Davis shouted, running up from the river with Mignon cradled in his arms. Her cream dress was wet, muddied, and torn on one shoulder. Her hair hung unbound and was tangled with twigs.

Leaving Ginette, I rushed to meet the two. Mignon wept against his shoulder. "Is she hurt?"

"I don't think so. Just shaken and wet. The bastard tried to put her into a canoe and take her. God, I'm so sorry. He took me by surprise."

I touched Mignon's shoulder and she turned to me. "She's safe now and that's all that matters. Let me hold her," I said, sitting on the ground. After a moment, Mr. Davis lowered her next to me. I wrapped my arms around her. Ginette joined us, putting her arm around us both.

"Nonnie, please. You must tell me if you're hurt," I said.

She calmed herself, taking deep breaths. "My . . . my . . . face. He hit me . . . when . . . I fought him."

I shuddered. "Thank God Mr. Davis stopped him."

The distant howl of a man in pain cut through the night.

"Where's Monsieur Trevelyan?" My heart hammered as I jerked my head around, desperately hoping to see him appear.

"He went into the woods?" Sounding worried, Mr. Davis spun around, looking too. "You three go back to the square where you'll be safe. I'll go look for him."

"Andre!" I remembered, urging Mignon to her feet with Ginette's help. "I left him with the clowns. We must hurry." With so much noise at the carnival, no one had realized what had happened. If Mr. Trevelyan hadn't pulled me closer to the river to dance, I wouldn't have heard Mignon scream.

Glancing back to Mr. Davis, I whispered a prayer that Mr. Trevelyan wasn't hurt.

We found Andre, still laughing with the crowd and cheering the clowns' juggling feats. By the time we pulled him to the side and found Mignon a crate to sit on, Mr. Davis and Mr. Trevelyan returned. Both men wore grim expressions. Mr. Trevelyan was muddy and wet.

I went to him. "*Dieu,* what happened?"

"I wrestled a man out of a boat and got an interesting confession before he escaped."

"What?"

"The scoundrel was hired to kidnap Mignon."

"How did he even know she would be here tonight?"

Mr. Davis cursed. "He either followed her or was told where to find her."

"He was told," Mr. Trevelyan said. "The man was hired less than thirty minutes ago, here at the carnival. He escaped before I could find out who hired him."

I grabbed his arm, locking my knees into place, determined to stand. I didn't know what evil was trying to harm my family, but I knew that I damn sure wasn't going to let it.

I wrote a letter to Mr. Goodson after I had everyone settled in bed. I demanded an explanation to his telegram and told him what had been happening in my home. I didn't know whom to trust. Everyone, Mr. Fitz, Mr. Gallier, Mrs. Gallier, and Miss Vengle, had been at the carnival. Mr. Trevelyan had been away from my side long enough to have hired a man to harm Mignon, and that bothered me. I didn't like questions and doubt, yet my life was filled with them. Even Mr. Davis could have had cause. How desperately did he want Mignon? What I didn't know was why. I didn't think the incident related to Mr. Latour's threat, but I couldn't rule that out completely. As I sealed the envelope, I heard the faint tones of music coming from outside.

Going to the French doors, I opened them wider, and the soft melody went from a whisper to the hush of a lullaby. Curious, I stepped onto the gallery, keeping to the shadows cast by the moon. The coolness of the night air rustling through the palmetto ferns and the sweet acacia brushed the tendrils fringing my face. It took a few moments for my eyes to adjust to the dimness, but my pulse already thrummed to what I knew I would see.

Across the courtyard, Mr. Trevelyan sat upon the

brick wall that overlooked the oak-strewn park. As usual, he turned my way, uncannily sensing my presence, strengthening the connection between us. I didn't think I would be able to sleep, as troubled as I was, and thought he might be suffering from the same. The doubts I'd had moments ago wavered as I relived the memory of dancing with him in the moonlight.

I wanted to go down the galley stairs and dance again. But to do so would be to succumb to the passions he awakened inside me with a single look, his brushing touch, or his softly spoken words. I had to go inside—yet I couldn't make my feet move. My need to gaze upon him burned stronger than any tenuous threads propriety still had on me tonight.

He was made for the shadows of the night. His dark hair gleamed in the moonlight, and his movements held a predatory grace akin to the black panther we'd watched at the carnival. I had the urge to reach out and stroke the sleek power I sensed in him as he slid off the wall and walked toward the house, looking up to where I stood in the shadows.

I could hear his silent plea, to join him, to finish that almost kiss. He stopped at the fountain where the statue of Saint Catherine of Siena beseeched the heavens for mercy with folded hands. I knew the words engraved in the stone at her feet: "Everything comes from love, all is ordained for the salvation of man, God does nothing without this goal in mind." Though I believed Saint Catherine meant well, life had taught me differently. Not all things came from love. The war hadn't. Betrayal didn't. What almost happened to Mignon tonight didn't.

I didn't know this man, and I couldn't go to him. I whirled about, ducking into my room, locking the French doors firmly behind me. For a long time I stood there, pressed against the cool doors until I heard the sound of him climbing the gallery stairs. I waited, straining to hear if he would be so scandalous as to climb the stairs to my room and knock upon my doors. I didn't draw an easy breath until his footsteps ended on the floor below.

Climbing into my bed, I stared into the darkness for a long time, trying to sort though the turmoil surrounding my family as well as the storm inside of me. I felt as if I had just drifted off when I awoke shivering, chilled to the bone. Thunder announced an approaching storm, and an icy chill filled my room. It was as cold as the cutting gust at Blindman's Curve, and the heavy sensation that had pressed on me then pressed forcefully upon me now, urging me from the bed. There seemed to be a shadow, blacker than the night there, fighting me. I wrenched back, striking blindly at it in the darkness around me. My fist hit nothing but air and tangled in the mosquito netting. I panicked, fought desperately to free myself, and jumped from the bed.

I heard no other sound but that of my harsh

breathing and approaching thunder. Lighting a lamp, I found myself alone, and knew I'd just wrestled with a ghost. There was no other practical explanation, for I knew I hadn't dreamed it. The lace curtains by my French doors rustled and my scalp tingled. I grabbed the poker from the fireplace, marching to the French doors, determined not to be afraid in my own home.

With the light behind me, I saw nothing but my reflection in the glass made black by the dark of the night. Just as I was about to turn away, a streak of lightning splintered the sky, silhouetting the shape of man staring at me from my balcony outside. He wore a western-style hat pulled low, obscuring his face completely, and he raised a wicked curved knife at me. I screamed, backing away and holding the poker like a weapon ready to strike.

The man disappeared just as the household erupted. I heard Mignon calling my name and a thunderous pounding of steps. Mr. Trevelyan burst into my room, followed by Mignon, then Ginette and Andre.

"What is it?" Mr. Trevelyan asked harshly.

"A man. Outside my French doors. He was staring at me. He had a knife."

Mr. Trevelyan ran to the door.

"*Mon Dieu,*" Mignon cried. Ginette crossed the room and wrapped her arms around me, shaking. I kept a firm hold on the poker with one hand and put my other around her, welcoming the comfort.

Swiftly unlocking the doors, Mr. Trevelyan stepped cautiously outside. He looked in both directions and then moved to the railing. "I don't see anyone. What did he look like?"

"I don't know. I didn't see his face. Just his shape."

"Then tell me that."

"He was tall, like you."

Mr. Trevelyan sent me a pointed look.

"I didn't say it *was* you. You're taller and broader across the shoulders than he was, but he was bulkier around the middle. He wore a hat, too."

"Good. We have bulky, not broad, and wearing a hat. Anything else? Did he try to open your door?"

"*Bon Dieu.* Isn't it enough that he was there and raised a knife at me!"

Mr. Trevelyan drew a deep breath. "Yes. Stay here and I'll take a look around the grounds."

"Don't go by yourself. Take Papa John."

Mr. Trevelyan shook his head. "He works hard enough as it is. I'll wake Mr. Fitz. Odd that neither he nor Mr. Gallier heard your scream—it was loud enough to wake the dead."

The search, which ended at daybreak, revealed nothing other than that Mignon had a bruised cheek, reminding everyone of last night's horror. I sent her and Ginette upstairs to press cool cloths to Mignon's face while Mama Louisa and I fixed breakfast. I also gave strict orders to Andre that he was to remain at home until I discovered who was terrorizing us. My son wasn't happy.

"We is doomed, Miz Julie," Mama Louisa said, pulling down a pot for gravy. "There's got to be a bad voodoo curse hanging over our head."

"Black magic has no power other than what your mind gives it," I told her firmly as I picked up an apron and tied it on. I refused to believe the cold dark shadow had anything to do with voodoo. Given the haunting ghost stories that flavored life in New Orleans, even my practical mind had accepted that there was a ghost in *La Belle*. But no ghost had shaken a knife at me, that had been a man.

I slammed a cast iron pot onto the woodstove, liking the heavy feel of the pan in my hand. It was a great deal more substantial than a poker, as if, I thought, I were David and could easily slay Goliath. I wished I could have hit the man last night with the pan. It angered me that he'd frightened me so.

Turning for the lard, I found Mama Louisa standing still, glaring at the pot before her, tears in her eyes. I'd been too curt. My nerves were frayed.

I went and hugged her. "Mama Louisa, I'll not believe in voodoo curses and the like. Now, let's set our minds to what has to be done and feed our boarders breakfast. It is a wonder they haven't left *La Belle*."

Sighing, Mama Louisa gathered the bowl of eggs. "Don't matter much if you believe or not, Miz Julie.

There's a grim reaper hiding in the attic, and ain't nobody can keep him out."

"Nonsense," I said, even as a shiver ran down my spine.

At breakfast, there was more interest in discussing the attack on Mignon than on eating. The boarders all seem shocked about it and about the man with the knife, but then, they were actors. I kept wondering the same question Mr. Trevelyan had raised. Why hadn't Mr. Gallier and Mr. Fitz come running when I'd screamed? The more I thought about it, both Mr. Fitz and Mr. Gallier were built like the man I'd seen, and I wondered if either of them owned a wide-brimmed western hat. I decided to investigate after breakfast.

I focused back on the discussion, and my agitation with Mr. Fitz grew with every word he spoke.

"There is nothing that Mignon could have done to prevent what happened last night and might still happen, if that is to be her fate. We're all puppets with no choice or control over our future." Mr. Fitz leaned back as if he'd just delivered God's word.

Mignon blanched as fear darkened her eyes.

"*Non,*" I blurted out, unable to accept that. "We choose."

"We don't choose tragedy. It chooses us," he said.

"You twist my words, Monsieur Fitz. We might not have control over what others do or over the forces of nature, but we can change the outcome of those things, by what we do before and after certain events. Our reactions determine our fate. It doesn't determine us."

"I agree with Mrs. Boucheron," Mr. Trevelyan added.

"I also, Mr. Fitz," Miss Vengle said. "By choosing to join the acting troupe, I escaped the untimely end the ravages of the war would have imposed on me."

"If I understand you correctly, dear," Mrs. Gallier said, "to change the course of one's life, all a person would have to do is to change their reactions to the people and the world around them, correct?"

"Correct," I said.

Mr. Fitz stood and tossed his napkin to the table, surprising me with his volatility. "You're all fools. Who among us would have chosen the ravages the war wrought? We have no individual choice, and it is folly to believe otherwise." His impassioned words echoed in the room as he left.

"I have to agree with Mr. Fitz," Ginette said quietly, speaking for the first time. "Our destinies are sealed and no matter how we will them to be different, we are all doomed to the lot life hands us, and not even love can save us."

"Ginette, surely you cannot believe in so tragic a future—" I gasped.

"Not necessarily tragic, but realistic," she said. From the shadows beneath her eyes, I could tell she'd slept as little as I did last night.

Just as breakfast finished, Mr. Davis arrived, upset and guilt-ridden by the attack on Mignon. He brought her a large bouquet of sweet-smelling pink tea roses, and actually spent his time listening to Mignon rather than talking about himself. After he left, I had a little time to investigate the boarders' rooms while they were out. Wielding a dust rag and beeswax for disguise, I went first to Mr. and Mrs. Gallier's room, polishing like a whirlwind, bringing a high shine to the armoire and desk. Then I peeked into the cabinet and drawers. Mrs. Gallier only had a few gowns, whereas Mr. Gallier had a multitude of suits—one of which was gray—but he had no western hat. I left incensed on Mrs. Gallier's behalf.

Continuing on to Mr. Fitz's room, I wondered if he lived in the room at all. There wasn't a crinkle in the bed coverings or any belongings in sight. The inside of the armoire was organized with military precision, every suit hung as neatly as if it had never been worn. A number of well-worn publications about the war filled one shelf, and that was it. No hat and nothing personal.

I stepped into Mr. Trevelyan's room, and dread filled me. Sitting on his desk was a western-style black leather hat. Could Mr. Trevelyan have disguised himself? Hunched down and worn a thick coat?

I dropped my rag and the tin of beeswax by the armoire, marched across the room, and snatched up the hat, outraged. When I did, papers under the hat went flying and slid beneath the bed.

Dieu! Setting the hat on the bed, I knelt, reaching for the papers. I could only get my fingers on one. As I held it up, I read it quickly.

Dearest Stephen,

I know you too well to believe the lies you told us to placate our concerns for you before you left us bereft. I'll not tolerate anything but the truth between us, no matter how difficult to face. How many of those who love you do you hurt with the guilt you carry? The living must forge ahead and leave those who've died, even tragically. . . .

The first page ended there, and though I knew I was utterly breaking the rules of propriety, I dived farther, reaching for the other paper. Under the bed to my waist, my chest flat on the floor, I caught the paper between my fingers.

The bedroom door opened, closed, and booted footsteps came to a halt somewhere in the vicinity of my derriere. I might as well have been naked in a tub. My scalp tingled and my leg muscles twitched as my mind shouted at me to scoot and run, or to crawl completely under the bed.

"Mrs. Boucheron?"

"Oui," I gulped, wondering if I should abandon his

letter under the bed. Then at least he might wonder if I had read it, but I wouldn't be caught with it in my hand.

"You make a rather interesting and very distracting sight. Are you stuck?" His hand outrageously brushed my left hip, then lingered exactly where it shouldn't.

"*Non*," I screeched, rearing up, banging my head against the wooden slats and biting my tongue.

"Whatever are you doing?"

"Having tea with the bed posts," I said, gritting my teeth as I scooted back.

I emerged to find myself face to face with him. He plucked the pages of his letter from my hand, his gaze unamused, his mouth grim.

"You have a hat," I cried.

"So?" His brows angled down, deepening his frown.

"The man last night wore a similar hat. I came to polish and found the hat!"

"Are you asking if I am despicable enough to threaten a woman with a knife, Mrs. Boucheron?"

He sounded so incensed that I felt utterly ridiculous for my suspicions. I exhaled. "*Non*. I don't know. I just saw the hat when I came into your room, and I grabbed it. The papers underneath flew off then, and—"

"And why don't we pretend this never happened."

He stood, extending a helping hand. I had no choice but to follow his lead and set my hand in his. Once I stood, his gaze dropped to my mouth and he stepped so close that his chest brushed mine, sending waves of fire to chase after my doubt and embarrassment. Sandalwood and spice grabbed at my senses, forcing them to clamor for more. The atmosphere in the room went from decidedly cold to overwhelmingly hot. Perspiration beaded my brow. When I backed to the door, he followed.

Reaching blindly, I found the doorknob and wrapped my hand around it. "Absolutely," I said. "This never happened."

But instead of twisting the knob to escape, my gaze settled on his lips. He groaned.

"And this didn't happen either," he whispered, lowering his mouth to mine. His lips brushed mine softly, as if savoring the exquisite feel of supple flesh, warm and welcoming. His tongue slid against my bottom lip and I opened to him, wanting to taste him and the dark pleasure he offered.

Lightning and magic bolted through me as his kiss went from whisper soft to a hard demand in a flash and his body pressed against mine, trapping me against the door. A hard thigh slid between my legs as his tongue delved deep, mating with mine in a sensual dance that set me afire inside. I groaned, arching my back, pressing my breasts deeper against the hardness of his chest as I wrapped my arms around his neck. I threaded my hands through the black silk of his hair and kissed him as deeply as he kissed me.

He moaned. His hands grabbed my hips, urging me closer to him until his arousal pushed intimately against my hip, then he slid his fingers up to brush the sides of my breasts, making every fiber of my being yearn for him. The overwhelming desire was almost more than I could resist.

"Please," I whispered as another searing kiss ended and he slid his hands closer to cupping my breasts. "I shouldn't be here." My breath came in quick, heavy gasps. My head spun, and my blood raced faster than my heart knew how to beat.

He exhaled deeply, his body trembling as much as mine, giving evidence of how he fought to control the dark fire consuming us both. "This is the only threat you face from me. I want you more than I want to breathe." He stepped slowly back.

My entire body burned to feel the hard, supple planes of his. My hands itched to explore, and I longed to taste a thousand kisses more. I had to leave or I would throw myself at him.

"This is far from over," he said softly. "It's just the beginning."

Twisting the knob, I bolted out of the room.

I ran into Mr. Gallier. His monocle went flying.

"What in the devil!"

"Oh, Monsieur Gallier, pardon me!" I backed up, spouting the first excuse that came to mind. "I've bread in the oven about to burn."

He sniffed the air. "Beeswax?"

"Mrs. Boucheron, you forgot your cleaning supplies." Mr. Trevelyan held up my rag and the beeswax tin.

"Thank you," I said, snatching them and hurrying downstairs, painfully aware of the gazes that followed me. Reaching the center hall, I drew deep breaths and looked for anything to do to keep me from thinking. I saw several letters on the marble table from Mrs. Gallier, waiting to be posted, and remembered that I'd put my letter to Mr. Goodson there this morning. It wasn't there now. Papa John was in the dining room, polishing the heavy wood mantel. "Did the post already go out today?"

"I believe it did, Miz Julie. Miz Vengle was talking to the postman earlier. The way they were laughing made me think they were well acquainted."

"*Merci*. Can I help you with the polishing?" I desperately needed to do something mundane, to regrasp my staid life.

"Not today. I'm feeling spry and the job is done. I'm heading to the attic now to see if I can't find those letters you were looking for. I'm still not believing the way those trunks fell."

"I'll go with you," I said, to escape seeing anyone. I had no idea what I was going to say to Mr. Trevelyan when I saw him, and having Mr. Gallier witness my flight from Mr. Trevelyan's room made my cheeks scorch.

"Are you all right, Miz Julie? You look as if you have a fever."

I shook my head. "It's just the heat."

"And the worst has yet to come," Papa John said.

I knew it down to the center of my soul.

I followed Papa John up the stairs and we started working our way through the attic. I kept looking for signs of the ghost, testing the air with my fingers, peering around objects for Jean Claude's letters. I found some blue boxes, but none of them held the letters. After searching through several trunks, I came to a gasping stop upon reaching a corner.

On the far side of the attic, near a neat stack of old papers, a cigar sat in the middle of a crumpled page of the *Picayune* newspaper. The newspaper was partially burned and had charred the edges of the large stack of papers nearby. It wasn't dusty or aged and was dated from two months earlier. Printed on it was an article about a radical political group.

Someone had been up to the attic. Someone who smoked a cigar and started a fire.

My stomach clenched, making me feel ill. The only boarder with cigars was Mr. Trevelyan. I told myself no, but doubt lingered. Then I forced my mind to Mr. Latour and his threat that he had other ways of getting what he wanted. A fire would have been one way to get me and my family out of *La Belle*. But why?

Years ago, just after Jean Claude and the gold disappeared, my home had been searched from top to bottom. Mr. Latour had led the search and had at least declared me innocent of being involved with Jean Claude's theft. I clung to the belief that Jean Claude wouldn't have abandoned me and Andre.

Slipping the cigar and what was left of the paper in my pocket, I felt as if I finally had a clue to help me discover who my enemy was.

I didn't have long to wait. An hour later, I noticed two men out on the street in front of the house. One man appeared to be photographing *La Belle,* his head tucked under a black cloth as he bent to look into the lens. The other man had a pad and alternated between writing on it and staring at *La Belle.*

I marched out of the house. "Gentlemen, I demand to know what you are doing."

The camera man peeped from his shroud, scowling. "Madam, please move to the side. You're disrupting the picture."

Moving quickly, I planted myself in front of the camera. "This is my home and there will be no photographs taken. Now state your business before I send for the authorities."

"There's no need to be unpleasant," the other gentleman said, dotting his sweaty brow with a handkerchief. "We're gathering the necessary information for the upcoming auction. We won't be but a minute more."

My body went numb. *"What* did you say?"

"The gentlemen have obviously made a mistake," Mr. Trevelyan said forcefully, as he stepped from the shadows of a nearby live oak and joined me, giving the men a hard look.

"Now, see here," the camera man bristled. "We have it on good authority from Monsieur Latour that this property will be up for auction shortly. We don't make mistakes."

"You have this time." Mr. Trevelyan's voice was deadly cold. "I suggest you leave immediately. Come back again and I'll take it as license to shoot."

The men blustered and huffed, but packed up their equipment and went down the street. Mr. Trevelyan didn't move a muscle until they were nearly out of sight.

"I could have sent them packing," I said, not ungrateful for his intervention, but feeling as if I were losing control of my life.

"I know. Unfortunately, I find myself unable to stand idle while you're being attacked on all sides. Do you know why someone would threaten your family and your home?"

"Not really." Yet I knew everything had to have some connection to Jean Claude.

Mr. Trevelyan's gaze turned cooler, and I missed the warmth of it. I had my doubts, and he could see that. I wanted to trust him, my heart cried out for me to, but there were too many dark shadows surrounding both of us.

"Who is Mr. Latour?" he finally asked.

"A former friend of my husband who has been trying to buy *La Belle* for the past two months. Since we won't sell, he's apparently trying to find a way to force the issue."

Mr. Trevelyan quirked his brow. "Mrs. Boucheron, do you have any friends?"

As I shook my head, I realized how alone I really was.

7

For the next few days the household settled into an uneasy routine with no "ghostly" events or trouble of any other kind. After the attack on Mignon, I wanted everyone close to home and did what investigation I could on my own. I went through all of Jean Claude's army papers that I kept in the study safe, looking for names or any information that might enlighten me to what danger Mr. Goodson found. And a discreet question or two slipped in at an unsuspecting moment to my boarders confirmed that neither Mr. Fitz or Mr. Gallier used cigars. Of course, that wasn't to say someone wasn't trying to frame Mr. Trevelyan by using one.

Nothing unusual happened, except that Mr. Trevelyan was strangely absent. He'd gone to town immediately after kicking the auction assessors off my property, didn't return until late, and had been gone from dawn to well into the night every day since. I found his behavior exceedingly frustrating. It was as if he'd kissed me and then I'd ceased to exist.

My family, Mr. Davis, and the boarders had gathered in the parlor after another Trevelyan-less dinner. Ginette was about to play the harp and sing when Mr. Trevelyan entered the room. Devastatingly handsome in a dark blue suit and an elegant shirt, he stole my breath in a heartbeat.

"Wherever have you been, Monsieur Trevelyan?" Mignon asked, getting up to greet him. "We've missed you."

Mr. Davis frowned at Mignon's enthusiasm. He'd been to call on her every day since the attack. I could tell his feelings for her were growing, but though grateful, Mignon's feelings for him hadn't changed.

"Attending to business." Mr. Trevelyan slid his gaze to me, and I saw cool doubt shadowing his eyes instead of heated desire. My smile faltered. He looked at Andre and held up a book. "I have a present for you, Andre."

"*Swiss Family Robinson?*" Excitement brightened Andre's face and he took the book reverently. "*Merci.*"

"You're welcome," Mr. Trevelyan said, his smile and his eyes warming.

"You're back just in time to hear Ginette play the harp. Come sit next to Juliet." Mignon led him to the empty seat beside me on the settee. Embarrassed, I shut my eyes and pulled the silver shawl he'd given me closer. Mignon's matchmaking had to stop. But I couldn't even begin to explain how welcome Mr. Trevelyan's warmth and presence was.

"You're in for a treat, Mr. Trevelyan," said Mr. Gallier. "We live to hear the blessing of Ginette's voice."

"We should have her sing as entertainment prior to the play. Wouldn't that be wonderful, Mr. Gallier?" Mrs. Gallier added, beaming at her idea.

"Not a good idea, darling." Mr. Gallier shook his head. "Miss DePerri would so enthrall our audience that our performance would be anticlimactic. Besides, the stage only corrupts angels, and Miss DePerri's purity should be preserved just as it is."

"The stage surely does not corrupt every woman, Mr. Gallier," Miss Vengle said, a sharp edge to her voice.

He smiled back at her. "There are exceptions to every rule, Miss Vengle, as you so often prove."

Mrs. Gallier stood, clearing her throat, peeved at Mr. Gallier. "I believe I will have to hear Miss DePerri play on another night. A headache is suddenly pressing upon me."

"Do you need me to come fix you a powder?" Mr. Gallier asked, apparently oblivious to his wife's anger.

"No, dear, I shall be fine. You stay and listen to Miss DePerri." She left the room.

Mr. Davis stood. "I need to be going as well. Mignon, would you see me out?"

"For just a moment. I can't miss hearing Ginette."

Mr. Davis looked as if he would object, but Mignon

didn't give him a chance. He had no choice but to follow her quickly from the room.

When Mignon returned, slightly flushed, Ginntte settled against her harp.

From the first brush of her delicate fingers over the strings, a hush fell over everyone. I'd heard people tell of mesmerists—men who took over the minds of their patients and wrought miracles—but Ginette's singing did more. She never failed to move her audience, making everyone yearn for love.

When she finished, she rested her head against her harp, drained from pouring her heart into the song.

"Thank you," Mr. Trevelyan said softly. "It would be irreverent to clap, but I must add a heartfelt brava."

"That was exquisite, Miss DePerri," Mr. Gallier said.

Ginette looked up, her face pale, her features drawn. "The pleasure was mine."

"I think I am going to retire on that perfect note and check on Mrs. Gallier," Mr. Gallier said. "Are you coming, Miss Vengle?"

Mr. Fitz stretched. "I think I'll retire, as well."

Miss Vengle waved her fingers at Mr. Gallier and Mr. Fitz. "Goodnight, gentlemen. I've a mind to hear more music."

"*Oui*," Ginette said. "I would love to hear someone else play. Andre?"

My son's cheeks flushed red and he shook his head. Though he was an excellent violin player, he lacked the confidence to play publicly unless he was purposely making a discordant racket. Then he could play for thousands.

"What about you, Monsieur Trevelyan? Do you play an instrument?" Ginette asked.

"Nothing nearly as astounding as you, but I can play a few tunes on the piano."

"Then will you treat us to one or two?"

"Certainly. I learned a number of fun sailing tunes on my trips abroad."

"Real sailor songs?" Andre asked, his eyes sparking with interest. "Can you teach them to me?"

"Aye, aye, mate. There is even a pirate ditty or two." Mr. Trevelyan moved to the piano, sat down, and ran his fingers over the keys. "The problem with these sailor songs is that they are not written down. The only way to learn them is by ear, and that is a very difficult thing to do."

"I can do that, monsieur. Let me show you." Andre quickly collected his violin from the corner of the room and went to the piano, where Mr. Trevelyan sat. "Play something and I will repeat it."

"If you are sure," Mr. Trevelyan replied.

Andre nodded.

A minute later, Mr. Trevelyan had my son copying a round of toe-tapping melodies without a care as to who listened. Mr. Trevelyan started out with a simple progression of notes that became more and more complicated, challenging Andre with each turn. I wondered what was it about Mr. Trevelyan that so easily bridged a gap I could not cross to my son.

Soon Mignon joined them on the harpsichord, while Ginette added a few notes with her harp, and Miss Vengle sang heartily. The evening spoke volumes about Mr. Trevelyan's enjoyment of life. I watched, relaxed, realizing that *La Belle* used to be filled with laughter and music all the time, but very little since the end of the war. I'd been too caught up in the tasks of the day, and over the years, had given little thought to the fun we all apparently craved.

Midnight had passed, and I still lay awake, troubled by Mr. Trevelyan's reserved behavior. Other than noting that I wore the shawl he'd purchased, he didn't make another personal comment or advance the entire evening. Lost in thought, I almost missed the creaking on the stairs. I sat straight up in the bed, my heart pounding at the sound of footsteps. I'd purposely left my door ajar and had the iron frying pan and poker nearby, but I hadn't truly expected there would be any intruder. For a moment I stayed frozen in fear, my gaze glued to the dark hallway outside my door. Another faint shuffle of steps bolted me into action.

I pulled on a silk robe over my cambric nightdress, snatched up the frying pan and the poker, and stole from my room, walking blindly down the corridor until my eyes adjusted to the light. I remembered that I did have a number of people in my home and any one of them might be awake. Before leaving the third floor, I quietly peeked into Ginette's, Mignon's, and Andre's rooms. They were all sleeping undisturbed.

Moving softly down the stairs, I went to the second floor, where the boarders slept. Their doors were all shut, with no light showing beneath. I assumed they were asleep as well, so I tiptoed down to the first floor, avoiding the creaking stair just before the landing.

The moment I stepped into the parlor, I felt a change in the air about me, as if a menace hovered nearby but remained hidden from view, like a hunting alligator beneath dark water. My palms dampened, and my mouth grew dry. I tightened my grip on the pan and the poker.

Nothing stirred but the soft click of the grandfather clock's pendulum in the center hall. Finally, I had to have air and drew in a deep breath. The acrid scent of cigar smoke hung in the air. Then the stair creaked.

Someone was headed toward me; the parlor was only a few steps from the end of the stairs. Mama Louisa always said there wasn't anything that God and a good frying pan couldn't set straight, and I aimed to prove her right. Moving into the shadows by the door, I set the poker aside, lifted the pan, said a prayer, and waited.

I wasn't sure what I expected to see edge around the door into the parlor, but it wasn't the barrel of a pistol. Instantly I realized how foolish I'd been. I had just one chance to hit the intruder hard and then run, screaming for help. An arm and a dark head appeared and I brought the pan down hard. I must have made a slight noise, because a second before I hit him, the intruder lunged toward me. The pan hit his head with a sickening thud and I heard a groan of pain, but instead of falling to the ground, the man fell forward, plowing into me, and knocking the pan from my hand.

One minute I was upright and the next I was flat on my back, with a dead weight pinning me down. White lights danced before my eyes as I fought to breathe. I would have screamed, but I couldn't draw enough air to do more than croak.

I squirmed, trying to dislodge the man and get help before he regained consciousness. Tears of frustration bit at my eyes. I couldn't budge him. Then I felt his body turn from dead weight to hard muscle.

Surprisingly, I grew calmer, determined to face this threat with dignity.

"Don't move," a familiar deep voice threatened.

Now that he had spoken, I recognized the scent of fresh sandalwood and mint in the air.

Shock flooded through me until even my toes tingled from it. I was suddenly aware of every inch of the firm body covering mine. Desire instantly heated my blood.

"Monsieur Trevelyan," I whispered.

He rose up on his elbows and looked at me, letting me draw a much needed breath. My breasts pressed against the warm muscle of his chest and I breathed again, enjoying the feel of him and the scent of him. Moonlight streamed through the window and cast a shadow across his face, adding even more dangerous appeal to his rakish good looks.

"Mrs. Boucheron, what in God's name did you hit me with?" His voice rumbled deeply, sending out vibrations that reached the very core of my femininity.

"A pan, monsieur. Are you all right?"

"A pan?" He groaned. "What sort of pan?"

Had the man gone daft? "What difference does that make?"

He shifted, leaning more of his weight to the left and raising his head a little higher.

"Just tell me," he said as if his teeth were gritted together. His right leg shifted and slid shockingly between mine. He was too close, too real, and too male. I could barely think.

"An iron frying pan. Um, since you have recovered your senses sufficiently to ask questions, monsieur, could you get off me? There may be an intruder in my home."

He just stared down at me, and my pulse leaped as a strange anticipation filled me.

"I am sure he is gone. I found the front door open and a dark shadow disappearing into the park when I came down the stairs the first time. I checked the house and was just leaving the storage room at the top of the stairs when I heard someone else, and thought the man hadn't been alone. It must have been you."

"How did he get in?"

"As best as I can tell, he entered through an open window on the fourth floor. Everything else is locked. The question is, who left the window open?"

"I did. We've been cleaning the attic. I did not think anyone fool enough to climb that high. Monsieur, I am *sure* you can move now," I demanded, trying to muster some resistance against the sensations growing inside me.

"I might, madam, if you will tell me why you are running around the house felling your boarders with a frying pan." He sounded miffed, which fueled my own irritation.

"My intent, monsieur, was to fell an *intruder*. If you had not been skulking around my house with a pistol, you would not have met up with my frying pan."

"Have you no sense, woman?"

"It worked, did it not? I knocked you out."

"Momentarily, but exactly where are you now, and where am I?" As if to emphasize his point, his hard arousal pressed intimately against my femininity, spreading a fire in my loins. "Don't you realize what an unscrupulous man might do if he found himself in a situation like this?" He stared down at me, burning me with the intensity of his gaze.

"Monsieur Trevelyan, I see no point in discussing the matter since you are not an unscrupulous man."

"You don't realize the danger you put yourself in." He shut his eyes as if pained. "You should have knocked on my door, anyone's door, rather than come downstairs alone. Given the right circumstances and enough desperation, any man is capable of becoming unscrupulous. You are beautiful, desirable, and if a man found himself . . ."

My eyes were riveted to the shadowed planes of his face, the full curve of his lip, then to his eyes.

"A man might . . . take liberties that he had no right to take," he said, almost whispering the last. "I warned you."

His gaze dropped to my mouth and his head dipped toward me, bringing his lips so close to mine that the heat radiating from him warmed my skin, making me tingle where his breath brushed my face. Even though I barely knew this man, I desired him like no other man before. My mind might carry doubts regarding him, but my body clamored for him. Something about him had slid beneath my guard the moment he'd spoken to me from the shadows of the live oaks. I had gone years wanting nothing, wanting no one, and in a mere breath of time he'd changed that to wanting everything . . . from him.

My hands gripped his shoulders to push him back, to save myself from this sudden, overwhelming temptation. Instead, I dug my fingers into the soft linen of his shirt, urging him closer, ready to give him everything.

"Monsieur Trevelyan, you must—"

"I must . . ." he whispered softly, then crushed my

mouth with his. His lips were warm and firm and I opened to his demand. He groaned deeply, pressing his arousal hard enough to caress me intimately though the soft cotton of my gown. His tongue slid enticingly against mine, making me moan from the heated caresses. Fiery pleasure sprang to life, rushing hot desire to every part of me. I met his kiss with fervor. He rolled to his back, bringing me with him so that I lay on top. His hands burned a trail down my back and up under my gown to caress my bare skin, and rhythmically pressed me even deeper against his demanding arousal.

As he groaned deep in his throat, his hands raced up my sides beneath my gown. I arched back, giving him access to my breasts. He slid his hands to cup them, brushing his thumbs over the sensitive tips, sending sharp bursts of pleasure deep inside me. The tension coiled to a feverish point that coalesced at the very place where his arousal insistently rubbed. I slid my hands into his hair and pressed my mouth to his in pure ecstasy.

My fingers slid into warm fluid. Lifting my hand, I saw blood. *"Mon Dieu,"* I cried, rolling off him.

He groaned. "Come back here."

"You're bleeding!"

"Yes, but I'm dying somewhere else."

I scrambled to my knees, peering down at him. I couldn't see the wound, for his hair was too dark, but I could tell generally where he was hurt. I gathered the hem of my robe and pressed it to his head. He groaned.

What sort of man practically made love to a woman while wounded? An utterly senseless man, my mind shouted. *A passionate man,* my heart whispered softly.

When a warm dampness seeped through the silk to my fingers, I grew worried. "Stay here. I will get help and send for the doctor."

"No." He grabbed my arm, his grip reassuringly strong. "I'm fine. I know what to do."

"But . . ."

"I studied medicine for a while. Believe me, it is not serious and I will be fine, but you will not fare as well. Human nature being what it is, the blow to your reputation would be worse than the little bump you've given me." Taking the bunched cloth of my robe hem from me, he pressed it harder to his head and sat up.

I stood, shrugging the rest of my robe from my shoulders so he could use it as a compress.

He wobbled when he sat up, and I caught his arm to help steady him.

"Not as steady as I thought I was," he muttered. "Your passion weakened me."

"Be serious. This isn't a joking matter. I've hurt you."

"Believe me, this bump is a lot less painful than sleeping in the room beneath yours every night, imagining you in bed above me, hearing you move about your room late into the night. Now *that* is painful."

"You're rambling nonsense. Perhaps you are hurt worse than you think. Do you feel faint? Do you need a drink?"

"No. I have sworn off liquor. Once I make it to my room, though, I may trouble you for a basin of water."

"I'll bring water plus bandages to put on the cut, and some salve, too. It will soothe the skin and help with healing."

"I'll tend to the wound myself. If you were seen in my room in the middle of the night, it would be disastrous for you."

"Nonsense. I am responsible for the gash, and I'll not rest until the wound is examined. If you won't let me help, then I will awake Papa John and send for the doctor."

Despite the dim light, I could see his gaze rake over me, rekindling the heat that consumed us, pulling the air from me.

"I'll apologize if I must, but I'm not sorry for touching you," he whispered.

"Nor am I," I said, my mouth so dry I could barely speak.

The desire I heard in his voice and the need I felt deep inside of me stayed with me as I helped him collect his pistol and walked him to his room. Then I hurried to my room, donned a thick robe, and got healing salve, bandages, and water. The moment I left my room, my pulse raced. I knew without a doubt that I was stepping beyond the safe boundaries surrounding my life.

He'd left his door ajar. Near the end of his unmade bed, he sat on a wooden footstool before a beveled mirror, trying to see his injury. When he saw me he stopped, watching my movements in the mirror. I set the basin of water, salve, and bandages on the counterpane, trying to ignore the tension between us, but it was impossible. He held my ivory robe and was softly brushing his thumb over its silken threads, making my palms damp and sending another wave of delicious heat thrumming though my body. I closed his bedroom door.

While I'd donned clothes, he'd shed them. He wore only his pants and had a towel draped across his broad shoulders. He seemed too muscular for anything as civilized as a suit and waistcoat. Black hair grew across his chest and tapered downward to the forbidden line of his trousers. I snapped my gaze to his smoldering one, feeling as if I were in the midst of a tug-of-war between the devil and propriety. I knew that were I to touch him, to splay my hands against his back and caress his muscled shoulders, we'd pick up where we had left off in the parlor.

But he'd still be a man whom I barely knew, and I'd still have my doubts. Besides, I'd yet to learn why he'd been so reserved and distant earlier tonight. I turned away and arranged my supplies and ministered to his wound. My hands trembled, making the task take longer than it should. The pressure he had applied to the cut had stopped the bleeding, and I saw that the gash was no longer than my thumb and not very deep. But surrounding the cut, his scalp was an angry, purplish color. He'd not only have a headache, but also a very tender spot for a while.

Every time I touched his dark hair, its silky strands wrapped intimately around my fingers, making me wonder if the black hair curling across his chest was just as soft. He'd touched my bare skin earlier, but I hadn't touched him. And I wanted to.

I hurriedly applied the lavender and mint salve to his cut and secured a bandage to the area. "I am done, monsieur."

He exhaled sharply, as if he'd been holding his breath for a long time. "Thank God." He slid the towel from around his neck.

Whirling about, I started gathering the supplies from the bed, every fiber of my being centered on getting out of his room before either of us acted any further upon the attraction sizzling between us.

"We have to talk." He spoke from just behind me. I could feel the whisper of his breath against the nape of my neck and the warmth of his body seeping though the thickness of my robe.

"There is nothing to say. It shouldn't have happened." I shut my eyes, fisting my hand around the bandages I held.

"Mrs. Boucheron, after tonight, I think you owe it to me to explain what you have that someone is willing to break into your home to get."

Everything within me froze as my pent-up desires fell utterly flat. He stood impatiently waiting for an answer.

"Well, Mrs. Boucheron? I deserve some answers. What are you hiding?"

The man had nearly made love to me in the parlor, and now he acted as if I had done something wrong!

"I have *La Belle*, Monsieur Trevelyan, and an iron frying pan—which I must be out of practice with, for I obviously did not strike hard enough."

Grabbing the salve, I pushed past him and sailed out the door, feeling satisfaction in the confusion that knotted his brow.

In the morning, I decided to send for the authorities after breakfast and inform them of the intruder. Then I would seek out Mr. Trevelyan and ask a few pointed questions about last night. I had no clue as to why this was happening, and I wanted to know why he'd been so adamant that I was hiding something.

When I went to wake my son, I discovered his French doors already unlocked.

"Andre?" Spinning around, I saw that what I had thought to be my son sleeping was only his bunched up counterpane and pillows with a note on top. A tentacle of fear squeezed my heart as I reached for the note, for a tiny part of me always worried that when he learned of the rumors about his father, he would try and find him.

I glanced at the names of Phillipe Doucet and Will Hayes on the note and read that Andre had left early this morning to meet his friends at the old military camp. Shoving the note into my pocket, I headed downstairs, determined to march out to the camp and pull Andre home by his ear. Ginette and Mignon were in the kitchen with Mama Louisa, and all three of them looked up at me when I stomped in from the breezeway.

"I knows trouble when I see it, sure enough, and them shadows under your eyes speak for themselves. Miz Julie, either the devil is at the door or you have got a bone bigger than the Pontchartrain to pick." Mama Louisa stopped rolling dough and set floury hands on her hips.

"Both." Not even the mouthwatering aroma of chicory coffee and beignets eased my ire. "Andre has already disappeared for the day. He left a note informing me of his whereabouts."

Ginette's eyes widened, but she didn't comment. In fact, I thought she appeared paler and her cheeks more drawn, as if she were in pain.

"At least he told you where he went," Mignon said.

"Thinking like that will have you thanking the alligator for taking off your fingers, because he left you your palm."

"But—"

"Nonnie, there are no excuses for Andre's behavior. He is on the brink of manhood. At almost thirteen, he needs to be filling shoes much more useful to this household than a frolic with his friends in the woods." I moved over to where Ginette sliced apples for breakfast. "Let me cut the rest of these. I desperately need to do something or I will start pulling out my hair."

"The juice is making my hands itch more, anyway." Ginette set down the knife, washed her hands, and sank back onto a nearby bench. "I will set up the sideboard in a few minutes."

That she let me take over spoke volumes. "Have you a headache this morning?"

"I have had one since yesterday."

"I remember you mentioning it when we were in the sitting room working embroidery. Has it not eased at all since?"

"*Non.*"

"I am sending for the doctor."

"Wait until after breakfast. It may just be that I did not eat much last night; I wasn't very hungry."

"All of you youngin's are going to make me old before my time," Mama Louisa said, shaking her head. "Not eatin' right, looking like a ghost. Miz Ginny, you go sit at the dining room table while I fix you a plate and some soothing tea."

"She is sick, isn't she?" Mignon asked softly, after Ginette left. "There is something you are not telling me. Is she going to die?" Tears flooded Mignon's eyes.

"No!" I dropped the knife and ran over to her. Setting my hands on her shoulders, I made her meet my gaze. "That is not true, do you hear me? Whatever made you think such a thing?"

"Beth died, and Ginette is so like her. And I have been so worried—"

"Beth? Whatever are you talking—" Realization dawned, and with it a tide of relief. "You are reading *Little Women*."

Mignon nodded, tears streaming down her face. "Jo knew before it happened. She realized that Beth would not recover. I don't want Ginny to die."

"Oh, Nonnie," I sighed, wrapping my arms around her, holding her tight. "Ginny is not going to die."

"You've a special delivery, Juliet," Ginette said.

Startled, I looked over Mignon's shoulder. Ginny stood in the doorway, whiter than the lace of her muslin day dress. She clutched the doorframe with one hand and held an envelope in the other.

"I don't want to die, either. What if Nonnie is right? What if she knows something I have yet to realize?"

The world around me kept trying to lurch off its axis, and I wasn't about to let it. "This is utter nonsense, and I'll not hear another word." I gave Mignon a little shake, and went to Ginette. "The way you two are carrying on, Monsieur Gallier and Monsieur Fitz will have you both on stage. Nonnie, you help Mama Louisa with breakfast. Ginette, you finish eating and then go lie down until the doctor arrives and puts your fears to rest. Remember when you were ten and Father brought *Mère* a bottle of perfume that had just arrived from Egypt? Remember the headaches you would get every time she wore it? I am sure this will be something just as simple."

I took the delivery note from Ginette's fingers and went to the one room in which I would not be disturbed, my father's office. I hoped the note was from Mr. Goodson, telling me when to expect him, or at least explaining what danger I was in. As I stepped into the office, I stared in a shock at the disorder before me. Every drawer was opened, papers were tossed to the floor, paintings had been pulled from the walls, and books dumped from the shelves. Someone had been in a hurry to find something. But what? And who?

I glanced at the missive in my hand and nearly fainted.

While I was out yesterday, Jean Claude collected his trunk, seeing only Father. When you see my brother, tell him to contact me immediately. Father has changes he wants to make in his will since Jean Claude has returned.

Regards,
Josephine Boucheron Foucault

8

I could not move, I could not breathe. After ten years, the husband I thought dead had resurrected himself and returned? It wasn't fathomable. My heart filled with dread. I'd believed with all of my heart that he hadn't abandoned us. That he hadn't stolen the gold and disappeared. Through my shock crashed a wave of anger so strong that it nearly blinded me. How dare the man hurt Andre and me like this!

Legalities and the Church might still bind me to him, but my mind, body, and spirit were mine, and I'd never subject them to the pain of abandonment again. There had to be something I could do to protect my family and home.

I was in definite need of legal counsel now, and had no choice but to consult Mr. Davis. I could already see Mr. Latour with his fleshy jowls flapping, informing everyone how he'd had the foresight to warn me of the woes I would have should Jean Claude return—a fact that was just too coincidental not to be investigated, along with the cigar in my attic.

Marching from the office while still looking at the note, I ran into a solid wall of man. Mr. Trevelyan quickly embraced me in strong, steady arms.

"Good Lord, woman. Where's the fire?"

"Fire, monsieur? I happen to be in a hurry and you are in my way." Pressing two fingers to his chest, I pushed him firmly back. As he released me, he slid his hands down my back, leaving a trail of fire that made me shiver.

"I daresay, Mrs. Boucheron, that were I a man of lesser stature and substance, I'd be sorely in need of a physician on a full time basis." He made a great show of straightening the cravat I had dented. "But I much prefer your person to an iron pan."

"Perhaps if you did not lurk in doorways, you would not have this problem. But you appear blessed. Either you have a very hard head or you recover at an astonishing rate." He wore no bandages, and the only sign that he had had an injury was the slight smell of the lavender and mint salve I had used.

"My recovery is due to the excellent care I received. What about you?"

"Nothing happened from which I needed to recover," I replied briskly, trying to ignore the heat he stirred in me and focus on why I shouldn't respond to him—that I was married was at the top of the list. But with him so very near, I had to force my gaze from the sensual curve of his lips and curl my hand around the note to keep from reaching out to touch him. "Did you wish to speak to me about something?"

"Yes, about last night. Whoever broke in was after something. What?" He seemed almost accusatory again, and something inside of me that I had had a tight rein on snapped loose.

Turning, I shoved the door to my father's office open. "Why don't you tell me, monsieur? You were the only person I saw about last night. Why should I take your word that there was an intruder? You're the only boarder who smokes a cigar. In fact, how do I even know that you are who you say you are? Why would a man from the famed Trevelyan Trading Company stay at my boarding house when there are luxurious new accommodations in the heart of the Vieux Carré?"

Mr. Trevelyan leveled his intense blue gaze. Frustration, hurt, and anger showed on his face. Then he surprised me by brushing his thumb along my cheek and over my lower lip. His gaze softened, and between that look and the fire of his touch, I melted.

"There is nothing that I can say that will induce you to trust me. And short of handing you my pistol and telling you to shoot, there is nothing I can do, either. Trust comes by choice. I can tell you this: if I had been the one to search through a room, you would have never known I'd been there. And the only thing I want in this house is you. I want to start off where we ended last night. It was a good thing you knocked me senseless—because if I had had my wits about me, I wouldn't have let you roll away from me." He turned around and left, but the need quivering inside me stayed.

I locked my father's office and went upstairs, where I rammed a bonnet on my head and collected my reticule and parasol. Then I gathered the official papers from the Confederate Army, citing my husband's crimes of deserting the army and absconding with seven hundred and fifty thousand in gold bullion.

I would have to show the papers to Andre. I closed my eyes, already feeling my son's pain.

Suddenly the papers flew from my hands as if ripped away by an arctic hand. My eyes flew open. A dark shadow hovered in the room. It seemed to have the form of a man, but I couldn't make out any features. I was so cold, my blood seemed to freeze. I knew that I'd come face to face with something from the spirit world, and I didn't want it here in my life, in my house.

"Go away," I shouted. The shadow moved against me, pressing me back from the door. Just as I opened my mouth to scream for help, it disappeared. I felt as if I had plunged into icy water and couldn't swim. My room, my bed, my things were just as they had been a moment ago, but I knew I would never be the same. The papers about Jean Claude lay on the floor. I quickly picked them up, stuffing them into my reticule, and left.

Downstairs, I instructed Papa John to send a request for Dr. Lanau to see Ginette today. I knew Mignon, Ginette, and Mama Louisa would give me the very devil for not telling them immediately about the note from Jean Claude's sister and the intruder last night, but I didn't want to be delayed. Exiting the house, I encountered Mr. Trevelyan, waiting for me. It didn't appear that he would be eating breakfast with the other boarders.

"Lurking again, monsieur?" I asked as I open my parasol.

"Seeking fresh air, actually. If you don't mind the company, I would enjoy a walk to town."

I was secretly relieved to have him with me. "If you are going to accompany me, I want you to tell me exactly why you are here in New Orleans and what that has to do with me. I also want to know what you think I am hiding."

Surprise flickered in his blue gaze before he smiled. "Words are a small price to pay for the pleasure of your company. But I have one condition. After last night, you must call me Stephen and I will call you Juliet when we are alone together, agreed?"

I searched his gaze a moment. "Agreed, Stephen," I said softly, relishing the feel of his name upon my lips. I descended the steps and he joined me upon the path. When we reached the edge of Rue Jardin's park and he still hadn't said anything, I took it upon myself to remind him. "You've yet to answer my questions. Are you having any untoward symptoms from your injury?"

"No." He sighed. The sound reminded me of when he'd spoken so revealingly about himself to Andre.

"I haven't lied to you," he said at last. "I came here to write and I am writing. But the truth of the matter is I needed a place to make a new start. I'd heard about New Orleans from a friend and decided to come here."

His tone, the sincerity in his blue eyes, left little room for doubt. So why did I feel as if there was something he wasn't saying?

"You have answered part of my question, Stephen, but have yet to explain why you are behind me every time I turn around. I do not believe it is mere coincidence."

"You are a fascinating woman surrounded by questions I can't dismiss from my mind." He shrugged. "It seems to me as if fate has joined us together."

Clenching my hands, I forced the truth from my lips. "It would seem we have a similar affliction, monsieur."

He caught hold of my elbow and brought me around to face him. His gaze focused on my mouth, a gesture that threw all of my senses askew as reminders of last night's kiss lay evident in the curve of his parted lips, the intensity in his eyes, and the sensual timbre of his voice. "After last night I—"

He jerked his gaze toward the park. Before I could ask what was wrong, he slid his hand to my back and spun around, effectively burying my nose against his spine as he pushed me protectively behind him. All I could see was the black of his suit coat. "What—"

"Who's there?" I heard him demand sharply.

Was I being followed? I peeked around Mr. Trevelyan's broad shoulders, surprised to see a man step from behind the trunk of a large oak on the edge of Rue Jardin's park. It took a second for my eyes to distinguish the man from the clumps of hanging moss, but as soon as he fussed with his cravat, I knew it to be Mr. Gallier, wearing a gray suit.

"A tip-top morning, wouldn't you say, Mr. Trevelyan and Mrs. Boucheron? Seems you two are *well* acquainted."

I opened my mouth, searching for a response that would nip the gossip I saw ready to leap from his tongue.

"Have you noticed what a good morning it is, Mr. Gallier?" Stephen's tone, though cordial, held an underlying menace. "To keep it that way, you may want to scrub the rouge from your shirt and straighten the twist in your trousers before returning to Mrs. Gallier."

Panic wiped the accusing gleam from Mr. Gallier's face. He looked down at his shirt, his eyes bulging to see a stain there as he simultaneously pulled at his pants.

"Tell Mrs. Gallier good morning for us," Stephen said, then cupped my elbow and escorted me away.

As soon as we were out of sight, I started laughing. I came to a stop, bringing Mr. Trevelyan to a halt beside me. "There wasn't any rouge on his shirt and his pants weren't twisted."

"Very observant of you, Juliet."

"But he really thought there was, so that means he must have been . . ."

"Illicitly occupied. Right again. You should laugh more often. It becomes you as well as the moonlight."

His words, his tone, evoked images of him lying upon me, his body pressed to mine, his lips claiming mine last night in the parlor, and anticipation wrapped around me. I wanted more.

I heard the sounds of an approaching carriage and waved down the hack. A brisk walk in the heat of the day and Stephen's stimulating company suddenly seemed too much to take.

Moments later, in the cushioned comfort of the carriage, I realized I had made a huge mistake. Stephen sat beside me and his long legs, stretched across the small confines of the cab, brushed mine. He slid his arm across the seat behind me, burning against my shoulders.

"I doubt Mr. Gallier will be mentioning to anyone what he overheard. There are only a few reasons for a man to skulk behind trees, and all of them are cowardly."

I shook my head. "Poor Madame Gallier. I wonder if she knows."

"I don't see how she can miss it. I would think having a wife and a mistress difficult enough, but having them both under the same roof would be murderous."

I blinked. "Monsieur Gallier is carrying on with Mademoiselle Vengle? But I thought that Monsieur Fitz was . . ."

"Enamored with Miss Vengle? I thought so myself."

"How can people betray each other like that?"

"Betrayal is not always so easy to avoid. Sometimes it can happen even when one doesn't mean for it to." The shadows of pain were back in his eyes, but then he shook his head. "Enough of that. You asked for answers. So what questions do you have?"

"The gold ring you wear, where is it from?"

He furrowed his brow. "I wear it to remind me every minute of a promise I made to a dear friend who died."

He sounded so sincere that I felt silly for my doubts. But the ring still nagged me, as did my questions. "You rounded the corner last night with a pistol ready, as if you're very familiar with one."

"A man born in the West knows his way around a gun, or he doesn't live to see the sunrise. And it seems to me that a woman who has been warned of danger and whose home has been repeatedly invaded would take her safety more seriously. She wouldn't search the house alone, and she wouldn't take off to town alone. Not unless she had something she was hiding."

"But—"

"Do you?"

Just a husband back from the dead, I thought. "No," I replied, irritated. "Why do you think I am hiding something?"

"It's a logical deduction. An intruder wouldn't invade your home and ransack rooms unless he wanted something you have."

"My home and my family are all I have. And more questions. How do you hear things that others don't? You'd shoved me behind your back before I could even blink. How did you know Mr. Gallier was there?"

"If you hadn't had me so distracted, I would have sensed his presence before I heard a twig snap."

"Sensed his presence? Explain yourself, monsieur." My heart beat a little faster. Though I didn't believe in such things, I had heard that there were men who practiced black magic. "Do you claim to have special powers?"

"Powers? Good Lord, no." He laughed so thoroughly that he immediately set me at ease, even brought a smile to my lips and had me feeling utterly ridiculous for my suspicions. "My sister Katherine is deaf, and when we were young, my brother Benedict and I would take turns being her ears, listening to the smallest of sounds and trying to describe them to her. By doing that, I think Benedict and I developed a keener sense of hearing than most people do."

"How did you do that for her? I mean, if someone cannot hear, how can you describe a sound to them?"

"By feel, mostly. Let me show you. Cover your ears and then close your eyes."

"Why must I close my eyes?"

"That will let you concentrate more on feeling."

Intrigued, I closed my eyes and covered my ears, and the moment I did, I had the strange sense of being vulnerable. "I am ready," I said, anxious to rid myself of the feeling. I was about to give up when I felt a bare brush of air against my cheek. It came in two warm mint-scented puffs. Then at the nape of my neck, I felt his fingers lightly brush across my hair, and I nearly sighed at the warm tingle that worked its way down my spine. I had relaxed into the gentleness of his touch so much that when he tapped me on the top of my head as if he was testing a ripe melon, I yelped.

"What was that for?" I opened my eyes and glared at him.

"You tell me," he said, with laughter twinkling in his gaze. "I gave you three sounds. You tell me what they were."

I had to shut my eyes again and imagine the sensations before I could answer him. "I would describe the first as a whisper, for it was soft and barely there. The second felt like a very light breeze, and the last one was a thump. You made me feel like a melon."

"You got them all right."

"I did?"

"Yes. Whisper, rustle, and thump. I have one more. This will be a new one for me. You don't need to cover your ears. Just shut your eyes, and give me your hand."

His warm hand clasped mine, immediately conveying both a sense of security and an anticipation of the unknown. But when he turned my hand palm up, my heart fluttered wildly. I knew what he was about to do, yet I didn't stop him, nor did I open my eyes. The kiss he pressed to the inside of my wrist sent a flood of desire right to the center of my body.

"Kiss," I said softly, opening my eyes to find him but an inch away.

"Yes, I believe I will," he murmured. He pulled the carriage curtains shut, then his mouth covered mine, urgent and demanding. I responded with equal passion, as hungry to feed his need as I was to satisfy my own. I wrapped my arms around his neck and pulled him closer. I wanted the feel of his body against mine and I groaned deeply, trying to get even closer. I wanted to touch him places that I hadn't last night. I was on fire, burning hot and more alive than I had ever felt in my life.

"Good Lord, woman. Come here," he whispered against my lips. He hauled me on top of him, slipping his hands beneath my dress to loosen my drawers and slid them down my legs. He cupped my naked derriere, pulling me firmly against his hardness, kissing me senseless. His rigid desire pressed insistently close to my femininity. The more he kissed, the tighter the exquisite tension became inside of me. I unbuttoned his shirt, sliding my hands over the supple warmth of his chest and through the silky hair matted there. I tasted his lips, kissed him deeply, and touched my tongue to the skin of his jaw and neck, relishing the salty taste of him. I drank in his scent, addicted to him.

He caressed me everywhere, pushing my dress and my chemise from my shoulders, exposing my breasts to his hands and lips. He nipped at my sensitive tips, driving my passion hotter, fueling my wrenching need. I reached for the buckle of his belt, desperate for him, to know him completely, to know everything that he could make me feel, wondering why his dark desire drew me so.

He hesitated a moment. "Are you sure?"

"Make love to me," I whispered, shutting my eyes so he couldn't see my turmoil.

"God help me. I cannot stop." He slid his pants down his hips and pulled me to him, his fingers easing into me, readying me. Then he arched up and heaven filled me in a hard, hot rush of pleasure.

I gasped, caught up in a storm that spun me out of control.

"I need . . . have never felt this . . ." I raked my hands up the muscled contours of his back, meeting each of his thrusts. The thundering of his heart beneath my cheek matched mine. Then his lips claimed mine again, his tongue sweeping my mouth as he drove deeper and deeper inside of me. He cupped my breast, tantalizing its peak with the brush of his thumb, and stroked me until intense pleasure tore through the very heart of me. I shuddered in his arms. He groaned, his pleasure peaking in one last thrust.

Tears filled my eyes and spilled to my cheeks.

"Shh," he said softly, pulling me into the crook of his shoulder. "Juliet, I am not a scoundrel. I'm sorry. I shouldn't have kissed you that way, touched you that way. I don't know what came over me."

His reassurances only made me cry harder. It wasn't his fault, it was mine. I'd knowingly reached for the forbidden fruit and now I had to tell him the truth. Somewhere in the midst of my tears I heard him tell the driver to make a tour of the city, and somehow a handkerchief ended up in my hands. He held me close until my tears were spent. It wasn't until I sat up and began tugging my drawers and skirts back into place, and he straightened his clothing, that he spoke again.

"I know what you are feeling," he said.

"You cannot possibly know," I whispered.

"Maybe I do a little. Because you are the ever-strong and kind Juliet Boucheron, who carries the burdens of so many, you will forgive me for kissing you and touching you—but you won't forgive yourself for responding. You shouldn't punish yourself for being human."

"You make it sound as if I am a saint. I assure you I am not. This time it is you who will need to forgive me, Stephen."

"What could you have possibly done to need my

forgiveness? I am at fault. If you're worried about pregnancy, I am an honorable—"

I pressed my finger to his lips. He was only making what I had to tell him harder. "The women of New Orleans have long known how to avoid pregnancies. Don't worry. What happened is my fault, and my sin *is* greater. The truth of the matter is that I am married. I learned this morning that my husband has returned from the dead."

His blue eyes turned so stark, they burned right through me. Whatever response I had expected to follow his glare, it wasn't the harsh bark of laughter so bitter that it scraped my soul.

"You are not a widow? Dear God. The irony. So much for making a new start."

"What do you mean?"

His fists were clenched and his words cut like jagged glass. "I'm damned. I was a weak enough fool to love my brother's wife, but too cowardly to claim her, and she died as a result. It would seem that we are both sinners beyond redemption, Juliet. Why don't you tell me about this husband of yours?"

There was a hard edge to his gaze. Beneath the sophisticated polish and laughing eyes lay a man to be reckoned with, and I stared at him a moment, completely shocked. "Your brother's wife? So she is the one you speak of? The person you did not save when you could have?"

"You can add her sister to that, as well."

"Why?" I asked, still unable to believe that he deliberately allowed another to die. The idea went against everything that I wanted to believe about him.

"It is a long story that I don't want to tell."

"Yet you expect me to confide in you?"

He exhaled, then looked out the window. "Let's just say my brother's first wife was a lost kitten in a huge storm. In trying to help her I grew to love her, and when she came to me wanting to physically consummate those feelings, I rejected her. That sent her on a path that resulted in her death several months later."

I puzzled over his words. "I do not see how that makes you responsible for her death."

"If I had left before my affection had grown past that of a brother for a sister, or if I had gone to my brother and forced him to understand what was happening, so many things would be different now. But I wasn't man enough for any of those things. I was caught up in my own anger, and then after Cesca's death, my own shame. That is all I can say about the matter. Tell me about your husband."

Surely there had to be more to his story, for him to feel so burdened. I stared at him searchingly, torn between wanting and needing to trust this man who could make me forget everything, and the tiny needle prick of doubt that still questioned why he'd come into my life. I pulled out the army papers from my reticule and handed them to Stephen.

"The last time I saw Jean Claude was in April 1863.

He came to see Andre and me in the middle of the night, dressed in a suit rather than his Confederate uniform. He said he was on an important mission for the army. As New Orleans was under Federal control, I feared he'd be captured as a spy. I'd no idea he'd be branded a traitor and a deserter three days after his visit. Then the official letter came, citing my husband's crimes in deserting the army and stealing gold. After the war was over, there were several newspaper reports recounting that Jean Claude had been seen abroad, but no one has ever been able to find him. I chose to believe he died in the war, rather than believe he abandoned us."

He read the papers, folded them, and handed them back to me.

"Then why do you think he is alive now?"

"This arrived, special delivery, this morning." I handed him the note from my sister-in-law. "I haven't any idea why he would return after so long."

"I do."

He spoke with such assuredness that I gaped at him. "You do?"

"Seven hundred and fifty thousand in gold would be reason enough for any man."

❦ *9* ❧

I didn't think the day could hold any more shocks. "If Jean Claude stole the gold, then surely he has it with him. The intruder—*Dieu*, Jean Claude smoked cigars!"

"Think about it. He visited you unexpectedly in the middle of the night. Then he and the gold disappeared. My guess is that at least part of the gold is at *La Belle*."

"Impossible. The army thoroughly searched the house afterward. Besides, there isn't a corner or a crevice that hasn't been cleaned over the years."

"I think there are a number of questions we both need to start asking. Exactly what errand has you rushing to town?"

I slid the curtain aside and glanced out the window. "I wanted to know what legal options I can take to protect myself from my husband's return. I also thought to confront Monsieur Latour. A cigar had been left amongst papers, causing a small fire that burned itself out despite all the dry paper around it. Fire would be one way to get my family out of *La Belle*."

"Or kill you." He leaned forward and took my hand. "What made you decide to handle this situation alone? Have you no conception of the meaning of danger?"

I opened my mouth to explain that there was no danger in a simple visit to town. But then I remember a man had been murdered on Rue Royale, and Mignon had been attacked in Jackson Square. If gold was indeed involved, then the danger was greater than I had imagined.

"I went through the whole of the war and Federal troops occupying my home without cowering in my room. I am not about to start now."

"So it's damn the consequences, full speed ahead?"

"Have you a better idea?"

He leaned back. "Tell me, am I right in assuming the Mississippi River touches your property?"

I nodded.

"Have you ever played the game of chess?"

Now I was even more perplexed. "I have played once or twice, but I don't see the relevance."

"It is a game of subtlety and power. I think our first move should be to let everyone in the game know the queen isn't alone."

A sense of wonder lit a warm glow inside of me. The man knew the worst of me, had seen the worst of me, and still wanted me. I had expected he'd leave the minute he heard about Jean Claude. But then a regretful pain scraped across my conscience—I could not have an affair with him. "Though most of New Orleans turns a blind eye to *affaires de coeur,* I could not do so, Stephen. I shouldn't have let it happen, but—"

"This offer has nothing to do with whether or not we share a bed, Juliet. We'll settle that later." I winced at the determined sensual glint in his eye, but given my response to his touch, I could hardly be scandalized by his bluntness. Learning of my husband seemed to have unleashed something inside of Stephen. I had the distinct feeling that whatever path of redemption he'd been seeking, he'd now abandoned it. Much like a man saying, "If I'm going to hell I might as well enjoy the journey."

"I have a vast number of resources at my fingertips. Using them will not only help protect your family, but might open legal doors to you that would at least put you on even ground when facing your husband."

I could not help but wonder what his motives were. I started to shake my head automatically, but he interrupted me.

"Before you answer, consider this. Mignon was attacked. A man threatened you with a knife. He has broken into your house more than once that we know of, maybe more. I smelled tobacco smoke last night, and you found a cigar in the attic that could have set your home ablaze as you and your family slept. You are dealing with a man desperate enough to chance lives and possibly even kill. What if Andre, or Mignon, or Ginette had interrupted him last night before I'd scared him away?"

When it came to the safety of my family, I had no choice. Whether I trusted Stephen completely or not, only a fool would turn down an ally in the dark. "I am not even sure what game is being played, so what do you suggest the first move to be, Stephen?" I asked, feeling like a pawn rather than the queen.

He smiled, easing my apprehension until he spoke. "It's time to lure your husband out of hiding. And I think I know exactly how to do it."

The carriage came to a stop in front of Mr. Maison's office and I stepped to the ground, feeling as if I had been on a thousand-mile journey. Stephen had redefined my world. Again. First by awakening my desires, and now, just as a landslide of disaster appeared as if it would bury me, he offered a plan that gave me some modicum of control. But I wondered what price I would pay.

Rather than rushing into my attorney's office desperate for advice, Stephen and I were about to use Mr. Davis's gossiping tendencies to flush out my husband.

I halted at the bottom of the steps. "It is hard to

believe that a man was attacked here and died. Stabbing a man in the back is so depraved, you would think you could spot the culprit in a glance."

"I have learned that there is no safe place, and that murderers wear many faces, some of them not as evil as you would suppose. And sometimes other people are just as guilty as those who commit the crime."

I knew he spoke of his past. I touched his arm lightly. "You shouldn't pay your whole life for one mistake."

"Are you willing to apply that leniency to yourself, as well? Why should you pay for what your husband did for the rest of your life?"

Startled, I dropped my gaze. He went up the steps, opening the door to Mr. Maison's office and leaving me to follow.

"Monsieur Davis," I called when I found the room empty. Mr. Davis appeared in the doorway of Mr. Maison's private office with an open humidor in his hands, his round spectacles magnifying the surprise in his blinking eyes.

"Mrs. Boucheron. Mr. Trevelyan. Is everything all right? Your sister—"

"Is fine. We're here to see you about a business matter."

His brows lifted. He snapped the humidor closed and tucked it under his arm.

I looked over his shoulder into Mr. Maison's inner office. "Has Monsieur Maison returned?"

"No. He will not be returning until the end of the month, remember?"

"Ah. I thought—" I glanced at the office behind him and shook my head. "Never mind. I have some very interesting news, and thought I would be the first to let Monsieur Maison know, since he will be representing my interests in Monsieur Trevelyan's business offer."

"A business proposal?" Mr. Davis moved to his desk, setting the humidor down.

"Yes. What brand?" Stephen asked.

"What?" Mr. Davis asked

Stephen gestured toward the humidor. "The cigars. What brand do you smoke?"

"Oh, no, never been able to afford the luxury. These Futas belong to Mr. Maison. I was just cleaning his office. What sort of business are you involving Mrs. Boucheron in?" His face creased in a scowl.

Mr. Davis's protective air surprised me.

"You are familiar with the reputation of Trevelyan Trading Company?"

Mr. Davis's brows arched. "Yes. It is a company of note. Am I to assume you are the owner of it?"

Stephen's smile fell short of genial, adding to the tension. "In a manner of speaking. My brother takes care of the everyday details. Recently, he has turned an eye toward steamboats and the railroad for intercontinental trade as opposed to international."

"I see," Mr. Davis said, then looked at me. "Are you investing in trade, Mrs. Boucheron?" He sounded astounded, as if a woman were incapable of such a feat. I wished I could disabuse him of that notion by saying yes.

"*Non.* I have been renting a room to Monsieur Trevelyan and now it appears I will be leasing some land to him as well. Or to be exact, to his family's company. They wish to build a wharf and warehouse on *La Belle*'s riverfront acreage."

"My . . . this is rather sudden," Mr. Davis replied.

"The Trevelyan Trading Company's lawyers will need to contact Mr. Maison. Can you tell me where he is staying in Washington?" Stephen asked.

"Not yet. I can put you in contact with him just as soon as I receive his post. When he left, he wasn't sure where he would be staying."

"*Merci*, we will anticipate your note, then." I nodded politely, thinking our business concluded, but Stephen spoke from where he stood by the door.

"Mrs. Boucheron told me of the attack out front. Did you happen to know the man?"

Mr. Davis cleared his throat. "No, not at all. Didn't know anything was amiss until I heard shouting on the street. It was a terrible thing."

"So you didn't see what happened?"

"No. It was a completely ordinary day, except for Mr. Maison's being gone, and I was here alone. I'd been to a lunch appointment and returned not long before the crime, but I had not noticed anything untoward on the street. Why do you ask?"

"Curiosity. As one of Mrs. Boucheron's boarders stated, it is a rather unusual crime to occur in the middle of the day on a business street."

"Criminals are becoming more and more outrageous. Just this spring, a man was hanged in his own yard by a political league merely for his republican fervor. I've told Mr. Maison a number of times to temper his views in public."

I did not want Mr. Davis to start one of his long conversations, so I cleared my throat. "These are difficult times. Please let us know as soon as possible where we can contact Mr. Maison."

"Uh, Mrs. Boucheron," Mr. Davis said. "I never did get to speak privately about Mignon. I've been waiting for her to feel better."

I bit back a sigh. "Why don't you join us for dinner tomorrow and we can speak afterward." I hoped that during the course of the evening, Mignon would make it clear to Mr. Davis that the discussion he wanted to have was unnecessary.

"Tomorrow, then," he said, smiling.

"Mr. Davis, one last thing," Stephen said as I exited the office. "Where is a good place to eat lunch in the city?"

"Antoine's is an excellent establishment. You will see both the famous and the infamous dining there."

"Thank you." Stephen followed me down the steps.

"Shall we walk to Mr. Latour's office?" I asked.

Stephen agreed.

Strolling down Rue Royale, we passed several shops, glancing at the wares displayed. I paused before the Emporium of Unusual Antiquities and nearly pressed my nose to the window to see what was new. "Look, they've a full suit of armor."

"We've two of them at Trevelyan Manor. One is a suit of metal; the other is Dobbs, the butler—though he isn't as stiff as he used to be. Ann, my brother's new wife, has managed to loosen up his starch a bit."

The warmth in Stephen's voice brought a smile to my lips.

"Every time you speak of your family, I can hear how much you care for them. Why did you leave?"

"They have a new baby, Elizabeth Ann, and they've built a happy family. They didn't need any reminders of tragedy," he said quietly.

Soon I would push past the stone wall of his past. For now, I glanced again through the window. "You look at the armor and you can almost feel the past, a time with knights and kings and quests. It's like there's a—"

"Story waiting to be told?"

"*Oui.*" I moved away, angling my parasol to block the sun. "You have never told me what you write."

"I'm working on a play right now, and finding it thoroughly satisfying."

"Tell me about it."

He smiled. "Not until it's done. Then I'll let you read it."

"I'm intrigued."

"Good. But you're not allowed to go snooping into my room again."

My cheeks burned. "I didn't snoop. I just glanced about."

He laughed. "You snooped. Twice that I know of. Was there more?"

"Certainly not."

"Blushing becomes you. So does making love," he whispered.

I shut my eyes, trying to escape the intensity of his gaze. "I shouldn't have let that happen."

He sighed. "We've discussed your husband, but we haven't talked about us."

I shook my head. "There can't be an *us*, Stephen. Jean Claude is alive. I'm married."

"As I see it, he forfeited his rights when he abandoned you and your son. Making love to you was not an ending to my desire, but a beginning of my passion for you."

"My mind is so muddled over everything that has happened, I don't know what to think or do."

He was quiet a moment. "Then what happened in the carriage? Were you making love to me, or trying to avoid a resurrected husband?"

I grabbed his arm, turning to him. Regardless of who might see, I pressed my fingers to his lips. "Never speak such a thing again. I've never wanted a man the

way I want you. Every sense cries out for the fulfillment that only you have brought me. When you touch
me, when I feel you, nothing else matters. But desiring
you isn't going to make my problems go away, nor is it
necessarily going to help me make the right decisions.
I have a son. I need time to think."

He kissed my fingers, brushing his tongue across
their tips, sending more heat and turmoil through me.
"I'll give you time. I'm not going anywhere."

I nodded and we moved on to Latour's office, which
wasn't as imposing as I thought it would be. The two-
story building off Lafayette Square, with its fancily
sculpted wrought iron and arched, beveled lead glass
windows, was in as much need of repair as *La Belle*. We
stepped inside to threadbare carpeting and tarnished
brass gasoliers.

Mr. Latour himself greeted us, beaming excitedly
above the rim of the spectacles sitting low on his puffy
nose. "Come in, come in, Mrs. Boucheron. Please have
a seat in my office." He directed us to his inner office.
"My assistant is away. Family emergency. May I serve
you a refreshment?"

"*Merci,* but I am fine. This isn't a social call. Let me
introduce you to Monsieur Trevelyan. Monsieur
Trevelyan, this is Monsieur Latour." They shook hands.

The first thing I noticed was the humidor on his
desk. Stephen did, too.

"I see that you smoke," Stephen said.

Mr. Latour turned red and flustered. "I, um, used to

indulge often. I haven't in a while. The humidor is empty, so I fear I can't offer you one." He turned a jovial smile my way. "Since you are here, Mrs. Boucheron, I assume you have changed your mind about *La Belle*. Fortunately, I have yet to commit Packert Investment Company's funds for another property. They will be so delighted."

I shook my head. "I have not changed my mind about selling *La Belle*, Monsieur Latour. I came today to ease your mind about our welfare, so that you won't be compelled to send any more auction representatives to my door."

Mr. Latour's widening smile froze. "That was a mistake. They misunderstood what I'd said."

"You have heard of Trevelyan Trading Company, have you not?"

"Of course." He shot a quick look toward Stephen.

"I will be leasing acreage on the riverfront to them for a wharf and a warehouse facility," I said with satisfaction.

Mr. Latour's mouth gaped. "But . . . but . . . can you legally do so? I mean, without permission from, well, you know?" He shot another glance at Stephen, then at me, twitching his eye as if trying to get me to understand a secret message.

"If you are referring to Mrs. Boucheron's husband, then your answer is yes. She can do so. I have a panel of lawyers that are going to make sure of that." Stephen's tone brooked no argument.

"If Jean Claude has a problem with my decision, he can tell me directly," I said.

"I am sorry, what did you say?" Mr. Latour squinted as if blinded by bright light.

"I said Jean Claude can—"

"That's what I thought. Are you feeling ill, Mrs. Boucheron? I mean, you do remember everything that has happened. You do know that this is 1874 and that, well, Jean Claude—"

"Has returned." I pulled out the note from Jean Claude's sister and showed it to him. "I thought he would have contacted you."

Mr. Latour snatched the note I held out. His face went stark white, then flushed purple. "He is back!"

I jumped at the force of his voice.

"Where! Where is he?" Mr. Latour demanded, standing and leaning over his desk at me. "He owes me for what he stole from my family, and I aim to get it back one way or another. Do you understand, Mrs. Boucheron! Now where is he?" He reached out as if he were about to grab my arm. Stephen wrapped his hand around Mr. Latour's wrist and pushed the man back. Off balance, he fell into his desk chair, knocking his spectacles askew when he slammed into the wall behind him. It all happened so quickly, I almost thought I had imagined it.

"Surely I misunderstood your intent, Mr. Latour. You were not about to manhandle Mrs. Boucheron, were you?" Stephen's tone cut like a knife through the air.

Mr. Latour shook his head, seemingly recovering his senses. "Certainly not! I, uh, was only reaching out to emphasize how important the information is. I would very much like to speak to Jean Claude."

"So would I." I retrieved the note about Jean Claude from his desk. "So if you do see my husband, tell him that for me."

❧ *10* ❧

As soon as Stephen and I returned home, I went to the kitchen. Stephen might have been giving me time to think, but the desire in his eyes wasn't. Every time I looked at him, I wanted to reach for him and damn all the consequences.

Mama Louisa stood at the counter, cleaning fish for dinner as Mignon shelled peas, but something was very wrong. I saw Mama Louisa swiping at tears with her sleeve and Mignon nearly mangling the pods she split.

"What is it?" I gripped the back of the chair, thinking that Jean Claude had come to *La Belle* while I was out.

"A miasma is claiming Miz Ginny," Mama Louisa said. "I told you I was feeling them bad spirits."

Mignon gave an angry snort. "I do not believe a word of it. I do not care what Dr. Lanau says. There is no poisonous effluvium floating through the air, draining the life out of my sister."

My breath caught. Twenty years ago, thousands had died from yellow fever, which many had claimed was a miasma of death hanging over the city. I sank into the chair at the kitchen table. "Does Ginette have a fever? Are others in the city ill as well?"

"*Non*," Mignon said. "I asked Dr. Lanau specifically if others were ill. Ginette does not have a fever, though he gave her a sleeping powder and told us to call him if she developed any other symptoms."

"Perhaps she has the ague."

"No chills. No fever. No pain. No cough. No congestion. He just does not know what is wrong with Ginny."

"I think you should call another doctor to see your sister. I have a recommendation, if you wish." Everyone jumped at the sound of Stephen's voice.

I whipped my head around, realizing that I had not even heard his approach. A person would have to walk on air to keep the old planks of the breezeway from groaning. "Ste—"

"And what would another doctor tell us, Monsieur Trevelyan?" Mignon's frustrated interruption saved me from blurting out Stephen's name.

"My friend specializes in exotic illnesses. The focus of his work is researching how to keep diseases from spreading, but he has treated a number of patients with unusual ailments, as well. I am sure he could be here tomorrow."

He had friends so close by? He had given me the

impression he was alone in New Orleans. Some things about Stephen didn't match up.

"That would be much appreciated, monsieur," Mignon said.

"I suppose it will do no harm," I agreed. "Is there anything else that you needed, monsieur?"

"I missed breakfast and find myself famished. Might there be any beignets and coffee left?"

I motioned for him to join me and he sat.

"I didn't realize you had friends in the city," I said, sliding the tray of beignets toward him.

He took a confection, avoiding my gaze. "I have friends in many cities." He shut his eyes before I could see more, then bit into the soft, sweet, fried dough. I watched pleasure ripple over his features and felt a responding vibration inside. Then he opened his eyes and looked directly at me, causing my insides to clench even tighter.

Mignon set two cups of chicory-flavored coffee on the table. "Ginette wanted me to get some boxes off the high shelf in her room, and I need Mama Louisa to help me. You will not mind if we leave for a few minutes?"

"Boxes? What for?" If Ginette was ill, why was she worrying about boxes?

"We will take care of it." Mignon patted my shoulder and grabbed Mama Louisa's arm, pulling her from the room before I could ask more. With very little subtlety, they'd left me alone with Stephen. Heat flushed my cheeks.

Stephen bit into another beignet, this time leaving a crumb of sugar at the corner of his mouth. Without thinking, I leaned toward him and brushed the sugar away. He grabbed my wrist, bringing my gaze to his.

"Tread carefully," he said. "A husband who has abandoned you for so long isn't proving to be much of a deterrent to me. He doesn't deserve you." It was all there—the desire, the want, the consuming passion that had blazed between us. Everything within me wanted to kiss him again, touch him again, and feel his hard body pressing so intimately into mine. It was too much.

"I must go," I said, jumping up, pulling from his touch. I hurried up the stairs.

Ginette's door hung ajar and I slowed my steps so that I could sneak by, but Mignon's voice brought me to a halt.

"I think my plan is working, Ginny. I left Monsieur Trevelyan alone in the kitchen with Juliet. Monsieur Trevelyan is so wonderful."

I stepped to the doorway, planning to admonish Mignon. But I saw she was indeed retrieving boxes from the top of the armoire and handing them down to Mama Louisa while Ginette lay on the divan.

"From the way they are looking at each other, I say they are already in love."

"Nonnie," Ginette said, before I could speak. "It will never work. I want Juliet to be happy, but as long as she is married to Jean Claude, she will never allow herself to be. Juliet's and my fate are already sealed. It is you who needs to find love."

Mignon turned around sharply. "What do you mean your fate is sealed?"

"Love will never be mine to hold, just as it is with Juliet, but your future is bright. Some young man will come along and find your beauty irresistible."

It pained me deeply to hear Ginette condemn herself to such a fate.

"I do not want a man. I am not ready for love or marriage. I want to travel and see places that I can only read and dream about. I want to reach out and make my own destiny. And you should, too."

Ginette sighed, more heavily than before. "It is too late for me. Can you bring me the blue-flowered box? I need it," she said, her voice wavering.

I moved from the doorway into the corridor and stole quietly to my room. Lying down on my bed, I stared up at the ceiling. How could I not know the hopes, desires, and despair of my own sisters? How did Mignon know of my feelings for Stephen? Were they so apparent? I shut my eyes to rest for a moment.

I awoke to darkness. Disoriented, I sat up wondering why I was fully dressed. Judging from the shadows, I must have slept the entire day. After lighting a lamp, I splashed my face with water, smoothed my hair, then went downstairs and I hurried to the kitchen. The boarders would be expecting dinner soon.

"This last tray is ready, Papa John," Mignon said. She didn't look up from where she was arranging fillets of baked fish on a platter of seasoned rice. Her back to me, Mama Louisa stirred a pot, shaking her head. "I don't know about this, Miss Nonnie. She's going to be awful mad we didn't wake her up."

"Mad or not, she will at least have had some rest. Once Monsieur Trevelyan patches up Andre, everything will be fine," Mignon replied.

Alarm wiped the last remnants of sleep from my mind. "What happened to Andre?"

Mignon jumped as if she'd been caught with her hand in the cookie jar. Mama Louisa whirled around, sending drops of sauce flying off her spoon.

"Where's Andre?"

"Up in his room. He got into a fight and Monsieur Trevelyan—"

I didn't wait to hear more. I rushed to Andre's door. He sat on the edge of his bed, face muddied, shirt torn, and lip bleeding.

"I have been in a scuffle or two myself over the years. You look well, considering," Stephen said as he dabbed a cloth to Andre's split lip. They both looked up at me as I entered.

"What . . . what happened?" I asked.

"Nothing." Andre lowered his gaze to the floor and stared hard. I'd never heard his voice sound so harsh. When I looked to Stephen, he shrugged, telling me he didn't know any more.

"Andre," I said softly. "I need to know."

He looked up then, his eyes already brimming with tears. "You lied to me. You told me never to lie, but *you* lied to me."

His words filled me with dread.

"I have a thief for a father and a liar for a mother. I wish I had never been born." He jumped to his feet and ran to the French doors.

I thought my heart would break. "Andre DePerri Boucheron! Don't you dare leave!"

He stopped at the doors. He didn't turn around, but clenched his fists at his sides and pressed his forehead to the glass. His shoulders shuddered with suppressed sobs. I went to him, setting my hands gently on his shoulders, and bowed my head until my cheek rested against him.

"Forgive me," I whispered. "I never meant to hurt you. Who told you?"

"Why? Why did he do it?" he cried harshly.

"I don't know. I have asked myself a thousand times. In his letters he spoke of you often, so proud that he had a son. He wrote of his plans for you, and had dreams of a great future. As soon as I find the letters, you can read them for yourself." In the reflection of the paneled glass, I saw Stephen leave the room and close the door.

My son pulled from my grasp, turning to face me. "Why did you let me believe that my father died fighting in the war? What about my grandfather? Did you lie about him, too?" He gulped for air.

"*Non*, Andre. It wasn't like that. Your father and the gold disappeared and nobody could find him. Until somebody could prove him guilty, I chose to believe he'd died in the war. You were too little to understand, when it happened. Then when you were older, I could never find the words to tell you. I am sorry. I wanted you to believe that your father was a good man, and I was wrong."

"What do you mean?"

"A post arrived this morning from your Aunt Josephine. It said your father has returned."

He walked away from me, grabbing clothes from the chest at the bottom of his bed.

"I cannot let you leave, Andre. This is your home. Your heritage."

"My heritage?" he asked harshly. Crumpling his clothes to his chest, he met my teary gaze. I could hardly recognize my son in the angry, bruised young man before me. "I am not leaving. I am going to take a bath. I feel dirty."

He left me standing alone in his room. I had stood by myself though the war, had fought every step of the way for my family since, but at that moment, I had never felt more alone. I left Andre's room by the French doors, silently moving along the gallery's shadows and down the stairs to the courtyard.

The muggy night closed in on me, oppressive and stifling. A gibbous moon hung low over the blackened silhouette of twisted tree limbs, clinging moss, and strangling vines. Night creatures thrummed a hungry beat into the darkness. Before dawn, it would storm. I could taste it in the air and feel it brewing inside of me.

I sank to the stones beneath St. Catherine's feet and leaned my head against the cool marble base of the fountain. The water trickled soothingly, and I wanted to do nothing but listen to its tinkling sound rather than hear the voice pounding in my head, telling me I'd failed my son. Threading my fingers through my hair, I loosened the strands, letting wavy curls fall about my face and shoulders to shut out the world.

"My darling, I knew you would come to me eventually. You are beautiful in the moonlight."

I snapped my head up. "Monsieur Fitz. Whatever are you doing?"

With one hand on the fountain, he stood to my right, leaning down toward me. He jumped and lost his balance, sending his hand into the fountain, splashing water everywhere.

I had to scramble out of the way to escape being drenched.

"Mrs. Boucheron, what in the devil are you doing here?" he sputtered.

"It happens to be my fountain, sir. Who did you think I was?" I knew he'd mistaken me for Miss Vengle.

"No one," he lied, swiping water off his drooping mustache. "My mistake. So sorry." He backed away and then went back inside the house.

"Whom have you been waiting for, Juliet?"

Whirling around, I didn't see Stephen at first. Then, in the darkest shadows cast by a lush camellia growing next to the enclosing stone wall, I saw him. He sat on the stone ground with his back to the wall, his long legs stretched leisurely out.

"How long have you been there?"

"Since before you came out. Come and join me." He motioned to the ground beside him. "There is more than enough room in my life for a friend, and the stars are quite humbling from my lowly spot."

Everything within me reached out to this man's offer. I went to him and settled my back against the wall beside him, adjusting my skirts to stretch out my legs as well.

"You remind me of myself, lonely, heartbroken, and lost. I once drowned myself in whiskey and sat by a fountain to mourn. A friend dragged me to my feet, and changed my fate. From your pain, I assume things did not go well with Andre. How is he?"

I didn't know what to say in the face of his revelation, so I tucked his story inside me in favor of what lay so heavily upon my heart. "He is angry. Hurt. Disappointed with me. He is taking a bath without being forced to for the first time in his life. This time, I have no doubt that he is actually in the water scrubbing rather than pretending to be. He said he felt dirty. He wouldn't let me touch him." Tears flooded my eyes again.

He took my hand in his and brushed his lips to my knuckles. "He needs time. One mistake won't cost you your family."

"Did it you?" I asked.

I couldn't see his expression in the dark, but I heard his sharp inhale. Rather than answer, he asked gently, "Why did you lie to him?"

I sighed. "How do you tell a three-year-old that his father is a thief and a coward? I asked myself the same question when he was five, then eight, then ten, and I still could not tell him. There was no proof Jean Claude was guilty, just gossipy rumors. I believed with my whole heart that he'd died in the war, and began calling myself a widow."

We sat quiet for a moment, his arm pressed warmly against mine, and I leaned his way.

"Why have you been hiding out here in the shadows?" I asked.

"It is cooler here than in my room. And I can watch the back of the house from here, see anyone leaving or going in, without anyone seeing me."

"Are you expecting Jean Claude?"

"Maybe. But he may not be our only threat. In chess, you never assume you know exactly what your opponent is going to do. You base your moves on a number of possible scenarios. Do you have another room to rent?"

"Only a small one next to the bath. I would hardly call it a room. Why do you ask?"

"As of tomorrow, you will have another boarder. His name is Phelps. I have hired him to help protect you and your family. He will be pretending to be a lawyer for Trevelyan Trading Company."

"Oh," I said, drawing a quick breath. "I hadn't realized that such lengths were necessary."

"With that much gold at stake, I am not willing to bet otherwise. Men have killed for less. Much, much less."

≪ *11* ≫

The crash of thunder awakened me and I sat up straight, a sharp pain cramping my neck. I'd fallen asleep in the large chair in Andre's room, clutching the soft, blue baby coverlet he'd always slept with. My gaze went immediately to his bed as yesterday's events washed over me, and only when I saw Andre still there sleeping could I breathe.

Last night, after leaving Stephen in the courtyard and speaking to Mignon, I returned to Andre's room and found him asleep. But when I saw the coverlet my mother had made him thrown into the empty hearth, I couldn't leave his room. The uncertainty that he would still be here when I woke had been too great.

Heavy rain and a lashing wind now whipped against the house, making the rafters groan in protest. I huddled deeper into the chair, resting my cheek on Andre's blanket, catching his scent mingled with soap. It would be all right. It had to be.

Lightning flashed a jagged swath across the room, and I looked up, startled. My throat convulsed at the ghostly figure swaying in the doorway.

"Juliet, Nonnie told me that Andre heard . . . I am so sorry."

"*Bon Dieu*, Ginette. You gave me such a fright. What on earth are you wearing?"

"My robe and a scarf. I am chilled and cannot seem to get warm. I am scared. For me. For Andre. For you. What is happening to our lives?"

I went to her, wrapping Andre's blanket and my arm around her shoulders. Shivers wracked her slight body, and my pulse leapt with alarm. Seeing her like a ghost in the night made me feel as if an omen of doom had slapped me in the face, telling me that this was fate and I could do naught to change it. I thought of those moments when a chilling cold had stolen into my body. Could it be possible that some sinister spirit stalked *La Belle* and had settled itself in Ginette? The thought was not just far-fetched, it was too horrible to contemplate during the hours of the night.

"Come sit with me for a little while and we can keep each other warm. This storm has brought a chill to the air," I said. We scrunched into the oversized chair together, much as we used to do when we were very little. The old chair had been the favored place for reading bedtime stories for generations. I'd spent many an evening in it myself with Andre.

"How long have you been awake?" I asked her.

"Only since the storm began. I left Nonnie sleeping on the divan. She was exhausted. I feel so bad for not doing my share of the work."

"Don't worry about such a thing. All of your thoughts need to be consumed with getting better."

Ginette didn't say anything and I hugged her tighter to me. "Did you hear me, Ginny?"

"Yes." Her whisper was a sob. "I can hardly work my embroidery anymore, and I wanted so much to finish the tapestry. It tells of my life, of so many things I can never say. It has been so long in the making that I swear it has collected dust."

Tears bit my eyes, blinding me as well. I had been so busy that I had yet to even look at the tapestry Ginette had been so diligently working on for almost a year. How could I have neglected someone I so dearly loved? I pressed my forehead to hers, pulling her even closer. "Ginny, my sweet Ginny. Don't cry, please."

"What if I do not get better, Juliet? There is so much of life I have yet to live. My heart cries for it all, yet every day my headaches are worse and I am weaker, as if life is slipping from my hands. As if death awaits me."

I opened my mouth to refute her doubt, but a cry from the doorway stopped me.

"*Non.* I won't let that happen," Mignon said almost angrily. "Do you hear me? I won't let it. It cannot happen."

I opened my arm to her and she clambered on top

of our laps. I gave them both a firm hug. "Nonnie is absolutely right. We are not going to let that happen. In fact, Monsieur Trevelyan has a doctor friend who is going to come see you. We are going to find an answer to this problem and solve it. And we are going to love Andre right through this hurt that I have caused him. We are going to be all right. I am sure of it."

But I had never been less sure of anything in my life. And I think my sisters felt the same, because for a long time afterward we stayed huddled together, listening to the storm and watching Andre, with his blackened eye and bruised cheek, sleep restlessly, as if nightmares edged in on his dreams.

Ginette's shivering eased and a sense of calm settled over us with the abating of the storm and the coming of dawn. Our arms and legs were cramped and our bottoms slightly numb, but our hearts had drawn comfort from one another. Mignon helped Ginette to her room while I stayed with Andre, waiting for the sun to rise before I woke him.

A tap on the French doors and a familiar dark silhouette brought me out into the early morning light on the gallery. I shut the door so I wouldn't wake Andre. A rumpled, unshaven, and bleary-eyed Stephen wearing a loose shirt, snug breeches, and scuffed boots stood there. My father, who'd been known to play a card game or two on the shady side of the Vieux Carré, would have said that Stephen looked as dangerous as a loaded six-shooter in a card game gone wrong. He'd been watching over *La Belle* as I slept. At every turn, he seemed to be standing between the enemy and me.

I prayed my desire for him wasn't masking truths I needed to see.

"My friend, Dr. . . . Marks, will be here sometime late this morning. I am going to sleep for a little. Would you send Andre to wake me when he arrives, or when Mr. Phelps arrives?"

"*Oui.* Thank you for watching all night. I feel guilty that you are expending so much of yourself and your time on our problems."

"Don't. My time was not wasted."

"Still—"

"If the roles were reversed and you could do something to help me, would you walk away or lay abed while I struggled?"

"*Non.* Absolutely not."

He brushed the pad of his thumb across my lips. "Someday we're going to make love again, and it won't be rushed. You can count on it."

His words grabbed at my heart and sent my pulse racing. He left before I could say a word. The day, washed anew by the storm, sparkled bright with promise, and I thought perhaps my optimism for the future was not misplaced. I touched my lips with my fingers and thought that perhaps I wouldn't be alone as I had been for so long.

Returning inside, I found Andre awake and lacing

on his boots. He'd dressed in his most worn clothes, as if he were leaving to join friends in the swamp.

"Andre?"

He looked up but didn't say anything. He didn't have to. The coverlet was back in the hearth. I had made a grave mistake in lying to him, but to leave him on what appeared to be his current path would be an even graver one.

"Good. I am glad you are dressed." I said briskly. "As you are the man of this household, there are a number of responsibilities that I have been negligent in sharing with you."

"I have other things to do."

"First," I said, ignoring his excuse, "you are going to retrieve the coverlet that my mother made for you. When she was dying, instead of feeling sorry for herself because life was not being fair, she spent some of her last days making that for you. You were to be her first grandchild, and her dearest wish in life was to hold you before she died. She did not get her wish, but I promised her that you would be a man she could look down on from heaven with pride.

"Then the second thing you are going to do is determine what damage was done to your grandfather's office. We apparently had an intruder the night before last, and we need to report the incident to the authorities. Meanwhile, Aunt Nonnie and I will tend the boarders, and await the doctor. Your Aunt Ginette is very ill."

He blinked with surprise.

"You would have known that if you had been here. You would have known that if those who have cared for you all your life were as important to you as you are to them."

Andre looked at me as if he wondered who I was, and I couldn't blame him. I hardly recognized myself. He didn't say a word, but he gathered his coverlet from the hearth and placed it carefully at the end of his bed. Then he followed me down the stairs.

After I set Andre to cleaning up the office, I walked into the kitchen to see Mignon, Mama Louisa, and Papa John looking at me as if I were condemned.

"Ginette needed another pair of woolen stockings," Mignon said. "When I got them from your drawer I found some disturbing things." She held up the telegram from Mr. Goodson. "Why did you not tell us about this?" Then she held up the post from Jean Claude's sister. "And Jean Claude is alive and he's back?"

"I haven't seen him," I whispered, unable to breathe.

"I knowed somethin' was wrong. And it ain't right you didn't tell us." Mama Louisa clutched a dish towel angrily, her eyes more troubled than I had ever seen them.

"She's right, Miz Julie. And I'm mighty disappointed. You should have told us, so we could help," Papa John said, shaking his head.

I found a stool next to the butter churn to sit on. "I planned to tell everyone when I knew more. Why cause all of you worry when I didn't yet know what there was to worry about?"

"That argument don't hold water, Miz Julie. That's like not telling your neighbor the Yanks are coming cause you don't know who's leadin' them to your door. We needed to know so we could be on the watch. Even after some scalawag done broke into the house, you didn't say a word."

"We are in danger and you did not tell us," Mignon charged.

"What of the cigar and the charred paper? What do they have to do with this?" Mignon held up those as well.

"I found them in the attic. I think our intruder might have tried to start a fire."

Everyone gasped. Mignon stamped angrily toward me, and I winced again. I'd never really considered how my actions would appear to them.

"You did not think to tell us? You do not trust us," she shouted, tears welling in her eyes.

Tears filled my eyes, too. I caught hold of her fingers as I took the telegram. "That's not true. I love you all dearly. Of course I trust you."

She pulled her fingers from my grasp. "*Non.* You may trust us not to cause you harm, but you do not trust us enough to share your burdens. Loving is sharing," she said, then ran from the room.

Mama Louisa shook her head and went back to the stove.

"She's right, and you know it in your heart, Miz Julie," Papa John said. "I am mightily disappointed." He left the room, shaking his head.

I stared down at the butter churn, tears falling. In my desire to protect my family, I'd brought them nothing but pain. My good intentions had paved the way to a Hades full of hurt, and reparation wasn't going to come easy.

Midmorning, I called a family meeting in my father's office. Bundled up in a quilt, Ginette lay upon the settee. Mignon stood to her right, Papa John and Mama Louisa on the left, and Andre sat on the hearth rug, lingering hurt in his features.

"We are waiting for one more person," I said.

"Who?" Mignon asked, puzzled.

A sharp knock sounded on the door, and I let Stephen in. He saw everyone gathered, lifted an inquiring brow, but didn't comment. He didn't look like a man who'd been up all night. Dressed in a suit that spoke more of business than elegance, the underlying edge to him seemed sharper than ever.

"Monsieur Trevelyan, please have a seat and I will get started." He joined Andre near the hearth, leaning against the mantel.

"In my desire to protect all of you whom I love so dearly, I have been the one to cause you pain. It is time for all of us to be truthful with each other. I have asked

Monsieur Trevelyan to join us, because as of yesterday, he has committed himself to helping us determine who is threatening our home and our lives."

I explained the events beginning with the telegram, and told them our suspicions that the gold Jean Claude had stolen might be at *La Belle*. When I finished, no one said a word.

Mignon recovered first. "For years I have prayed for excitement and adventure, but this is too much."

"My father is here and he hasn't come to see me!" Hurt and anger filled Andre's voice.

Stephen settled a hand on Andre's shoulder. "We don't know that, lad. Not until Jean Claude is actually seen. All we know is that someone is threatening your home. Everything else is supposition, but we have to start with the facts."

"How does pretending that your family will be leasing land from *La Belle* help?" Ginette asked.

"Power," Stephen said. "By blending the financial and legal resources of Trevelyan Trading Company with your family, you will be perceived as being less vulnerable. Your sister's reputation remains untarnished, yet she will no longer be seen as destitute and alone or easy for someone to take advantage of."

"But if this is just pretend, how will it make a difference?" Mignon asked.

I stepped forward. "Because only we know it's pretend, and nobody is to tell anyone otherwise. Not even your friends, Andre."

"They are not my friends anymore."

Before I could question him, a knock sounded at the front door. Papa John went to answer it and quickly returned with a man.

Stephen left Andre's side, holding his hand out. "Thank you for coming. I know this is a difficult time." They shook hands as if they'd known each other for years.

The man glanced around the room and his eyes settled on Ginny's pale face. "I hear you have a special patient for me."

"Yes. I will let Mrs. Boucheron make the introductions." Stephen turned my way. "Mrs. Boucheron, this is Doctor Marks. He is the physician I mentioned who specializes in exotic ailments."

Dr. Marks appeared young, but scholarly and somber enough to inspire confidence in his abilities. After I introduced him, he followed Ginette and me to her room to examine her.

Dr. Marks was so meticulously thorough during the exam that he instilled a kernel of hope inside me. The only comment of note that he made concerned a faint red rash Ginette had on her hands. I remembered her saying her hands itched when she was cutting the fruit yesterday morning.

"What is your opinion, Dr. Marks?" I asked, with my heart in my throat.

"To be honest with you, Mrs. Boucheron, I am rather perplexed. There is definitely a degenerative condition in progress, but there appears to be no determinable cause at this point. I'd like to have a few days to do some research into her symptoms. For now, can you tell me for sure that you are not taking any patent medicines, any healing tonics or such?"

Ginette shook her head, her eyes tearing. I, too, felt her disappointment. I had hoped he would have an answer. "Other than an occasional cup of sassafras and lemon verbena tea, and the headache powder Dr. Lanau gave me once, there has been nothing," Ginette whispered.

"Who prepares the tea?"

"Mama Louisa."

"Good," he said. "I will want to ask her exactly what ingredients she uses."

Stephen waited outside for Dr. Marks and as soon we exited, they launched into a conversation. I excused myself to go to Ginette.

Rather than staying in her room, Ginette asked to go to the courtyard. Papa John set her up a comfortable chair and I gave Andre the task of reading *Swiss Family Robinson* to her while I helped Mama Louisa and Mignon prepare the noonday meal.

In the kitchen, I had just put a thick bouillon sauce on the chicken when I heard the jaunty notes of a song being played outside. We all hurried over to the window to see. Stephen, with apparently little care to his dignity, marched around Ginette's chair like a comical pied piper. Andre followed, looking just as silly as he smacked two stones together, punctuating the beat of "Jim Crack Corn" and then "Yankee Doodle." Ginette's laughter rang out. Stephen always seemed to know exactly what to do to help.

"There's just somethin' about that man that does a heart good. Does a mighty favor to the eyes, too," Mama Louisa said, pointedly. "Somethin' you should be a takin' note of, Miz Julie."

"Mama Louisa!" I said, scandalized. "I am a married woman."

"Marriage ain't no written words, and it ain't no church's fancy ritual. It's lovin' and helpin' between a man and a woman. You ain't been married for a decade, if you ask me. And you've done been alone too long. That man is here, and it looks to me like he's wantin' to be lovin'."

Mignon spoke up. "Every month, you go to your suffrage meeting to discuss the rights and independence of women, yet for years you have kept yourself imprisoned, because you weren't sure what had happened to Jean Claude. I would not sit idle for ten years accepting a lifetime of loneliness as my fate. I would choose a quiet *affaire de coeur*, be it right or wrong in the eyes of an unforgiving Church."

"Mignon!" Heat flushed my cheeks. I felt as if I'd been stripped bare and exposed. Were they right? I'd worried that Mignon would let a man rule her because she feared to hurt his feelings, but in truth, it was I who had enslaved myself.

I needed to think and quickly excused myself. When I reached my room I went to the balcony, where I could watch Stephen with Andre and Ginette. I was there but a moment before Stephen turned my way. The intensity of his gaze told me that if I went outside tonight, or the next night, or the next, he would be waiting for me in the sultry light of the Louisiana moon.

12

"Mr. Phelps is doing remarkably well, don't you think?" Stephen whispered from behind me.

We'd all gathered in the parlor for refreshments, including the boarders, Mr. Phelps—Stephen's hired guard posing as a Trevelyan Trading Company representative, who'd arrived an hour ago—Mr. Davis, whom I had invited, and unexpectedly, Mr. Latour. Apparently Mr. Latour's conscience wouldn't let him rest until he'd apologized again for his unseemly behavior at his office yesterday. He'd brought me an armful of spring flowers. Thankfully, he'd spent most of his time speaking to Mr. Phelps about Trevelyan Trading Company's interest in leasing land on the river.

"What I think is that this dinner has the makings of a nightmare," I whispered back, pulling my silver shawl tighter.

"I wouldn't miss a minute of it," he replied.

"Oh? Why is that?"

"Except for your ever-absent husband, everyone whom you might consider a player in the game is present."

"Does that include you?"

Stephen brought his searching gaze to mine. "I thought we were beyond that."

I smiled softly. "Perhaps. I am reserving judgment on some things, though." I was half teasing, but some part of me still questioned what had brought him to *La Belle.*

He lowered his voice and spoke intimately close to my ear. "Was I on your mind this afternoon? I enjoyed you watching me from the gallery, much as Juliet must have looked down upon Romeo. 'Were I silk upon your skin, Juliet, O what pleasure would be ours.' " He slid his hand beneath the shawl to the small of my back and softly caressed my spine.

My pulse sped and heat coiled inside of me.

"You take liberties, monsieur," I gasped. "I believe Romeo said glove, did he not? 'O, that I were a glove upon that hand, that I might touch that cheek.' "

"That, too," Stephen said, sliding his finger up my spine, making my toes curl. "Or a slipper upon thy foot, a stocking upon thy thigh—"

"Enough! Someone will see."

He laughed. "I think your beauty has indeed addled my wits. I quite forgot myself."

"I am beginning to think that there isn't anything you would not dare."

His eyes darkened with passion. "When it comes to you, you are right."

I fled to the kitchen, but before checking on the dinner preparations, I shut my eyes, remembering the feel of him, the taste of him, and the power of him inside me. My body burned for him, leaving a long, hot night ahead of me.

On my return to the parlor, Miss Vengle stood in the doorway.

"Mrs. Boucheron, I hope you don't mind, but might I have a word with you?"

Her molasses drawl made me cautious. "Of course."

She glanced about and lowered her voice. "This negotiation with Mr. Trevelyan to use your land. I wondered if it was well—wise, to be blunt."

I was so surprised that I stood frozen for a few moments before I collected myself. "Miss Vengle. Not to be rude, but my business matters are hardly of concern to you."

"You are right, but I did overhear the men speaking of it. You should know there is a great deal of speculation going on in regards to your, uh, reputation. I also heard them say that once you lease land to a large company, you might as well will it to them, since they take everything over. Before you know it, the Trevelyans will have your house, too."

"That's utter nonsense." Yet was my attraction to Stephen blinding me? Was I so busy looking for a wolf that I missed seeing one wearing sheep's clothing? "But

I thank you for the warning, Miss Vengle. Whom did you overhear?"

She fluttered her hand. "Just the men. Oh, I forgot to tell Mr. Fitz something. Excuse me," she said, and hurried across the room.

Scanning the room, I noticed Mignon and Mr. Davis were absent. Stephen stood at the French doors, looking out. I went to him.

"Mignon?"

"She and Mr. Davis stepped outside for a moment. He brought me Mr. Maison's address in Washington, D.C.," he replied.

"Good." Peering through the glass, I saw my sister and Mr. Davis by St. Catherine's statue. Mignon was talking in an animated way, using her hands expressively. She appeared to be entreating Mr. Davis to understand. "Miss Vengle just warned me that our land-leasing association was not only compromising my reputation, but could cost me my house. She believes you will take over everything."

"Interesting that she would approach you. I've found myself questioning the legitimacy of that acting troupe on occasion. Their method of putting on a production seems highly unusual, and now they are expressing far more interest in our land-leasing proposal than I had anticipated. The deal seems to be the topic of the evening. Mr. Latour has monopolized Mr. Phelps with questions about it. And a moment ago, I heard Mr. Fitz and Mr. Gallier elbow into the conversation."

Though concerned about what Stephen had to say, I kept my gaze glued to Mignon and Mr. Davis. Mr. Davis said something else to Mignon, and she shook her head adamantly. She definitely meant no. I hoped Mr. Davis would realize that Mignon regarded him as a friend and not a suitor.

"There is a problem with Mr. Davis?" Stephen asked.

"His interest in Mignon has deepened and she does not reciprocate his affections. She is telling him so now."

Mignon soon entered the house, frowning, and Mr. Davis was beaming.

"*Dieu*, this does not look good," I said under my breath. "His persistence is taxing."

Stephen smiled at me. "I can well understand his attraction to the DePerri beauty, though."

"Your sympathies are supposed to be with me," I said, exasperated.

Thankfully the dinner bell rang, and I urged everyone toward the dining room. On the way in I whispered to Mignon, "What happened?"

"He's convinced that once I have more time to know him, my feelings will change." Mignon smiled sweetly. "I agreed and promised to sit with him at dinner."

I watched her cross the dining room, worry weighing on my heart. She wasn't being very successful at discouraging Mr. Davis.

We had just started to eat when Mr. Fitz spoke to the table at large. "We have settled our argument over which play to do."

Since finding me at the fountain and mistaking me for another, Mr. Fitz had avoided speaking to me, whereas Mr. Gallier, who had to know I suspected something after seeing him in the park, didn't show the least bit of discomfort. He was smooth as honey with his wife and his mistress at the same table.

"Yes, a delightful compromise," Mr. Gallier added.

"We are going to do two plays, both rather appropriate for the times," Mr. Fitz continued. "*Julius Caesar*, and *Romeo and Juliet*."

Mr. Davis cleared his throat. "Sorry, gentlemen, but I find it hard to believe plays written centuries ago have any great relevance to the complexities we face in today's world."

Cheeks puffing, Mr. Gallier bristled. "No relevancy?"

Stephen spoke up. "From *Romeo and Juliet*, it's a mere step to speak of the North and South—from a long-held grudge, the spilling of civil blood, and a rage that only death could remove. Enough life has already been lost, enough blood already shed, enough young men have died. The continued strife between the North and the South needs to be buried."

"If you had been in the war, Mr. Trevelyan, you would not be speaking so," Mr. Latour said forcefully.

"I take it you were in the war, Mr. Latour?" Stephen asked.

"Every God-awful moment of it." Mr. Latour spoke so passionately, that an uncomfortable silence hovered over the group. "I gave everything I had to win it, and then Lee left us hanging dry by surrendering."

"Did he abandon the cause, or did he realize the price of winning was too high to pay?"

"He betrayed us."

"The war was thick with it on both sides of the battle lines," Mr. Davis said darkly.

"Did you fight as well, Mr. Davis?" Stephen asked.

"I would have to say I was neutral at the time, being as young as I was. But I wasn't too young to understand that any man would have stabbed me in the back for a slice of bread." Mr. Davis's voice rose, then he seemed to realize it. "That was a long time ago."

"But if you were so young, perhaps you are remembering it wrong. To think there is no honor, but only self-serving greed, seems so cynical," Mignon said, batting her lashes at Mr. Davis.

I realized that Mignon was deliberately being unlovely and unamenable and from the shock in Mr. Davis's eyes, she was succeeding rather well.

"That brings us back to the topic of our choice of play. *Julius Caesar* is an old story of betrayal," Miss Vengle said, entering into the conversation.

"Reminds me of the conspiracy behind Lincoln's assassination," Mr. Fitz said.

"I wouldn't call Booth and his ilk a conspiracy." Mr. Davis appeared amused.

"It's laughable to think otherwise." Mr. Fitz looked at Mr. Gallier. "Edmund, you've been in the acting business for almost thirty years, correct? During that time, how many actors have you met who were driven enough about politics to murder a president? A casting director, or a lead actor, maybe. But a president?"

"Nary a one," Mr. Gallier said. "I even met several of the Booth acting clan, and my answer would still be none."

"Then who would you say is responsible?" Mr. Davis asked, his brows rising.

"Booth may have pulled the trigger. And others, like the Surratts, Paine, Herold, and Atzerodt, were paid to be involved. They were men desperate to avenge a fallen South. But I say to you, the power most likely behind the conspiracy is no less than the men Lincoln called his friends: Stanton, Baker, even Vice President Johnson."

"Betrayal always comes from those you trust most," Mr. Latour said, looking directly at me.

A shiver went down my spine. I had never been the recipient of so much hate and anger.

Suddenly the lights flickered. The same bone-cold breath that had accosted me several times darkened the room, and a gray mist seemed to hover over Mr. Latour. Then I blinked and it was gone. But Mr. Latour's face drained to a pasty white, and Stephen's sharp gaze searched the room as if a predator lurked nearby.

Everyone appeared tense, and the sensation that evil was but a whisper away grew.

I heard Stephen's haunting music well after midnight, as I stood waiting with my cheek pressed to the glass and my hand on the lock. My heart beat wildly as I stepped cautiously into the moonlight. I went to the gallery's railing, but saw nothing except for St. Catherine's statue. The music had stopped the moment I appeared, so I knew Stephen had to be there.

"Stephen? Where are you?" I whispered.

"Here, fair Juliet." He leaned out from his own balcony, looking up at me, a mere six feet below."

"Whatever are you doing there?"

"Getting closer to you."

"We can't," I said, even as I thought back to what Mignon and Mama Louisa had said. Why shouldn't I have an affair? My eyes widened as he raised himself onto the railing of his balcony and climbed up the decorative wrought iron framing the pillars. He didn't stop until his shoulders were well above the floor of my balcony. I got down on my knees to face him as he hung onto the bars.

"What is this insanity?"

"I cannot stay away. One kiss," he whispered.

"Just one," I said.

He laughed. Climbing over the rail, he pulled me to my feet. I barely caught my breath before he backed me up against the wall into the shadows and kissed me hard. His body pressed to mine, making me feel the hot yearning of his desire with every part of me. He trailed kisses down my neck, then whispered into my ear, "The silk of your skin, the scent of your body, the taste of your kiss, makes me hunger even more for you."

I shivered with pleasure. "What is a woman to do with such impassioned flattery?"

"Silence me with another kiss. Then I will go," he said, nipping my mouth with his.

"One more." Groaning, I leaned into him and he deepened the kiss, drowning me in the heady elixir of desire. My robe fell open to his insistent touch as he cupped my breasts. He brushed the hardened tips with his thumbs, driving a sharp pleasure through me. I arched to him, lost in the feel for him, but he soon stepped away, leaving me bereft.

"Stephen," I whispered, reaching out my hand.

He took my fingers and brushed them with his lips and tongue. "When you're ready to damn the consequences, come to me," he said, desire roughing his voice. "I swore I wouldn't sweep you away with my own desire. You have to want this as much as I do." Releasing my hand, he backed away. "Good night, Juliet." He swung over the rail and disappeared from sight.

I went to the railing, my whole body throbbing for him. He could not leave me on this piercing edge of desire. I yearned for him, and nothing else mattered.

"Stephen?" I whispered, and waited. Nothing. I

called again and still no answer. I went inside and tip-toed to the second floor, but just before I reached his door, I heard a sound. I slipped into the shadows at the end of the corridor.

A door opened and I saw Mr. Gallier tying his robe closed over his naked body. He let himself out of Miss Vengle's room, tiptoed down the hall, and entered the room he shared with his wife. He did not see me, but someone else did.

Mr. Fitz stood outside his doorway, his gaze stark. I couldn't tell if pain or anger twisted his features. He stared at me, not saying a word, until I felt my jumping skin crawl.

"Sorry, Monsieur Fitz," I whispered. "I thought I heard a noise. Have you seen anything unusual?"

"Not at all, Mrs. Boucheron," he said, then shut his door.

I returned to my room, torn by my desire for Stephen and my need to choose the right path. Whatever decision I made would affect my entire family.

The next morning, after looking for Jean Claude's letters again, I finally resigned myself that they were lost. I had wanted Andre to read them so he would at least know how his father felt about him at one time. Andre's hurt had lessened since I had confessed to everyone what I knew about the sinister shadow in our lives. He may have been angry, but when his family was threatened, he closed ranks.

Walking into the parlor, I found Stephen and Andre playing chess. Their dark heads were bent over the board, deep concentration on their faces. My heart swelled. Rather than going back to my chores, I picked up a book and settled into the parlor with it, deciding to enjoy a few minutes just relaxing with them nearby. I'd read no more than a page when I felt Stephen's smouldering gaze, setting me afire. The words on the page blurred as images of being with him filled my mind.

"Monsieur Trevelyan," Mignon said, bustling into the room. "Might Ginette have a moment of your time?"

"What is it?" I straightened, slightly alarmed. "Is she worse?" Ginette had sat in the sun of the courtyard for a while, working on her embroidery, but another painful headache sent her to her room.

Mignon shook her head. "*Non*, she is the same. She is rested now and has asked to see Monsieur Trevelyan."

"Of course. I will be glad to speak to her," Stephen said as he stood. "Our game can wait a few moments, can it not, Andre?"

"Certainly. But I must warn you, I am strategizing your demise, and the more time I have to think, the worse it will be for you." Andre smiled.

Stephen laughed. "I am looking forward to the challenge, sir."

After he left, I went to Andre. "*Mon petit*, we have to talk."

"I do not want to talk." He looked away, but not before I saw the light in his eyes dim.

I swallowed hard. "I have to know what happened. Whom did you fight with? Phillipe or Will?"

"*Non*. Neither."

"Then who told you of your father? I have been meaning to tell you for months now, but I was waiting on a report from an investigator, Monsieur Goodson.

"Why? Would you have let me go see my father?"

"*Oui*," I whispered. "For though I do not know what the war did to him inside, I know at one time he loved you dearly. And I could not stand in the way of you finding out your own answers to your questions about your father."

Andre regarded me with surprise. "Then you did not purposely let me believe he was dead to keep me from him?"

"*Non*," I said emphatically. "I only wanted you to believe good things about your father and your heritage. Now please, Andre. What happened?"

"Monsieur Hayes and several of his friends were at the camp, showing us how to shoot rifles."

I gasped.

"They said a man has to know how to protect and feed his family. Everything was fine, and then the more whiskey they drank, the wilder they became. They started shooting at squirrels and birds, laughing. I told them I was going home, and Monsieur Hayes called me a coward just like my father, and told one of his friends that he better check the silver at the house before I left. The friend said he'd check me right now and grabbed me, ripping my shirt. He asked me what I did with all that gold. I tried to hit him, and he punched me in the face. Then they told me how my father stole everyone's gold and deserted the army."

"Where were Phillipe and Will?"

"Hiding in the trees."

Grown men had done this to my son! Why, after years of silence, had Mr. Hayes spoken so cruelly to Andre? First thing in the morning, I'd pay his family a visit. How dare he treat my child so!

"Andre, I would have given my life to save you from this."

He took a deep breath. "I didn't need your life. All I needed was the truth."

"Will you ever forgive me?" I whispered.

At first I thought I was imagining his hand upon my tightly fisted one. But as he increased the pressure of his fingers prying mine open, I realized he was reaching out to me. I opened my hand and he slid his into mine. Only then did I have the courage to meet his gaze.

"I am angry about everything. But I love you, *Mère*. I love Ginette and Nonnie, and Mama Louisa and Papa John. Anger does not make the love go away, but it does make me want to be alone right now. Do you understand?"

There was more substance to my son than I had

known. "*Oui.* Just know that when you are ready, I would very much like to hug you. You have become a man who will make me very proud."

His eyes widened.

Stephen returned then and his smile appeared forced, his eyes more shadowed, adding fuel to my apprehension. After he and Andre finished their chess game, I approached.

"Would you care to join me in the courtyard for a few moments, Monsieur Trevelyan?"

"Certainly. I am in need of a bit a fresh air. Andre has just beaten me soundly."

"Really?"

"*Oui, Mère.* When might we play again, Monsieur Trevelyan?"

"Tomorrow evening, after dinner. I need time to strategize."

Andre laughed, then excused himself, saying he had to finish reading *Swiss Family Robinson*.

"He has never shown an interest in literature before. You are quite the miracle worker," I said as we exited through the French doors, leaving the coolness of the house for the steamy heat of the sun. By unspoken agreement, we headed toward the fountain.

"Just a matter of tweaking the lad's interest. Sometimes that requires having been a boy yourself."

"Tell me about Ginette. What was so urgent?"

He glanced away from me, looking at the fountain for a long moment, then sighed. "She wanted to know if I could do her a favor, and she wanted to know more about Dr. Marks. Now, tell my why you look upset."

I told Stephen what had happened to Andre at the camp. "The incident with Mr. Hayes and his cohorts would have never happened if it weren't for me."

Stephen slammed his fist against the hard marble of the fountain's base. "The hell it wouldn't. Men like Hayes are a disease in society. You cannot blame yourself for the vileness of others."

I took my silk handkerchief, dipped it into the cool waters of the fountain, and reached for his hand. He sucked in air as I pressed the silk to his torn knuckles.

"I fear that my wardrobe is unlikely to survive all your injuries, Stephen."

He wrapped his fingers around my wrist. "Just as I am unlikely to survive your touch or my desire for you, Juliet. I want you." Desire darkened his eyes.

"I want you, too," I whispered.

"Enough to come to me? I want you to touch me. To trust me. To let me fill your every desire." Releasing my wrist, he slid his fingers tantalizingly down my arm, awakening my senses, touching my heart.

I had to close my eyes to keep from reaching for him. "I am not a free woman."

"So?" he asked harshly. "Must you pay for your husband's crime by spending your life alone? Could you go back to being his wife after all these years?"

I shook my head. "Legally I should, but I could never do so." My heart belonged to Stephen.

He exhaled with relief. "That's a start."

"What do you mean?"

"It means I want more than a tumble in a carriage. I want all of you, every sweet inch of you, inside and out for a long, long time. Even if Jean Claude turns up alive, I'm not going anywhere, Juliet. I'll try and be patient for a short time, because of everything that is happening, but we haven't even begun to explore the pleasure between us."

❧ *13* ❧

The next morning, after a long discussion with my family about my course of action, I traveled in the safety of a carriage to speak to the Hayes family concerning their treatment of my son. I thought to ask Stephen to go but he was strangely absent from his room, his bed still made as if he hadn't slept there.

On the way to the Hayes Plantation, I had the driver stop at the post office and the telegraph office, where I inquired if there was any word from Mr. Goodson. I was irritated and worried over his continued silence, and thought I might have to take a trip to Baton Rouge in the near future.

Before long, the busy streets of the Vieux Carré pulsed outside the carriage's window. The bustling city in the early summer morning shimmered with life. Everyone hurried about, trying to get as much done in the cool of the morning before the sun would steal the breath from the air.

Suddenly, on the street corner I saw a disheveled Stephen with a fully turned-out Miss Vengle at his side. They were standing close together, talking. She appeared to be hanging on his every word, and a stab of pain and jealousy shot through me. Had he been with her during the night?

I wanted to stop the carriage and demand to know what was happening. Then it hit me that I thought Stephen guilty of being with another woman, with no real reason to believe that. He'd been talking to her, not kissing her. And honesty made me face what I had been doing to Stephen for days: I'd led him to make love to me, then I'd held Jean Claude like a barrier between us.

I could no longer avoid a decision about our relationship.

My thoughts dwelt on that during the long ride to the Hayes Plantation on River Road. I didn't take note of my surroundings until the sharp, repetitive report of gunfire snapped me from my thoughts.

"Monsieur." I rapped on the roof of the carriage with my parasol and peered out the window. "Whatever is going on here?"

The driver leaned over the side, his bleary blue eyes troubled. "Sounds like the White League to me, ma'am." He pointed to the woods flanking a huge, sprawling lawn with an equally impressive mansion sitting in the middle of it. A haze of smoke hovered over the trees, and I heard the rhythm of precisely timed gunfire.

"The White League is mighty restless these days. They aim to take down folks they think are too uppity for their own good. They especially hate you if you don't have the right color skin."

"I didn't realize Mr. Hayes was associated with such a despicable group." In fact, there had been some discussion at my suffrage meetings about the group. The league had vociferously opposed the Women's Right to Vote movement. *Dieu*, what had Andre involved himself in?

"Mr. Hayes leads a vigilante group, and no one dares oppose him or they are likely to be found hanging."

I shuddered.

"You still interested in going to the Hayes Plantation?" He nodded at the mansion and my eyes widened.

The Hayes family had done extremely well since the end of the war. They'd been well off before and now it appeared they were doubly so, if the expansion of the house was an indication.

"Oui," I said, tightly. "But you had better wait for me."

When the driver pulled to a stop, I exited the carriage with determination and rapped the brass door knocker soundly.

The butler opened the door immediately. "May I help you?"

"Oui," I said, marching in past him. "It is urgent that I speak to Madame Hayes."

The butler looked down his nose at my rudeness. "She is indisposed. If you'll leave me your card, I will see that she is notified."

"Then Monsieur Hayes will have to do."

"He is indisposed, as well."

"I am not leaving until you tell one of them that Madame Boucheron is here."

"Very well." The butler turned and left me standing in the center hall. I walked about the foyer, surprised to see valuable statuettes and gilt-framed paintings filling every possible space.

Moments later, a red-faced burly man hobbled into the room. I could hardly recognize Mr. Hayes; he appeared to have grown monstrously overweight and had developed an unseemly disposition to match.

"Come to gloat over your lover's handiwork? How dare you come to my house?" he said, standing menacingly in front of the doors.

Shocked, I straightened my back, wondering what in God's name he meant. He appeared crazed, and I tightened my grip on the bone handle of my parasol. "You dared to harm Andre! Grown men beating up and cruelly taunting a child—I'm appalled by your cowardly abuse."

He laughed. "Abuse? You dare say that after what you had done to me? I'll show you what abuse is." Fist raised, he came limping toward me.

"No! We will be ruined if you harm her," Letitia Hayes cried, running into the hall behind him. She had a bruised cheek, her hair spilled from her bun as if she'd not fixed it in days, and terror glistened in her gray eyes. Mr. Hayes turned and knocked Letitia back, sending her to the floor.

My gasp of disbelief turned to pure outrage. He turned toward me again, raising his fist. Heart pounding, I hit him firmly between the legs with my parasol. He doubled over and fell to the floor, grabbing his unmentionable parts and yelling for help.

I pressed the pointed end of my parasol against his throat. "If you dare hit me, or my child, or any child or any other woman again, not even Satan will want what's left of you."

Turning, I went to Letitia, reaching out to help her up. Though she'd spurned me for years, she was once close to me, and my heart cried for her. Her home was richly grand, unlike mine, but her life was a travesty, and so poor compared to the fullness of mine.

She shifted away from me, hiding her face. "Go away."

"Let me help you. How badly are you hurt?"

"Just go away," she whispered.

I dropped my hand but leaned close enough to whisper, though as loudly as Mr. Hayes was screaming, he couldn't have heard me. "Come to the suffrage meeting. There are women there who can help. Don't let him do this to you."

She didn't say anything and didn't look my way. The sound of approaching footsteps urged me to leave before Mr. Hayes found someone willing to carry out his threats against my person.

"You're always welcome at *La Belle*," I said softly to Letitia, then left. Mr. Hayes was screaming for his army from the woods, so I quickened my step and told my driver to hurry.

All the way back, I feared that Hayes would come barreling into the carriage and extract revenge. My driver was about to turn onto my street when he stopped, alarming me.

"What is it, Monsieur?" I asked, peering out.

"Something in the road, ma'am. Appears to be an injured puppy. I'll go see what it's about."

Hearing faint whimpering cries of pain, I reached for the door, only to have the latch snatched from my hand. A man covered in a white-trimmed dark cloak, wearing a ghoulish mask with two slits cut for eyes, grabbed me and wrenched me from the carriage. I screamed, and a brutal hand clamped over my mouth and nose, cutting off my air. Struggling, I fought against the man's grip while a dizzy haze threatened to consume me. I saw the driver lying in the road, bleeding, and I fought harder. I twisted violently, managing to dislodge the attacker's gloved hand enough to draw precious air into my lungs.

"What's wrong, dear wife? Do you not remember your loving husband?" the unfamiliar voice rasped harshly. "I've returned, and you'd better run for your life, because I am going to come for you and you will never know when. In the middle of the night when you and your lovely sisters sleep, when you tuck my son into bed at night . . ."

"*Non!*" I cried, throwing my entire weight forward and kicking back at him with the heel of my boot. He grunted and I broke free, running for the live oaks and their thick cover of heavy moss. I heard the report of a pistol, but I didn't stop.

Branches and twigs stabbed at my face, digging into my skin. I ran and ran until Stephen's voice jerked me to a stop.

"Juliet! Where are you! Answer me!"

I gulped for air. "Here," I tried to say. "Here," I called again, louder this time.

Dense foliage rustled and Stephen burst into view. He limped toward me, favoring his left leg as if he were injured.

"Dear God." He wrapped his arms around me and pulled me hard against his thundering heart.

"There's a masked man. We must hurry," I urged him.

"I shot at him. He left. How could I do this to you?"

I pressed my hands to his chest and pushed hard. He stepped back, releasing me immediately.

"What do you mean?" I asked.

"When you told me what happened to Andre at the Hayes Plantation, I swore to myself that I'd make sure those who were responsible paid, and I went looking for them last night. By morning I'd found them all and gave them a thrashing they won't forget. Now it looks as if I've brought the wrath of the White League down on you. Christ, I'll never forgive myself. And I'll never forgive you for putting yourself in danger! What were you thinking, to go there alone?"

"I was accompanied by a driver. Letitia Hayes used to be my best friend. I knew I wouldn't be welcomed there, but I didn't know there would be danger." I should have been appalled by the violence in his story, but I wasn't. He'd fought for my son and me, which touched me deeply. Brushing at the tears on my cheeks, I drew a deep breath. "I left Hayes on his back, and it is going to be a lot longer before he walks." I told Stephen what happened at the Hayes Plantation, then said, "The masked man claimed to be Jean Claude."

"Was it?" Stephen tightened his hold on me.

"No. I didn't recognize his voice. Oh, the driver and the puppy! We must go help them." When we exited the trees, I saw the carriage parked in front of *La Belle*. The coachman was in front of the house, pointing down the street. Papa John and Andre had rifles in their hands.

Stephen called to them as we hurried their way. The moment Andre saw us, he ran. I opened my arms to him and he hugged me tighter than I had ever been hugged before. After a moment, I felt Stephen's hand on my back.

"It would be better if everyone went inside. The man left, but that does not mean he won't come back."

I shivered, remembering his threat. Keeping an arm around Andre, I hurried into *La Belle,* bringing the driver and the injured puppy. There was no doubt in anyone's mind that the animal had been harmed on purpose. I wondered if I would find the evil lurking in the shadows of my life before it destroyed me.

"No matter what the man said, it wasn't Jean Claude." I paced in front of the French doors of my father's office. Two hours had passed since the attack. The authorities had come, spoken to the driver, and taken my story. Though I told them that the man threatened me and my family, I didn't tell them the man claimed to be Jean Claude. I knew it had not been my husband, and I had assured Andre. Now Stephen and I were alone.

"What makes you so sure?" Stephen stood in the shadows next to the hearth, appearing wholly dangerous, as if the day's events had stripped all semblance of civility from him.

"The attacker was larger than Jean Claude. He did not speak with a French accent as Jean Claude would have. And no matter what Jean Claude's crimes were, he would not threaten me, my sisters, and Andre."

"I agree with you, but for different reasons. A man declaring who he is has no need of a disguise. And were he here to torment you as he claimed, would he tell you to run for your life? The attack was meant to frighten you into leaving your home. You said Mr. Latour has been trying to buy *La Belle*, correct?"

"*Oui*. Do you think it was he?"

"You tell me. Did anything the man do reveal himself to you?"

"No. But I kicked him hard in the shin."

He smiled. "Then we will simply go around and pull up everyone's trouser legs, looking for a bruise. Add my name to the suspect list, since I have a nasty bruise on my leg."

"It was not you."

"How do you know?"

I drew a deep breath, and sent my mind tumbling in the direction my heart had fallen in. "I know it was not you, for I know your touch, and your scent."

"Is that the only reason?"

"No. I know without a doubt you wouldn't hurt me or mine. I trust you." At that moment, I realized that I loved him, deeply, irrevocably. "Stephen," I whispered, my heart in my voice.

He stared at me so intently that I thought he'd cross the room and kiss me. I wanted him to. But he cleared his throat and turned away instead, his hands fisted. "All of this conjecture regarding your husband's return is based on a note. How do you know it was really your sister-in-law who sent it?"

I shook my head, shocked by my feelings and his

question. "It appeared to be Josephine's handwriting. I never even thought to doubt the news," I said with surprise. "I think it is time Andre saw his grandfather again."

Stephen crossed the room and took hold of my shoulders. His gaze searched mine, as if he were trying to reach my thoughts, my soul, the very heart of me. More gently than the feathery brush of soft down, he slid his finger along my cheek.

"I never again want to feel the fear that ripped me apart when I saw you being attacked and was too far away to help. You cannot go anywhere alone. I am now your shadow."

I nodded, swallowing thickly. I didn't want to know that terror again, either.

During the journey down River Road, Stephen regaled Andre and me with so many lively stories that I felt as if I'd lived his childhood with him, his sister Katherine, and his brother Benedict. We entered my sister-in-law's home in a jovial mood that quickly dissipated.

Josephine Boucheron Foucault had never been known for her hospitality, and a decade of postwar struggle had dried any kernel of kindness she might have once possessed. Her butler escorted us to a chilled parlor that held only straight-backed wooden chairs without cushions. The few decorations dotting the room were sparse and dull.

"You were asked to never come here," Josephine

growled as she marched into the room, her mouth and face as grimly severe as her home. "My post in no way hinted otherwise."

"So you did write the note about Jean Claude." Part of me had hoped the note a forgery, for I did not want to believe Jean Claude was responsible for the menace stalking us. Yet part of me had hoped that Jean Claude would walk through the door with her. I could then confront his wrongs and move on with my life.

"Since you contacted me, you have no one to blame but yourself, Josephine. We have several questions and then, once Andre has seen his grandfather, we will leave."

"Father is unwell."

"All the more reason for Andre to see him," I said. "Have you seen Jean Claude since you wrote to me?"

"No," she said dourly. "He came while I was at church, spoke to father, collected his trunk of belongings, and then left without speaking to me."

"He has not contacted me, either."

"I am not surprised. What man would want a wife who abandoned his family's home when he had to fight?"

I gritted my teeth. Josephine believed that if I had stayed on the Boucheron Plantation, the renegade Federal troops that burned the house and killed Jean Claude's brother would have been more lenient, and subsequently, Jean Claude wouldn't have stolen the gold. "Have you had any contact with him at all since he left the army?"

"I have not."

"Then if you will direct us to Andre's grandfather, we will leave shortly."

"He is in the solarium," she replied tightly, and quit the room without ever looking at Andre or Stephen. We went to the back of the house and through a glass door. The bright sunshine transformed the dullness of the small room. Near the windows, a uniformed nurse sat beside a feeble man in a wheeled chair. He did not resemble the vital man who had carved a successful plantation out of the untamed wilds of Louisiana's swampy land. Sliding my hand into Andre's, I urged him forward. Stephen stayed close behind, making true his shadow promise.

The old man looked up and beamed at us, but instead of looking at Andre, his cloudy eyes were focused on Stephen. "My son, I knew you had not forsaken me. Come sit with me for a while. It was very naughty of you to leave so quickly on your last visit. I have waited so long to see you."

Stephen returned my look of shock.

"What does he mean, Mère? Do Monsieur Trevelyan and my father look alike?" Andre murmured.

"No," I whispered, feeling uneasy.

The nurse said, "Don't take mind of his ramblings. He is often confused, and these past few days have been worse."

Leaning down, I met the old man's bleary gaze. "Monsieur Boucheron, do you remember me? I am Juliet, Jean Claude's wife."

The old man looked at Stephen, a broad smile on his face. "You married well, son." He looked at Andre, beaming with pride. "This must be your boy then, my own grandson. Come closer, lad. These old eyes can barely see anymore."

Andre stepped forward awkwardly and held out his hand. "*Grandpère,* I am Andre."

Taking Andre's hand, his grandfather pulled him into a surprisingly strong hug and patted his back with a gnarled hand. "You are a fine boy. The spittin' image of your father when he was a lad. Bet you are a devil at chess, aren't you?" he asked as he released my son.

"I enjoy the game very much," Andre said modestly.

"You have done well, Jean Claude. Thank you, my son, for coming back and for bringing Andre to me." The old man kept his gaze on my son.

I swallowed the lump in my throat as I realized Jean Claude's father held no hatred for Andre and me, despite what Josephine had claimed years ago.

The old man's expression became somber as he looked at Stephen again. "Be careful. I will die before I breathe a word of what little you have told me, but this plan is a dangerous one, and greed is stronger than loyalty to any cause. Watch your back, son."

My heart skipped a beat, but Stephen didn't even

blink an eye as he replied, "Tell me what worries you. Would you have me do anything different?"

"The whole setup bothers me," the old man said, his agitation growing. "A spy for us or not, that lad, the ... Shepherd Boy, does not have the experience to help you and Roth, should things go wrong." He coughed heavily. "No one is going to believe you innocent, and a man's honor is a hard price to pay for any victory, much less a minor one. But I agree with you: if you are sure our salvation is safe, then at least the families who sacrificed will not starve, no matter what the outcome of the war."

Jean Claude's father lapsed into another coughing spell, suddenly exhausted.

"What are you doing to him?" Josephine shouted as she stomped into the room. "Is your intent to kill him for what little inheritance remains?"

Andre gasped, clearly horrified. Laying a protective hand on him, I faced Josephine. "I pity you. You have so little joy yourself that you try to steal it from others. What has it gained you to keep Andre from his grandfather?"

"I will not have anyone poison my father against his only daughter."

I shook my head sadly. "We will leave, but Andre will be back to see his grandfather, now that I know the truth of things."

I ignored Josephine's ranting as I ushered Andre out of the house with Stephen close behind us. The cloud of Jean Claude's theft and desertion that had hovered darkly over my life now roiled with questions.

"Well, that was enlightening," Stephen said the moment the carriage door shut.

I drew a deep breath. "As confused as Jean Claude's father is, anyone could have claimed to be Jean Claude and collected his trunk. I am beginning to wonder if anything I believed about Jean Claude's betrayal is true."

"You mean my father might not have stolen the gold?" Andre asked.

"*Non*, but it is clear from what your grandfather said that your father did not act alone. And there was a plan and a purpose for the gold."

"I hate to say this, but I must," Stephen said. "What we have is Jean Claude, a man who has never been seen by anyone he cared about since he went on a mission for a cause that he was willing to sacrifice his honor for, so that others would not starve. And we have a plan for seven hundred and fifty thousand in gold that was never put into action."

"You think my father is dead. That he really did die in the war," Andre said, his tone so bleak that my heart wrenched for him. I held my hand out to him and he slid his hand into mine.

"Yes," Stephen said.

The sounds of the creaking carriage, rolling along the rutted road, and an occasional screech of an owl above the low hum of katydids filled the silence.

"I am curious," Stephen said after a time. "Why did your sister-in-law have Jean Claude's belongings and not you?"

"Josephine claimed everything had been destroyed in a fire."

"If your sister-in-law was any smarter, I might suspect her as being the power behind the malevolent forces darkening your life."

❧ *14* ❧

Upon waking Tuesday morning, I had one thing on my mind: the man who'd filled my hot dreams during the night. I couldn't solve the mystery of Jean Claude's disappearance, but I could reach out for the man I now loved. I went to the French doors with an anticipation for the coming night that not even the heavy rain outside could dampen.

Opening the doors, I almost screamed at finding a man lying at my feet. He rolled over in a flash. *"Bon Dieu,"* I gasped.

"Morning," Stephen mumbled, sitting up, damp from the rain.

"What are you doing?" I whispered.

"Guarding the gates of heaven while the world sleeps," he said with an impish smile.

Warmth filled my heart, and I leaned down to cup his beard-roughened cheek in my hand. He brought my fingers to his lips, then turned my hand over and brushed a kiss to my palm and my wrist.

"Stephen," I whispered as he kissed his way higher, rising to his feet. My knees nearly gave way when his lips reached mine, brushing softly at first, and then delving deeply.

"Juliet," he said softly, when he ended the kiss. His gaze sought an answer from me.

"Please," I said. A gripping anticipation captured my pulse as he set his hands on my shoulders.

"Please what, dear Juliet?"

"Love me."

"Yes," he said, swinging me into his arms as his mouth covered mine. He walked to the bed and set me on my feet. "I have longed to touch you again, to feel all of you, to love you."

Taking the hem of my gown, he lifted it over my head, leaving me naked in the lamplight.

He groaned as he raked his gaze over me, his eyes burning. He reached for me, but I stepped back.

"I want to see you, too."

"Whatever the lady wants. Touch me. Feel me. See how much I want you."

I brushed his hand from the buttons of his damp shirt. With each button I loosed, I slid my fingers over his supple skin, feeling his silky hardness, and the warmth of him. Pushing his shirt back from his shoulders, I trailed kisses from his firm jaw down to his chest, tasting his saltiness, breathing in the heady elixir of his scent. Then I slid my fingers to his belt, unbuckling it. His erection burned hotly and I brushed my hands over the bulge of his pants, relishing the pulsing heat and power of his body.

"I need you now," he rasped, sliding his fingers through my hair and bringing my mouth to his for a searing kiss.

"Let me finish," I gasped.

"Next time you can torture me," he growled, pushing me back onto the bed. Lying beside me, he cupped my breasts in his hands and covered one tip with his mouth, then the other, laving his tongue over the hardened peaks until I squirmed.

I reveled in his hot passion, pouring over me with every stroke of his silken tongue. He slid between my legs and rose to his knees, looking down at me.

"You are pure heaven." Sliding his hands from my breasts, he brushed his fingers over the dark curls of my femininity, pressing his hand against my yearning flesh, then caressing me. Fire burned. I rocked my hips to him, wanting more, wanting *him*.

He reached for my pillows against the headboard. "I must have a taste of heaven." Then he lifted my hips up, placed the pillow beneath, and spread my legs wide.

Pure sensual vulnerability rippled through me at having my secret flesh so exposed. "Stephen, what are you doing?"

"Praising you with my silver tongue." He pressed his

hands against my thighs, holding me still, and kissed me right at the center of my aching need for him. The instant pleasure launched a storm so wild and intense, I could do nothing but give myself over to its passionate wind. Stephen drove me almost to the peak of madness with his lips and tongue. Then he rose up and entered me, driving his erection deep. I arched up, gasping for more.

"Yes," he whispered. "Let yourself go, Juliet." His gaze locked on me as he thrust harder and deeper and faster. "Feel me," he rasped.

I wrapped my legs around him, matching the power of his thrusts, yielding to his consuming passion. "I do," I cried, fevered from pleasure so intense that I thought I would die from the hot ecstasy of it. Suddenly heaven burst inside of me, and I cried out and shuddered uncontrollably.

"More," he demanded. He slid his finger over the very spot his tongue had lashed and teased my nipple, sending me out of my mind as he shuddered into me. I screamed as fulfillment shattered through me.

In mere moments, I heard the rumble of feet in the room next to mine.

"Mignon! She must have heard my scream," I said, panicked.

"Hell," Stephen muttered, rolling from me. He threw my robe at me, grabbed up his pants and shirt, then he ran naked out my French doors. Scrambling, I pulled on my robe and kicked Stephen's boots under the bed just as Mignon burst in on me. She looked wildly about, then focused on the bed.

"Did you have a nightmare? You screamed."

I nodded, unable to speak from the embarrassment burning me.

"By the looks of your bed, it was bad."

I drew a deep breath. "I'll be fine."

Then I heard noises from downstairs—knocks on doors, the shuffle of feet, voices calling out.

Ginette showed up next, wavering in the doorway like a starved street urchin. "Juliet," she said. "Are you—"

She fell over. Mignon and I barely caught her before she hit the floor, looking as lifeless and gray as death itself.

"Nonnie, was Ginny worse last night?" I cried.

"I thought her better. We spent a good amount of time in the sitting room, she with her embroidery, and I with my writing tablet."

"Help me get her back to bed and we will have Monsieur Trevelyan send for Dr. Marks. If he cannot come immediately, we will send for Dr. Lanau."

When the smelling salts failed to revive Ginette, we carried her to her room, alarmed not only by the lightness of her frail body, but by her continued unconsciousness. Nonnie ran immediately to fetch Stephen, Mama Louisa, and Papa John.

I knew Ginette breathed, for I counted every rise and fall of her chest. The pulse at her neck thrummed faintly beneath my fingertips. Her skin was cold and clammy. I rubbed her hands, her face, her feet, and covered her with blankets, trying to warm her. She didn't respond, didn't move, and I held onto her hand and prayed.

"Juliet?"

I looked up to see Stephen in the doorway, pale, somber, and still dressed in his damp and rumpled suit. "I am going for Dr. Marks. Give me thirty minutes. Please, don't leave the house while I am gone."

"I am not leaving Ginny's side."

He nodded, started to leave, then turned back. "Did Miss Vengle tell you she was going anywhere?"

"No. Why do you ask?"

He ignored my question. "When did you see her last?"

I swallowed the sudden lump in my throat. "Yesterday morning. I saw her standing on the corner of Canal and Chartres. She was with you."

He sucked in air, as he stared intently at me a moment, then left. I felt very much alone at that minute, as if the intimacy of this morning was nothing more than a wild dream. Why hadn't Stephen offered an explanation?

Mignon brought me clothes and I quickly dressed. Stephen soon returned with Dr. Marks, both of them soaked from the heavy rain.

Mignon followed them into the room with an armful of towels.

"We rode horseback," Stephen said. "It was faster."

Dr. Marks shed his sodden overcoat, dried his face and hands with a towel, and came to Ginette's bedside.

"She fainted this morning and hasn't awakened." I told him.

"Has she been worse since I was here, exhibited any other symptoms?" he asked as he examined her, listening to her chest, checking her pulse, and then opening her eyes.

"She seems more chilled all the time."

"After I am done, I want to know everything that she did, and everything that she ate and drank yesterday and last night."

"Mignon can speak to you about that. I was away last evening and did not return until late."

Mignon and I waited hand in hand. Dr. Marks's examination was thorough, and when he finished, I nearly cried at the grim expression on his face.

"Mrs. Boucheron, might I have a private word with you?"

"Of course."

He looked hard at Mignon. "Miss DePerri, stay with your sister. If she awakens, call me immediately and do not give her anything to eat or drink. Do you understand?"

"*Oui*, Dr. Marks."

The doctor then motioned for me to join him in the corridor. "I have been thoroughly investigating her symptoms and trying to match them to a cause. There are two things that bother me immensely: the inconsistency of her attacks and the rash on her hands. Mrs. Boucheron, I believe your sister is being poisoned."

"What?" I grabbed the wall behind me for support.

"Whether by accident or on purpose, I cannot say. But usually accidental poisoning occurs as a single incident. Is there any reason someone would poison her but try and make it appear to be an illness? An inheritance, maybe?"

"*Non.* We have only what you see here, Dr. Marks. My sisters and I equally share *La Belle.*" *The gold,* my mind shouted. *The intruder.* But why poison Ginette?

"Can Miss DePerri be trusted?"

"Nonnie? *Oui.* A thousand times so."

"Your sister cannot be left alone with someone you do not trust implicitly. She is in a very vulnerable state. Any more exposure to the toxin could kill her."

His warning echoed alarmingly in my mind as I called for Mignon to speak with Dr. Marks.

How could I have let this happen? Maybe if I hadn't kept Mr. Goodson's telegram a secret, everyone would have been more alert. From the expression on Stephen's face when he entered Ginette's room, it was clear Dr. Marks had divulged his suspicions.

"I cannot believe someone would do this," I said.

"I can."

"But why?"

"The gold."

I threw my hands up. "But we do not have the gold! We do not know anything about it!"

"That doesn't matter. Someone *thinks* that you do."

"What does poisoning Ginette have to do with it?"

"Were one of you to die, how long would the rest of you hold on to *La Belle*? At what point would the memories become too painful to face?"

Never, my heart wanted to cry. But was that true? "Oh, Stephen. If something happened to both Ginette *and* myself . . . Mignon and Andre are but babes, susceptible to anything. . . ."

Stephen grabbed my shoulders, his eyes fierce. "Something has already happened to Ginette *and* to you. Remember the attack yesterday? The trunks in the attic? The man with the knife? My guess is that whoever is behind this is just waiting to come back and finish what was started."

Stephen left to confer with Dr. Marks and Mignon as they searched the house for the source of the poison, while I examined Ginette's room, looking for anything she might use on her hands. Before long, I had accumulated half a dozen bottles of hand lotion and set them aside for Dr. Marks to see. Then I settled in a chair by Ginette's bed to keep vigil.

Spying the stack of decorative boxes Mignon had taken down for Ginette the other morning, I opened them one by one, searching through ribbons and buttons and old keepsakes. I found nothing odd until the last box, the blue-flowered one Ginette had asked Mignon to get for her. My fingers tingled as I reached for it and slid off the top. Inside I found a bundle of letters, and when the endearment at the top of the first page caught my attention, I froze.

My Dearest Love,

I thought I was strong enough never to speak aloud what my heart has whispered to me day and night since the moment I met you. I thought I would never succumb to the overwhelming desire to write you, for wisdom tells me that your youthful heart may feel you love me now, but in time, maturity will prove it to be a passing fancy.

Yet as I look across this hellish battlefield strewn with the slain bodies of men I called my friends just yesterday, and those of men who were our brothers before this godforsaken war, I find that I can remain silent no more on what matters most.

When the bugle sounds on the morrow, I will leave this tent. I fear, I too, will fall victim to this dark tide of senseless maiming and killing, and if such is to be my fate, then everything decent and good within me demands that I not spend my last hours huddled in fear, or spewing false hate toward the Confederate camp across this crimson valley in hopes of building enough bravado to face the dawn.

Instead, I choose to dwell on the richness and depth of the love I hold for you and to draw my courage from that endless well. I had to tell you at least once before I died exactly what you mean to me. With each rise of the sun across God's land, I remember the light of your smile, the warmth of your kindness, and the depth of your soul, which my words fail miserably to describe. I remember every word you spoke to me when you secretly tended my wounds. I remember your every touch and your every prayer.

And had I the power to call forth the angels that ring in your voice and resonate in your harp, I would have no need to fear the future, for salvation would surely be mine.

If by some miracle this letter should reach you and I survive the battle that will rage, I ask you, nay I beg you, to write to me of your life. I will fight tomorrow in hopes that a letter from you lies in my future, and that the affection you declared to me before I left still lives within your heart. I will pray that someday, when this great, sorrowful war that has divided hearth and home and blood and brother is over, our love can *heal each other and what devastation man has wrought.*

> *Eternally Yours,*
> *James*

My fingers trembled as I stared at the worn page, blotched by what surely must be tears.

There could be no doubt that the man who had declared himself to my sister was Federal Army captain James Edwin Jennison. The letter was dated six months after his regiment had left New Orleans.

As I refolded the first letter and opened the second, my hands were shaking so badly that I had to lay the letter upon the floor to focus on it. Guilt pricked at me, but I had to know more; I couldn't leave anything unknown until I determined who was poisoning her.

Heart of my Heart,

How can I accept that your love, which has kept me alive and sane through the depths of hell, may never be more than written words on a page? We have waited years, torn by war and death. Can we not find a way, now that the promise of peace has held out a loving hand?

I beg of you, sweet Ginette, to reconsider. Come to me and be my wife. If there were any other way, I would forsake all worldly goods to be with you. But the lives of those I love just as dearly rest in my hands. I understand the struggle you and your sister wage against these desperate times, and I know how much she needs your support. But I beg you again, bring all those you love here to my humble home in the hills and marry me. I will care for your family as my own. We will build a new life for us all out of the ashes of this war.

> *My heart is yours for eternity,*
> *James*

The letter was dated a year after the war had ended. Eight years ago, this man loved Ginette.

Carefully, I retied the notes with their scarlet band, set them back into the box, then placed the blue-flowered lid on top. I went slowly to the chair at Ginette's bedside, numbed by the enormity of what I had just learned. Every hauntingly sad song she had sung, I suddenly understood and felt more deeply than ever before. Music had been the outpouring of my sister's heart, and though I had cared for her, laughed with her, dreamed with her, struggled with her, and cried with her, there was a secret part of her that loved, suffered, and sacrificed without her ever having uttered a word.

"Ginette, please. Can you hear me? You cannot

give up. You have to fight. You have to fight." She didn't move or respond. A sob caught in my throat.

"*Mère?*"

Biting my lip, I turned to see my son hovering in the doorway. He held the injured puppy in his arms.

"Come here. Ginette is sleeping." I held my arm out to my son, and he stepped into my embrace. It was a minute before I could speak again. "It appears that the puppy has received more doctoring."

"Dr. Marks gave Mama Louisa and me a box full of real bandages to care for *Mon Amie.*"

"So you have named her already." The puppy was a curly mass of black fur with shiny eyes, a button of a nose, and a pink lapping tongue. She smelled warm and snuggly. Andre glanced at Ginette.

"Ginette is very sick," I said, not bothering to brush away my tears.

He tightened his hold on me. "Don't cry. She is going to get better. I am sure of it." He spoke so fiercely, I believed him.

"I hope so."

"Monsieur Trevelyan believes it, too. I heard him tell Dr. Marks just a few minutes ago. He said, 'Mark, she is not going to die. Do you hear me? Whatever you have to do to assure that, do it. I'll not have her death on my conscience, as well.' They are even having a special lady who helps Dr. Marks come to nurse Aunt Ginette."

Mon Amie wiggled in his arms and whimpered.

"She might be hungry. I need to take her back to Mama Louisa to feed her." Having to care for a little one who needed him so badly brought out a wealth of responsibility Andre had never exhibited before.

Mignon marched into the room a short while later, anger bristling her every movement. "Her tapestry," she cried. "What vile, evil monster could do such a thing?"

"What is it, Nonnie?"

"Ginny's tapestry, which she has been putting her heart and soul into. Apparently she has been putting her life into it as well. Dr. Marks has found a fine powder dusting the tapestry and her threads. Not so much that would make anyone suspicious under normal circumstance, but considering Ginette's hands, he is almost positive it has been poisoned. We were searching the house looking for anything Ginette did with her hands, when I remembered her embroidery. And the more I thought about it, I realized that anytime she became worse, it was shortly after working her tapestry. He has taken it with him to his laboratory to see if he can determine what kind of poison. Meanwhile, he is sending back a nurse who has experience in tending to patients with exotic illnesses. Dr. Marks wants Ginette to drink as much water as possible."

"How? She has yet to awaken."

"That is why he is sending the nurse. She has a way to help Ginette drink. But I fear we have another problem. Monsieur Gallier and Monsieur Fitz are waiting for you in the parlor. No one knows where Mademoiselle Vengle is, and they are quite upset."

By four o'clock that afternoon, Ginette still remained unconscious. I had contacted the authorities about Ginette's poisoning, and when they came to investigate the situation, Miss Vengle's name and circumstances were also brought to their attention. It was suggested we check her favorite stores in town and contact the police again later in the day. Mr. Fitz, the Galliers, and Mr. Phelps had departed for town to search and had yet to return.

Dr. Marks had been back twice to check on Ginette, but hadn't determined what poison she had been exposed to. He seemed to think that every hour she passed without her condition worsening was a good sign, yet my worry for her deepened. I knew once Ginette awakened, I could not allow her to imprison herself in my life any longer.

I'd just left the nurse with Ginette, and found Stephen with his hand fisted against the window frame as he stood looking out at the rain, tension filling the parlor.

"If you want to go look for Mademoiselle Vengle, I am sure we will be fine here."

Stephen looked over his shoulder as I came into the room, tenderness easing into his shadowed eyes. "And be so far from you? No. You look exhausted."

This was the first moment we'd been alone together since this morning in my room, and an odd awkwardness washed over me. The intimacy we had shared was unlike anything I had ever known.

I moved to the rosewood armchair and nervously fingered the delicately crocheted threads of a throw. "Andre overheard your conversation with Dr. Marks about Ginette earlier today. Why do you think yourself responsible for Ginette's illness?"

I turned to find Stephen directly behind me. I cupped his chin in my palm. "You carry too much guilt, blaming yourself when you shouldn't."

He closed his eyes and turned his head to press a kiss to my palm. "Juliet," he said, "I need to tell you that I—"

The front door opened so forcefully that a bang reverberated through the house. Stephen rushed to the center hall, his hand burrowing quickly into the pocket of his coat and pulling out a pistol. I stood shocked. He'd armed himself.

I followed to find Mr. Fitz, Mr. and Mrs. Gallier, Mr. Phelps, and Mr. Latour all dripping rain onto the center hall's polished wood floor and Eastern rug. Stephen returned his pistol to his pocket.

"We have had no luck in town," Mr. Phelps said when he saw Stephen. "We are going to search the area around *La Belle* and the park. Mrs. Vengle could have fallen and injured herself during a walk."

"In this rain? We can only hope," Stephen replied

gravely, making me wonder why he would hope such a thing until I read the undertones in his voice. Dread snatched my breath away.

"We encountered Mr. Latour in town at Antoine's Restaurant and he has offered to help," Mr. Phelps replied.

"Yes," Mr. Latour said, adjusting his waistcoat. "This is really most disturbing. A young woman missing."

I studied him a moment, wondering why he looked different, and I realized he didn't have his spectacles on.

Stephen lifted a brow at Mr. Latour. "At Antoine's, you said?"

"Yes," Mr. Fitz replied. "Mrs. Gallier thought Miss Vengle might have gone there for lunch."

"The dear girl loved the place and planned to return at the first opportunity." Mrs. Gallier shook her head so sadly that I studied her closer. It was almost as if she had cause to pity Miss Vengle—an emotion I suspect she would not have felt if she knew Miss Vengle was her husband's mistress.

"Well," Mr. Gallier said, rubbing his hands together and puffing his cheeks importantly. "I say we get on with this search, but I still think we are wasting time. Miss Vengle is most likely at a dress shop or out having tea with one of the cast members we have yet to locate."

I frowned. The man did not sound in the least concerned about Miss Vengle.

When I cut my glance to Mr. Fitz, I noted he had his fists and jaw clenched as he glared at Mr. Gallier. Then Mr. Fitz looked at me, reminding me of the night I saw him staring at me from his doorway. An eerie feeling crept like a spider over my skin, for I wondered if Miss Charlotte Vengle had fallen victim to the web of deceit she had spun.

✎ *15* ✎

Since Stephen requested that we stay together while he helped search the grounds for Miss Vengle, Mignon, Andre, and I remained in the parlor with Mrs. Gallier. *Mon Amie* slept in a box at Andre's side, basking as contentedly as any puppy ever could, despite her injuries. The loving care my son constantly gave the bundle of fluff was a balm to my heart. All of us tensely waited for news from the searchers and practically jumped at every sound, be it the chime of the grandfather clock in the center hall, or the lash of the wind against the house. The devilish rain continued to pour, making it difficult to see more than a few feet out the windows. Mignon and Andre sat at the card table close to the door, playing whist. I sat with Mrs. Gallier, trying to do something constructive.

"I think it would be good to make a list of anyone in New Orleans who Mademoiselle Vengle might know well enough to go see, and then we can check off each person you have already spoken to," I said.

"If we were to count the cast for the troupe, there would be ten people. Five are staying at another boarding house on Toulouse Street, and the others had the remarkable good fortune to be acquainted with a Williams family and were invited to reside in their town house on Dauphine."

"Then we will start with their names. Were you able to speak to all of them about Mademoiselle Vengle today?"

"With all of them running about to get things ready for production? No. We were only able to contact four out of the ten."

I was surprised. "Then Mademoiselle Vengle could very well be out with a friend?"

"Mr. Gallier is sure of it and wanted to keep looking for her in town."

"Then why did you return to *La Belle*?"

"Mr. Fitz was adamant that we were wasting our time in the city."

A hardy knock resounded on the front door, and Mignon jumped up to answer it.

"See who is there before opening the door," I called out as I followed.

"It is Monsieur Davis," Mignon said, before she opened the door.

"Mignon, dearest, I came as soon as I heard. I am so sorry," Mr. Davis said, stepping into the center hall.

"*Oui*, it is most terrible," Mignon said.

"Who would do such a thing to your sister?"

"We have yet to determine the—"

"Nonnie," I said, interrupting her, for I did not want Ginette's delicate state discussed outside our family.

"Mrs. Boucheron?" Mr. Davis peered at me, blinking as if his vision was blurred, and I noted he did not have his spectacles on.

"Monsieur Davis, is there something wrong?"

"No," he said, tossing his wet coat onto the settee. "It is just that I did not see you standing there and you caught me by surprise."

I hurried over and removed the wet coat from the settee, giving it a vigorous shake so that I could hang it on the coatrack with the others. "Nonnie, why don't you escort Monsieur Davis to the parlor and then help me fix tea in the kitchen? I will take some to Ginette's nurse, as well."

"Ginette's nurse?" Mr. Davis said.

"*Oui*," Mignon replied. "She is ill, but Dr. Marks is going to save her. The nurse is already helping."

Mr. Davis shook his head. "Oh. I hadn't realized she was so very ill."

The sharp rap of the brass doorknocker startled everyone.

Mignon turned to pull the door open. "I hope this is good news about Mademoiselle Vengle," she said.

I hurried forward.

"Miss Vengle?" Mr. Davis gasped.

I froze in my tracks. A stranger wearing a long, black coat, black hat, and an equally somber expression stood on the doorstep.

"May I help you?" I asked firmly, before Mignon could invite the stranger in from the rain. Handing her Mr. Davis's coat and hat, I took hold of the door.

"I need to speak to Juliet Boucheron about an urgent matter."

"What do you need to see her about?"

"I have a packet from Mr. Goodson for her, and I have strict instructions that it may not be delivered to anyone else."

"Your name, monsieur?"

"Zacharias Hall. I am executor of Mr. Goodson's estate and his attorney."

Executor for Mr. Goodson's estate? I opened the door wider, hanging on to it for support. "Monsieur Hall, are you saying something has happened to Monsieur Goodson?"

"I am afraid so . . . Mrs. Boucheron? I am sorry it has taken me so long to get to you. Your envelope was mixed in with some other things and has just now been sorted out."

I stood staring at the man as the blood drained from my head, leaving me dizzy and disoriented.

"Come in, Monsieur Hall," Mignon said, stepping forward and motioning the gentleman inside. She slid the door from my numb fingers and started to close it.

"This obviously is not the best time for a visit," Mr. Davis said. "I will return later."

"That would be best," I said, finding my voice. "Monsieur Hall, would you mind stepping into my father's office?" I motioned down the corridor. "I will be with you momentarily."

The moment he left, I turned to Mignon and whispered, "Stay with Andre and keep Madame Gallier busy. I do not know how long this will take."

Mouth dry, I turned to join Mr. Hall in my father's office. I found him standing by the window. "How did he die?"

He turned, surprise arching his brow at my abruptness, but I didn't have the time or the patience for pleasantries. "Please, I must know," I added.

"It is a rather indelicate subject, Mrs. Boucheron. I would not want to offend you."

"Monsieur, you offend me more by not being forthright with me. Now please tell me."

"He was stabbed on the street in broad daylight."

I didn't have to ask where Mr. Goodson died, for I already knew. He'd been murdered outside of my attorney's office just a few weeks ago.

"Juliet," Stephen rapped on the door to my father's office. I could hear concern and alarm sharpening his voice.

"Come in. Anything yet?" I asked as I turned to him.

"They are gathering everyone to come back here. Thank God I decided to check on you first and not wait for the others. Lord, woman, not even an hour has passed and I find you alone in a darkened room where anyone could cause you harm."

With Mignon, Andre, and Mrs. Gallier in the room next door, close enough to hear me call, I thought his reaction overly protective, but I appreciated his concern.

Water had slicked his dark hair back from his brow and clumped his lashes, making his expression starker. It was hard to see the sophisticated stranger in the rugged man before me. It was as if the events of my life kept stripping away his superficial masks, leaving a flesh and blood man who called to the very of heart me. "Stephen, this is my home."

He marched toward me and clasped my arms, pulling me toward him. "Damnation, don't you understand the danger? If something terrible happened to you, I would never forgive myself."

I splayed my hands against his damp chest and met his gaze. "Jean Claude is dead," I said softly. "Murdered two days after he came here to see Andre and me, before his mission."

I still felt numbed by the enormity of what I had read in the papers Mr. Hall had left.

"How do you know?" The words seemed almost torn from him.

"A written confession from a man in prison who

was part of the plot to kill Jean Claude and take the gold. No gold was ever found. And now another man has died, and this time it is all my fault."

Stephen's grip on my shoulders tightened. "Juliet, calm down. Start at the beginning and tell me what is going on."

"Monsieur Goodson, the investigator I hired to find Jean Claude, was the man murdered in town. His attorney brought me a packet of information Monsieur Goodson had kept for me in his safe. He'd uncovered the truth about Jean Claude, and he died because of it."

"Uncovered what truth? Did he mention anyone else being involved?" Stephen's voice sounded odd. I pulled slightly back to see him better, shrugging my shoulders against the intensity of his grip.

He sighed heavily, loosening his hands, and dipping his forehead to touch mine. "Dear God, I cannot protect you if I do not know every detail of what you have learned. I am sorry for what happened to Jean Claude. I am sorry Goodson is dead, but you have no idea what this has become for me, being here with you yet powerless to stop what is happening."

Releasing me, he turned away and faced the French doors with his hands fisted. A man so painfully alone that I wanted to reach for him, but he spoke before I could move. I stayed still. I wanted to hear what he had to say, needed to hear it, to put to rest any doubts I harbored.

"I suppose you are wondering how I can even claim that I love you, given what I told you about my brother's wife. But to save your life, I would pay any price. Do you doubt that a man can fall in love with a woman in so short a time? Do you think I am a fool bent on nothing but seduction?" He stared out at the rain and spoke softly, almost to himself. "It is ironic, given the way I have lived most of my life. You might be right in thinking those things. It was a sorry way to be a man and I paid the price for that folly. Even my affection for Cesca was more to save her from the tragedy of her life than a passionate love. What happened was inevitable. She lived seven years in our family's home, and my brother spent much of that time gone, building the family's fortune. I find I am incapable of living with others and ignoring their troubles, needs, or happiness. Then I came here, saw you, and learned from your sisters how you have fought every day with a valiant courage that shames the frivolity with which I have lived.

"So how can a man love a woman so quickly?" he asked, still facing the rain. I moved closer to him; he watched my ghostly reflection in the glass. "He can love her because her heart is so big; she would give the last of her strength to help her family. He can love her because she stands so strong and beautiful against overwhelming odds. He can love her because her wit hones his, her smile softens his, and her laughter restores his."

I could not hold back any longer; I set my hands on his shoulders and pressed my cheek to his wet back. He stood within my embrace a moment, then turned to face me, cupping my cheeks in the palms of his hands. "Juliet, how can any man look upon you and not love you? It is impossible for me not to. Did Jean Claude see what I see?"

Tears filled my eyes, and I shook my head. No one had ever loved me so.

He slid his thumbs along my cheeks, threaded his fingers through my hair, and leaned down, pressing his lips softly to mine. His kiss was an entreaty I could not refuse.

"I believe you, Stephen, for who am I to question the ways of a heart? Mine was yours long before I had the right to give it. I love you."

He encircled me in his arms and I pressed myself to him.

A bolt of lightning startled us both, and we looked out the window into the courtyard. Something on the ground caught my attention. It glistened for a moment and then was gone, mingling with the rain.

Stephen looked at me intently. His blue eyes, so dark with passion, glowed like the midnight sky under a full moon.

"I do not deserve your love or your trust, but I am too weak a man to deny myself anything when it comes to you." He kissed me firmly. I could feel the power of the passion he held in check, the heat of it, the strength of it, and I trembled in response. Then he backed away from me and breathed deeply, as if he had expended every ounce of his strength.

"Everyone should be returning momentarily," he said at last. "May I see the information Mr. Hall brought?"

"Of course." I went to my father's desk and gathered the papers, handing them to Stephen. "Monsieur Goodson made a thorough investigation. The confession is from a man named Roth Hubbard. I do not know him."

He lifted a brow. "Your father-in-law said the name of Roth when he spoke of Jean Claude's plan. What other names are mentioned?" He quickly scanned the letter, answering his own question. "Just two others. John Rache and the Shepherd Boy. Who is that?"

"It doesn't say, but I think he must be who we are looking for. Roth Hubbard is still in prison, and you will find a death certificate among the papers for John Rache."

Stephen shuffled through the rest of the papers. "Killing your husband and framing him for stealing the gold had been their plan all along. The only thing that went wrong is that your husband did something with the gold before they got to him. That indicates to me more than ever that the gold is here at *La Belle*."

"I have no idea where it could be, for I swear to you, over the past ten years there has not been a corner, nook, or cranny at *La Belle* that hasn't been cleaned."

"No secret rooms or passages? Gold bullion is not easy to hide. It would require a considerable amount of space."

"How do we even know it is here? He could have left it anywhere. In fact, he could have buried it at the army camp near the Hayes Plantation. That would explain how they have prospered so abundantly during these times," I replied.

"It's possible," Stephen said. "In my investigations the other night, I got a fairly ugly picture of how Hayes has been prospering."

"How?"

"He and his army of followers are being paid a lot of money by important people to keep the political and social situation in an uproar. The White League is doing everything possible to intimidate anyone they do not want in public office. They consider themselves above the law."

I could readily believe it. I moved back to the French doors, noting that the rain had slowed. "Until the war tore my world apart, I did not realize how much hate and evil flourished around me." Again, I saw something glint on the cobblestones across the courtyard. "Stephen, twice now in the past few minutes I've seen something silverlike in the courtyard."

He was at my side in an instant. "Where?"

"Over by the camellia bush."

"I do not see anything."

"Neither do I now, but, I swear I saw it."

"You sure you're not just imagining that the gold is floating up from the ground after all this rain?"

I smiled and shook my head. "The only things that come floating up out of the ground around here are coffins. I am going to go see."

"You really think there is something there?"

"Yes."

"Then I will go. You stay here." Opening the door, he stepped outside. I followed him a foot or so, standing beneath the cover of the second floor gallery. When he reached the camellia bush, he bent down and picked up something. As he stood, I realized what it was and ran out into the rain, dismayed.

"That is my silver shawl!" I took it from him, clenching its sodden threads close to my heart, heedless of the dirty water staining my gown. I doubted that the fragile silver threads would ever be as beautiful as they had been.

Looking up, I was surprised to find Stephen on his hands and knees peering under the foliage of the old camellia bush. I bent down to see what he could possibly be doing but he quickly rose and grabbed my hand, pulling me.

"Come with me," he said harshly, urging me back toward the house.

"What is it? What is wrong?" I looked back over my shoulder at the camellia.

"I assure you, Juliet, you do not want to see."

I dug in my heels. "Stephen, at least tell me what is wrong." I pulled my hand from his and saw blood on my fingers. "You are bleeding."

He held his palm up, surprised. There was a cut on his palm. "It feels as if I have a piece of glass in my hand, but that is the least of our worries. Miss Vengle is dead."

Everyone gathered in the parlor.

"Mrs. Boucheron, you said that the last time you saw Miss Vengle was yesterday morning in town with Mr. Trevelyan, correct?" the criminal sheriff of Orleans Parish asked me for the third time.

"*Oui.* I saw Mademoiselle Vengle speaking with Monsieur Trevelyan. They stood on the corner of Canal and Chartres." A nightmarish two hours had passed since Stephen discovered Miss Vengle's body stuffed beneath the shrouding foliage.

"Did it seem to you, Mrs. Boucheron, that they were well acquainted, out for a stroll, enjoying the morning together?"

This was a new question, and I frowned at the implied intimacy he tried to establish between Stephen and Miss Vengle. I wanted to tell Sheriff Carr of the improper relationship between Miss Vengle and Mr. Gallier and Mr. Fitz's apparent feelings for Miss Vengle, but to mention that in front of everyone, including Mrs. Gallier, would have been too indelicate. I would have to seek out Sheriff Carr privately to address the matter.

In the meantime, I was not going to allow him to impugn Stephen's character. "I would not say they were together at all, Sheriff Carr. Mademoiselle Vengle was well turned out, whereas Monsieur Trevelyan was quite rumpled. I learned later that he had been in a minor altercation that morning with a man who had harmed my son, and that he'd happened to meet up with Mademoiselle Vengle on his way back to *La Belle*."

"So you say Mr. Trevelyan is a man given to violent tendencies?"

"*Non!* Not at all." Frustration tightened inside me and grew. Every word I said was being twisted to paint Stephen in a bad light. Other than his grim expression, Stephen appeared undisturbed by Sheriff Carr's remarks. But everyone else except Mr. Phelps eyed Stephen as if he'd grown a horn in the middle of his forehead.

Sheriff Carr paced across the parlor, then whipped around to face Stephen. "Mr. Trevelyan, you *claim* that the last time you saw Miss Vengle was in town yesterday morning as well. That was about eleven o'clock, correct?"

"Yes." Stephen's reply was curt.

"And when you saw her, she said she was in town to do what? I need you to refresh my memory."

"Shop for a particular dress that would, in her words, capture the passion and innocence of Juliet— her part in the upcoming play."

"Have you met with Miss Vengle on any other occasion away from this boarding establishment? Either a planned meeting or an accidental one?"

"No."

"Mr. Latour, you were acquainted with Miss Vengle?" Sheriff Carr asked.

Mr. Latour puffed out his jowls importantly and cleared his throat. Without his spectacles, he looked heavier. "Yes, I met the young woman last Saturday night at dinner here."

"And that was the only occasion you saw Miss Vengle?"

"That is what I just said."

Sheriff Carr raised his brows. "It is very neighborly of you to spend your entire working day searching for a woman whom you had just briefly met."

Mr. Latour straightened his back as if offended. He fumbled in his pocket, put on his spectacles, and scowled with outrage. "See here. I resent what you are trying to imply. I am a respectable attorney from a noteworthy family. I consider it my civic duty to help."

A knock sounded at the front door and after a minute Papa John came to the parlor door and motioned to me. He informed me that Mr. Davis had returned to see Mignon.

"Have him wait in the sitting room, and she will see him as soon as we are through—"

"Mrs. Boucheron," Sheriff Carr said. "My apologies for being so rude, but if whoever is here had any occasion to know Miss Vengle, I would like for him to join us."

"Oh, of course," I said.

Papa John brought Mr. Davis to the parlor. Mr. Davis came to an abrupt stop when he saw so many gathered.

I made the introductions. "Monsieur Davis, this is Sheriff Carr. Sheriff Carr, Monsieur Davis; he is Monsieur Maison's assistant."

They shook hands and Sheriff Carr nodded. "We've had the opportunity to meet, though not under these circumstances."

Mr. Davis looked about the room again, puzzled. "Is there something wrong?"

"Mrs. Boucheron says that you were acquainted with Miss Vengle."

"I had the pleasure of her company here several times when I called on Miss Mignon DePerri. Is Miss Vengle still missing?"

"Then you know of the search for her?"

"Yes, I stopped by earlier. This is very disturbing, Sheriff Carr. A young woman disappearing."

"It is even more disturbing than you intimate, Mr. Davis. Miss Vengle is dead. She was strangled with a cord."

Mr. Davis frowned. Without his glasses, his face was leaner, more rugged. "Murdered? Good Lord. The authorities must do something about the crime in this city."

"When did you see her last?" Sheriff Carr asked abruptly.

Mr. Davis blinked. "The last I saw her was at dinner Saturday evening. Surely you cannot think that I had any connection to Miss Vengle."

"I question everyone, Mr. Davis. Why don't you have a seat, and if you think of anything else, you can let me know." The sheriff turned quickly and addressed Mr. Gallier, and I realized he was deliberately keeping everyone off balance to trick the guilty party into making a mistake.

"Now, Mr. Gallier. The last time you saw Miss Vengle was at dinner last night?"

"Quite right," Mr. Gallier said. "She claimed she was worn out from her shopping excursion and retired early, as did my wife. Mr. Fitz and I spent several hours after dinner discussing details about our upcoming productions. Then we retired, as well. After that I did not leave my room."

"But—" Mrs. Gallier said. Mr. Gallier patted her hand and she dabbed harder at her eyes with a handkerchief, her face crinkling into a look of frustration. Could it be Mrs. Gallier knew something and was being forced to keep silent?

"But what?" The sheriff's gaze narrowed at the couple.

Mr. Gallier cleared his throat and acted as if he was being sorely put upon. "If you must know, occasionally I have difficulty at night. I have bilious attacks that require lengthy use of the water closet. Sometimes not even my Dover's powder helps. I had such an attack last night."

I wondered how many times the water closet ended up being Miss Vengle's room.

"When did you notice anything wrong?" the sheriff asked Mr. Gallier.

"This morning, about six. Mr. Fitz heard a woman cry out and knocked on our door, rousing my wife and me."

"Mr. Fitz, do you think you heard Miss Vengle? Was it a cry for help?"

My face burned and I had to fight to breathe normally.

Mr. Fitz ran his fingers over his mustache to make sure his handlebars weren't askew. "I couldn't say for sure what sort of cry it was. I was awake, heard the rain, and then the cry. I decided to investigate the source of the noise."

Sheriff Carr narrowed his eyes. "You said earlier that you went to Miss Vengle's door first. Therefore one can assume you thought she'd cried out."

Mr. Fitz's face flushed red. "I thought that it might have been."

"And when Miss Vengle didn't answer her door, what did you do?"

"I assumed she was still asleep. I then knocked on Mr. Gallier's door and Mr. Trevelyan's. When Mr. Trevelyan answered, he was already dressed . . ." Mr.

Fitz looked at Stephen in shock. "By God, he was wet, too! As if he had been out in the rain."

I stood. "It was I who cried out."

"I can attest to that," Stephen said, giving up his relaxed position against the mantel and walking determinedly toward me. "I was out on the gallery, enjoying the first cool morning there has been since I arrived in New Orleans. Being from San Francisco, I rather welcomed the rain. I heard the cry from up above me, and I stepped out into the courtyard to view Mrs. Boucheron's balcony. Then I heard Mr. Fitz's knock and hurried back into my room. After speaking to Mr. Fitz, I immediately went upstairs and learned from Miss Mignon DePerri that Mrs. Boucheron had cried out during a nightmare, and that Miss Ginette DePerri had fallen seriously ill. I then left to get the doctor." Stephen didn't take his gaze off me, making it very clear that I was not to contradict him.

"Does this coincide with your recollections of what happened this morning, Mr. Fitz?"

Mr. Fitz frowned. "I suppose."

"Mrs. Boucheron?"

"Monsieur Trevelyan has been most helpful."

Sheriff Carr nodded. "And you say that Mr. Trevelyan was with you and your son last evening, returning well after midnight?"

"That is correct. The fog was so heavy, the carriage had to move at a crawl," I said, thankful to be truthful.

The sheriff paced across the room, and everyone sat

silent, waiting for him to speak. "Then, given everyone's testimony, including yours, Mrs. Gallier, sometime between nine last night and six this morning Miss Vengle was murdered. And yet with a household of people, some awake late into the night, no one heard or saw anything usual. Does anyone have anything to add to that?"

"I do," Stephen said. "Considering the thickness of the fog, the menacing events surrounding Mrs. Boucheron and her family, and the fact that it appears Miss Vengle was wearing Mrs. Boucheron's shawl and resembled Mrs. Boucheron in size and hair color, I believe Mrs. Boucheron was the intended victim."

My heart went cold. Which of the people sitting in my parlor was a murderer? Which one knew about the gold?

≪ *16* ≫

"Juliet?"

I snapped my eyes open and sat up, surprised to find someone had draped a light coverlet over my shoulders. I'd fallen asleep in a chair at Ginette's bedside, her hand in mine. Her skin had lost its cold, clammy feel and I thought her color better. The new nurse sat attentively on my sister's other side. Turning to Stephen, I blinked. "What time is it?"

"After midnight." His hair was damp, as if he'd just bathed. He wore a loose white shirt and dark breeches that were faded and soft looking. They appeared to have hugged the contours of his thigh muscles for a long time.

"Where is Dr. Marks?" I asked.

He'd arrived just before dinner and I had gladly made my excuses to the boarders. No one had said much of anything since Sheriff Carr's questioning. Before the sheriff left, I told him privately of the relationship between Mr. Gallier and Miss Vengle, and of Mr. Fitz's interest in Miss Vengle. To my surprise, he was already aware of the situation. He left, giving strict instructions that no one was to leave the city until the investigation into Miss Vengle's murder had been concluded.

"Dr. Marks went home and will return in the morning. I thought his news positive that Ginette is in a restorative sleep."

Rubbing my stiff neck, I moved toward Stephen. Dr. Marks had determined that the powder on Ginette's embroidery was most likely a botanically derived pesticide. Many such substances were for sale on New Orleans's darker streets, where a coin could buy a potion to cost a man his life. "It is late. You should not have let me sleep. There is still so much to do—"

"Everything has already been done. Andre and Mignon are in Mignon's room with the puppy. Papa John is watching the first floor, and Mr. Phelps is outside. The house is completely locked and everyone is under strict instructions not to unlock any doors or windows until morning. Now it is your turn for someone to take care of you. Come with me." He held out his hand, and I let him lead me into the corridor and down the hall.

I sighed. "If Mademoiselle Vengle hadn't worn my shawl, she would still be alive."

"You do not know that for sure. And there is no way you could have known that ahead of time. You should not blame yourself. I have learned the hard way that the only thing you can do in the face of tragic events is to determine not to waste a moment of your own life."

"Was not Monsieur Phelps guarding last night while we were gone?" I looked up at Stephen, realizing that having a guard had not secured Miss Vengle's safety.

"At my orders, Mr. Phelps kept watch inside the house in the corridor on the family's floor until we returned last night. So, if anyone is to blame for her death it is I," he said, bringing his voice to a whisper.

I whispered back, feeling odd at the necessity to do so in my own house. It was another reminder that my enemy might not be at the gate but in the very next room. "Then that would mean something happened to Mademoiselle Vengle before we arrived back at *La Belle,* which clears you completely as being a suspect. Why did you not tell Sheriff Carr?"

"As long as the murderer thinks that I am under heavy suspicion, he will be less on guard."

I shivered. "What if I was not the target, Stephen? What if Monsieur Gallier or Fitz strangled Mademoiselle Vengle? What if my shawl was thrown out there to make it appear that I was the intended victim?"

"I have considered that, but we would then have to rule out Mr. Fitz."

"Why?"

"Let me put this as delicately as I can. There is a distinct difference in the cry of a woman being pleasured and a woman being hurt. From Mr. Fitz's embarrassment during Sheriff Carr's questioning, I think it safe to assume that he suspected Miss Vengle and Mr. Gallier were together and that he wanted to interrupt them, perhaps even rouse Mrs. Gallier and expose the affair. That is why he went directly to the Gallier's room when Miss Vengle did not answer her door. If he honestly thought Miss Vengle had cried out in distress, needing help, he would have just opened her door. It was not locked."

My face burned like fire. Stephen leaned down and brushed his lips across mine.

"You need to rest. Go take a bath. Mignon has already placed your nightgown, robe, and slippers inside. I'll stay right here to make sure you are safe."

I opened the door to the bath to find a steamy tub, smelling heavenly of rose oil. Undressing, I slid into the water with a sigh. The languid heat eased into my body, chasing away tension and the dampness of the day's rain. Rather than growing sleepy though, my senses seemed to come alive, beginning at the tips of my toes and steadily climbing until my breasts ached with anticipation. I was acutely aware of Stephen waiting just outside the door.

When I finished, I slid on only my robe and slippers, leaving off my nightdress. I had never been so bold.

I found Stephen pacing in front of the door, looking

a great deal more ragged than he had fifteen minutes before. Anticipation curled hotly inside me and grew as he wordlessly accompanied me down the corridor to my room, where I noted a chair just outside my door.

"Keep the door ajar so that I can hear the least noise. You get some sleep now. Tomorrow I need to talk to you. There is something I need to explain." He brushed a kiss against my forehead, then held the door open for me. My moment to reach out to him was fading, and I could not let it slip through my fingers. Halfway to my bed, I turned to face him.

"Stephen," I said, emotion thickening my voice. "There is a problem."

He darted his gaze over my shoulder to search the lit room. I didn't hesitate. I slid loose the silk ribbons tying my robe and shrugged it from my shoulders.

"I need you tonight, Stephen. I want you."

My breath caught at the intensity in his blue eyes. He stepped into the room and kicked the door shut as he grabbed the hem of his shirt, stripping it over his head. The broad expanse of his chest and shoulders gleamed in the lamplight. He covered the distance between us and backed me up to the bed, setting his pistol within reach on the bedside table. Then he stripped off his pants and stood before me naked, a mixture of vulnerability, power, and desire.

I drank in the sight of his dark beauty, the roughly hewn angles of his jaw, his jutting arousal, and the passion glittering in his eyes. He took hold of my robe, sliding the silk from me as he raked his gaze over me.

"I do not deserve what you offer, but I die for you, Juliet," he rasped.

He pulled me into his arms, his mouth covering mine in a kiss so searing that it reached deeper than my soul, opening and exposing my every need with the brush of his lips and the stroke of his tongue.

I slid my hands along the hard velvet contours of his arms and back, up into the silk of his hair, delving into its thickness and warmth. I reveled in the seductive scent of sandalwood and spice enveloping me in a haze of desire.

"Tonight, I get to touch you and to feel you. To awaken your senses like you do mine," I said.

"They are fully awake. You only need to glance down to see that."

"There's more," I said, and slid my fingers lightly over his arousal. "Lie down and let me touch you, Stephen."

He drew a deep breath. "I don't know if I'll live through your sweet torture."

I smiled and nodded toward the bed. Reluctantly, he went and lay down. Propping his head up, he raked his gaze over me so hotly that I knew I wouldn't be able to resist his dark desire for long. Judging by his sensual smile, he knew it, too.

"Turn over and shut your eyes," I whispered.

His gaze widened with surprise, bringing a secret

thrill to me. I could almost feel his body warring with his mind as he turned to his stomach. I went to the bed, standing over him a moment, drinking in the sight of his hard curves and supple muscle. Starting at his shoulders, I slid my hands over the broad expanse of his back, softly pressing my fingers into his warmth and strength, feeling the power of him. Then I followed my touch with soft kisses that made him groan. With each touch, with each sensation, my blood heated and hot desire pooled in my center, making my breasts ache for him. I moved lower, easing down his spine to the fascinating firmness of his bottom and the hard contours of his thighs. When I pressed kisses there, his body jerked taut.

"Juliet," he gasped, his breaths as ragged as mine.

"Turn over."

He moved in a flash and tried to reach for me, but I stepped away.

"Put your hands behind your head."

"What are you doing?" he demanded, complying but looking dangerously close to rebellion.

I wanted to love every inch of this man. I wanted to make his fantasies unwind. I ran my fingers up his leg to his arousal, wrapping my hand around him, feeling the throb of his pulse, and the burning heat of his desire.

"Developing a silver tongue," I said. Leaning forward, I put my mouth upon his erection, brushing my tongue over the hot velvet of his desire. His whole body arched. Four more kisses and he groaned, grabbing me.

"Heaven help me," Stephen cried as he pulled me down on top of him. He brought my knees to his sides, held my hips in place, and buried himself inside me in a single hot stroke. Then he reached for my breasts, teasing them mercilessly with his deft fingers, making their tips ache until my hips rocked with the need to ease my desire. I burned hotter with his every upward thrust, until he brought my world to a shattering pinnacle of pleasure and I shuddered with fulfillment. Then I watched as his body went taut, his breath came in a deep rasping moan, and his eyes lost focus in a shuddering release.

I collapsed on his chest and he pulled me close to his heart.

"I love you," I said softly.

"I have never been loved so well, nor have I ever loved so deeply." He kissed my forehead, then my lips, and wrapped his arms tightly around me. The tenderness, the warmth, and the love in his voice shook me, bringing tears to my eyes.

"Neither have I," I whispered.

"All of life pales to the beauty of being in your arms," he said softly.

I knew exactly what he meant.

Stephen spent most of the night with me, though I awoke alone to the dim light of dawn and the memory of heated passion. Rolling from the bed, I pulled on my robe and went to my door. Stephen sat in the chair outside of my room as I expected, looking rumpled and wonderful.

"Mornin,' angel," he said softly, his eyes telling me that last night was no dream.

"Have you slept at all?"

"And miss any moment of heaven?"

"You are an impossible romantic."

He lifted a questioning brow. "Doth the lady protest too much? Or"—he reached for the front of my robe—"does she need reminding?"

"What the lady needs is not to have her head all a muddle, a condition you induce with a mere look. I need to see about Ginette."

"The nurse has good news. Ginette moved restlessly in her sleep last night and spoke, as if she dreamed."

"Then she is regaining some level of conscious-ness?"

"That is what the nurse thinks. Dr. Marks will be here in an hour. Everyone else still sleeps, and there was no trouble during the night."

"I had best bathe and dress, then."

"Quickly, or else temptation is going to win over my common sense. There is something about you in silk that not even a saint could resist, and we both know I am far from saintly." He reached for my robe again, tugging it just enough to expose a breast to his view.

"Stephen," I gasped as he stood, a familiar, determined gleam lighting his eyes.

Snatching my robe to my chest, I decided prudence the better part of valor and ducked back into my room.

The door flew open and then closed again behind Stephen. "Heaven can't wait," he said. "Fortunately, it will only take five minutes to get there."

My eyes opened wide. "*Dieu*. Five minutes?"

"Make that four," he said, pulling my robe open.

I think it took seven. I rushed down the hall a short while later, my body still tingling from the pleasure he brought me. I'd gone from famine to feast in a night's span and thought I might expire from the bounty of it.

Mama Louisa, Mignon, and Andre were all in the kitchen when I arrived. Breakfast was well on its way and *Mon Amie* yipped a greeting from the comfort of her padded box. Dawn had given way to the sun of a bright day in a world washed new by the rain. The cool air drifting into the window carried a hint of blooming jasmine to mingle with the scent of baking biscuits and sliced oranges.

"I need to show everyone something important. Mama Louisa, where is Papa John this morning?"

"At the market, but he'll be back before long."

"Then I will let him know later." I motioned for everyone to gather around the kitchen table, where I placed the papers from Mr. Goodson. "What we have here is proof that Jean Claude never deserted us or the army, but that some evil men betrayed him on his last mission." I put my arm around Andre's shoulders. "Your father was killed two days after braving capture to see us."

I hugged my son tighter as I saw tears gather in his eyes. Though this was painful, in so many ways it was a release, as if the dark cloud over our lives had finally moved on.

Andre picked up the letter, holding it as if it was his most precious possession. He walked over to the light from the window and silently read it, tears falling down his cheeks.

As I went to him, the gold wax seal that had been on the back of the letter fell off and I stopped to pick it up from the floor. When I looked at it in the light from the window, something about the intricate pattern struck me.

"He was innocent of stealing!" Andre exclaimed. "He wasn't a coward!"

I put the wax in my pocket. "He was no coward, Andre. I do not know what to say about the gold. The men who killed your father never found it. And we know from your grandfather that there was a special plan for the gold."

"Then the gold could really be here at *La Belle*." Mignon looked stunned.

I shook my head. "I do not think it likely. Monsieur Trevelyan says that much gold would require a considerable amount of space. We would have found it."

"How do you know for sure? Have we really examined every trunk in the attic?"

"I . . ." Some of the trunks in the attic *had* been moved, and Papa John said he hadn't moved them. Had our intruder been up there searching? And the ghost that I had determinedly tried to forget that I'd seen—was it here for a reason? Was it possible?

"We will begin a thorough search of the house later today."

Andre and Mignon smiled widely. Eager for the task ahead, they quickly helped prepare breakfast.

Mr. Fitz and Mr. Gallier declined to join us for breakfast. Instead, they left immediately for town to make arrangements for Miss Vengle's funeral. I offered to help with whatever they needed, and Stephen did as well, telling them that the expenses would be taken care of and to choose nothing but the best. Mr. Gallier had nodded. Mr. Fitz had tears in his eyes, and I thought Miss Vengle had made a poor choice with her affections.

The shadows I saw in Stephen's eyes stayed, and every now and then I would find him studying me. I asked him several times if there was anything wrong, but he only shook his head and said that it would have to wait until a better time.

Stephen and Andre played chess in the parlor while I dusted, and Mignon swept the center hall free of the dirt and mud that had accumulated from yesterday's rain and visitors. We awaited Dr. Marks's arrival, hoping that Ginette's continued restlessness was indeed a sign that she was on her way back to us. Andre was in the middle of admonishing Stephen for making the game too easy, when Mignon cried out. Anxious, I ran for the center hall behind Stephen. We both came to a relieved stop as we saw Mignon standing unharmed, holding something in her hand.

"It is a cigar, Juliet! Here on the settee!"

"Let me see, Nonnie." I went over to her and took the cigar she held out to me. "I have the other upstairs. I am going to see if they match."

"Good Lord, you never said that you had evidence," Stephen said.

I looked back at him. "Well, you didn't ask." I hurried on, anger fueling my steps. I pulled the stub from my drawer along with the crinkled newspaper and set them on my desk. Everyone gathered around it.

"They are a match," Stephen said, even before I had focused on them.

"How do you know?" I asked.

He picked up the cigars. "Same quality and color of paper wrapping the cigars. And see this mark here?" He pointed to a faint line of script written about two finger's width from the bottom. "These are a very expensive brand and are signed by the maker, Carlo San Fuenta from Havana. Fuentas sell for twenty dollars apiece in San Francisco."

"Twenty dollars!" I gasped, shocked that someone would spend so much on something so frivolous.

"We still do not know who we are dealing with,"

Stephen said, looking at me with concern. "Everyone was here yesterday in the center hall and in the parlor. And truthfully, I have three of these cigars in my room as we speak. I smoke occasionally."

Mignon picked up the newspapers, spreading them out. I noticed for the first time that they had at one time been folded neatly into fourths, as one might do when putting a paper into a pocket. "The date on these is from two months ago," she said.

"*Oui*, I noticed that."

"*Mère*, wouldn't that mean the person who is trying to hurt us has been here for two months?"

"Or longer," Stephen added. "Good deduction." He nodded at Andre.

Mignon shook her head. "Why anyone would carry papers around about a political party is beyond me."

"It's about the White League," I said, looking at Stephen.

"You are thinking it's Mr. Hayes. I don't think the man patient enough or calculating enough to involve himself in skulking around."

I frowned. "You're right."

"What does the article say about the White League?" He picked up the newspaper.

"I didn't read it all. Part of it is burned, anyway."

"It's an editorial piece suggesting the White League had a heavy hand in hanging a man to warn ardent republicans what fate awaits them. I've heard that before. Where?" Stephen asked.

"Miz Julie." Papa John stood in the doorway; he looked aged and tired, and very upset.

"What is it?" I turned, immediately moving to him and setting my hand on his shoulder.

"We've a visitor."

"Who?"

"It's Captain Jennison. He has asked to see Miz Ginette."

The man I held as an enemy was standing on my doorstep? "*Bon Dieu.* However did he take the notion to come here?"

"I telegraphed, asking him to," Stephen said quietly.

❧ *17* ❧

I turned from Stephen, too shocked by his action to speak to him. He'd secretly invited an enemy to my home?

I could hear Captain Jennison loud and clear.

"Stand aside, sir. I have no quarrel with you, but nothing and no one will keep me from seeing Ginette, except her own word."

The deep, emotionally wrought voice boomed up the stairs, and I quickened my pace. I had to face this man from my past who had taken over my home. A man who'd fought for the army that killed my father. A man my sister loved. I would deal with Stephen later.

At the top of the stairs, I saw Mr. Phelps blocking the way of a man that I hardly recognized. The youthful, dark-haired Federal officer had been replaced by a man who'd aged a score in a decade. There was gray streaking his hair and a dark somberness to his rugged features. I felt Stephen come up behind me, but I ignored him.

"Monsieur Phelps, Captain Jennison has a history of intruding rudely into our home, but this time he has been invited by Monsieur Trevelyan—whose liberties, it would seem, are as boundless as his glib tongue." Even if Ginette had asked Stephen to send for Captain Jennison, the fact that Stephen hadn't told me hurt.

Captain Jennison looked up the stairs, his handsome face starkly haggard. "Where is she? I have traveled four days without stopping, and I will not wait any longer. Shoot me if you must."

I drew a deep breath. "There has been too much bloodshed already. She is in her room. You may see her, but then we will talk."

Mr. Phelps stepped aside, and Captain Jennison took the steps two at a time, his determined chin set at a grim angle. "What happened to her? A fever?"

"Someone poisoned her."

He blanched and a knife-sharp glitter hardened his gaze. "Who?"

"We don't know yet."

"Why?" His voice rang sharply, as harsh and stark as his eyes.

"We think it was because of missing gold from the war. Men killed my husband for it, and apparently haven't found it yet."

"Will the curse of evil upon this country never end? God help whoever did this."

Captain Jennison took one look at Ginette, swore as

he crossed to her, then lifted her, covers and all, into his arms.

The nurse jumped up as if she was going to battle for her patient, but sat back down when Captain Jennison settled into the large wing chair, cradling Ginette against his chest. He kissed her reverently on her forehead and began talking to her in so low a voice that I could not make out his words. Given the tears flowing down his cheeks, I knew I was not meant to. Tears gathered in my own eyes and I turned away, quietly leaving the room.

Pulling the door closed behind me, I motioned Mignon, Andre, and Stephen down the hall so we would not be overheard.

"Yesterday, I inadvertently learned through some correspondence that Ginette has affections for Captain Jennison, and that for a number of years after Captain Jennison left our home, they wrote to one another."

"I knew it!" Mignon's face lit with interest. "I knew there was someone, but I could not figure out who. This is wonderfully scandalous. Dear, quiet Ginette and a Federal Army captain, no less."

"Mignon, your enthusiasm is not very heartening at the moment," I said, feeling at odds. How could Mignon have suspected Ginette's secret when I hadn't? "Though I think Ginette better, her recovery is not assured."

Mignon shook her head. "I think it more assured

now than ever. How could love like that fail to save her? *Dieu*, it has been years since they have seen each other."

"I agree, Mignon," Stephen said. "How can love fail to save?"

"He's a Yank?" Andre said, his brow furrowing. "Monsieur Hayes says they are taking everything over and need to be hang—uh—sent home."

"I have to see Mr. Phelps about a matter. I will be right back," Stephen said suddenly, his voice grim.

I focused on my son. "Andre, you were four years old when the war ended. There were many reasons, good and bad, for both the Confederate cause and for the Federal cause. Until you know what those reasons were, you cannot rightly make judgments. Monsieur Hayes and his ilk are looking for an excuse to further their own importance, by demeaning, defaming, and destroying others. You are a better man. You need not follow in the steps of another man's poor choices."

"Are you not angry over what they did?"

"*Oui*, but to what end? I've no wish to be like your Aunt Josephine. When all the issues on both sides of the war were brought to light, there were more wrongs on the Confederate side when it came to the rights of human decency. Yet it was in the Southern states in which President Lincoln abolished slavery, long before he did so in the North, which makes his reasons at the time related more to the war than to the just rights of men to be free. It is time we all move beyond the past, especially grown men like Hayes, who are still caught up in their own petty importance. Now—as it is getting close to lunch, would you go help Nonnie and Mama Louisa in the kitchen? I need to have a discussion with Monsieur Trevelyan."

"Come along, Andre," Mignon said. "We can even fix a special puppy treat for *Mon Amie.*"

I found Stephen in the center hall. "Monsieur Trevelyan, might I have a word with you in my father's office?"

He lifted a brow at my curt tone and steered me toward the parlor. "I am in need of much more than a discussion with you," he said, "but unfortunately, unless we can talk while we stroll in the courtyard, it will have to wait."

"Why?" I felt miffed. Didn't he realize how important this was?

"It concerns a hanging and a chunk of glass," he said. "I think I know who killed Mr. Goodson and mistakenly murdered Miss Vengle."

I stared at him a moment, my eyes wide and my mouth open. "Who?"

"I may be wrong, and this would ruin a man's reputation. I'll know more if I find what I am looking for in the courtyard."

He hurried through the French doors and I barreled into the courtyard after him.

He began searching the ground by the fountain. Already the humidity threatened to make the day unbearable, but not as unbearable as my frustration. I thumped him on the head as if he were a melon.

"Reputation be damned, Stephen, tell me right now! Who killed Monsieur Goodson and Mademoiselle Vengle?"

He held up a rounded piece of glass to me. The sun glinted off the ring on his finger, and I suddenly realized where I had seen the design on the ring before. Shock slammed into me, making my heart plummet. "That's Monsieur Goodson's ring, Stephen. He sealed his letters with it. Why do you have his ring?"

"Yes, Stephen, I think it is time for us to tell Mrs. Boucheron all, don't you?" came a voice from behind me.

I whipped my head around to see Mr. Davis step out from behind the camellia bush, a pistol in each hand and a thick rope hanging over one arm.

"Nice of you two to make this so easy for me. I was just about to go to the attic and wait for the night. Drop your pistol into the fountain, Stephen, unless you'd like to see a bullet between Mrs. Boucheron's pretty eyes." Mr. Davis aimed his pistol at me, and the blood rushed from my head. I grabbed for the edge of the fountain behind me. Then I heard a splash— Stephen's pistol was now useless.

"Both of you, move toward the gate. And don't even think about calling for help. We wouldn't want dear Mignon or Andre to come running into a bullet, would we? We are going for a nice walk in the park."

Putting one unsteady foot in front of the other, I nearly stumbled over the courtyard's stones. Stephen set a steadying hand to my back, drawing me close to his side. His chiseled features were frozen in a grim mask.

"You are never going to get away with this," he said harshly.

Mr. Davis laughed. "Oh, I think I will. The White League is going to have a little lynching party. Too bad Mr. Hayes won't hear about the fun until it's all over, but I think he'll feel sufficiently avenged. The gossip of Stephen attacking Mr. Hayes is all over town. Nice of you to wrap this up so neatly for me."

We exited the gate. Ahead were the mossy eaves of the rambling live oaks and the dark shadows of the park. The moment I reached the cover of the trees, I would run. The ghostly moss might be able to save us.

"Stop here and turn slowly around," Mr. Davis ordered, just before we reached the trees.

Six more feet, I thought. So close.

Mr. Davis had exchanged one of his pistols for a long knife during our walk from *La Belle*. "I need a little insurance that you two aren't going to take the notion to run in opposite directions." He tossed the rope to Stephen.

"Put the noose around Mrs. Boucheron's pretty little neck."

Stephen threw the rope on the ground and stared at Mr. Davis.

Mr. Davis's face flushed red. "You just bought her some fancy artwork before she hangs. I only have to decide what to carve up first: her face or—"

"Sheriff Carr will be here shortly." Stephen's voice cut across the ugly threats with deadly calm. "He knows it's you: all of the pieces fit. You called the cigars Flutas rather than Fuentas when Mrs. Boucheron and I came to your office, finding you with the humidor. But Sheriff Carr will undoubtedly find them to be Fuentas that belong to Mr. Maison, and to match the butt Mrs. Boucheron found in the attic.

"Then there's the matter of the White League hanging during the spring. You mentioned it that day, too—perhaps forgetting that you had left the article about the incident with the cigar to set a fire in *La Belle*'s attic. Then there is the matter of your age and your comments about the war. You are the spy known as the Shepherd Boy, who worked with Jean Claude. You met Mr. Goodson for lunch at Antoine's and then killed him on the steps of your office afterward. You must have hired someone to attack Mignon at the carnival. Playing Mignon's hero fit nicely into your plans, except she didn't fall lovingly into your arms. Your plan to poison Ginette, kill Juliet, and marry Mignon didn't quite work out, did it?"

Stephen was right, the pieces fit with horrifying perfection.

"Not a jury in the world will convict a man on such flimsy guesswork."

"No, but the lens of broken spectacles at the scene of a murder is evidence enough. Your glasses broke in the scuffle you had with Miss Vengle."

"That is why you were so surprised to see me," I gasped. "When you came yesterday, you came to comfort Mignon because you thought you had killed *me*. A cigar fell out of your coat when you threw it on the settee. Is Monsieur Maison alive or dead?"

"His ardent republican views caught up with him on his way to Washington. I'm sure his body will be identified as soon as they find it. Just think, I'll have a prominent business, a lovely wife with a prestigious house, and the bloody gold, for I'll not give up until I find it. The clue is in his journal, and I am sure once I live in *La Belle*, I will figure out what he wrote."

"What journal?" I asked.

"Your dearly departed husband's. I know some very intimate things about you."

My skin crawled.

"Sheriff Carr knows," Stephen said again, his voice like shards of glass.

"No, he doesn't." Mr. Davis nodded to the trees. "Mr. Phelps met with an unfortunate accident with my knife before he made it to town, and will likely bleed to death before anyone finds him. So I now have part of the lens and the letter you wrote to Sheriff Carr, and I will get the rest of the lens from your pocket after you swing."

Mr. Davis laughed, enjoying his game. "Since we are

hanging men on circumstantial evidence, let's give you your trial now, Trevelyan. I'm sure it would interest Mrs. Boucheron to know you were acquainted with Mr. Goodson. She would love to know that he told you about the gold, wouldn't she? Why else would you come here under false pretenses? Why else pretend you'd just arrived, when you'd been in New Orleans for a month?"

"Stephen?" My voice cracked.

I knew he wasn't guilty of murder, but deep in my heart I knew he had lied to me about why he was here. I yearned for him to explain, say anything to refute what I feared to be true—but he didn't say a word.

"Stephen," I begged softly.

"The little lady is heartbroken, because she can see that everything you put at my door can be placed at yours, even an acquaintance with Miss Vengle. Poor Mrs. Boucheron, doomed to love traitors. You're as gullible as your husband was, madam. He never even saw my blade coming. I didn't expect that he'd already stolen the gold."

"You bastard."

"Don't sound so disgusted. Your lover here is no different than me. I would have married Mignon to get the house and eventually the gold. All Trevelyan had to do was get into your bed. Perhaps I picked the wrong sister."

A crow flew from the oaks and gave a mournful cry, catching Mr. Davis's attention.

Stephen lunged for Mr. Davis, who glanced back and feinted to the side. Stephen caught hold of his pistol hand, wrenching it. Mr. Davis slashed downward with the knife in his other hand, cutting a deep gash in Stephen's arm and knocking him down.

I cried out in horror at the blood soaking Stephen's sleeve. Mr. Davis jammed the pistol against Stephen's temple. "Put the rope around your neck or he dies now, Mrs. Boucheron."

"Don't do it, Juliet. Run, damn it! Get the hell out of here."

I picked up the rope because I had no doubt Mr. Davis would end Stephen's life the very second I ran. I slid the noose over my head slowly, my heart fluttering wildly. Cold terror seeped into my soul, and I firmly resolved that I would defeat the odds even in the face of this evil.

"Tighten the noose."

"No. Damn it, run!" Stephen cried.

Mr. Davis cocked the pistol.

I reached for the knot and fumbled with it. Then a deep chill struck me, causing me to shiver. The ghost! I couldn't get the noose tightened. Stephen's life hinged on my ability and I was failing. A gray mist seemed to hover over Mr. Davis. "It is stuck. I cannot budge it."

"Tighten it or he dies."

I jerked at the knot, forcing tears to my eyes as I struggled. "I can't, I tell you! You do it," I said, stomping toward him, holding the end of the rope out in both of my hands.

Mr. Davis's eyes widened, but before he could react, I tossed the rope over his head and jerked it hard, pulling him off balance. Stephen came up off the ground, knocking the pistol from Davis's hand and slamming his body against Mr. Davis. As I fell backward, Mr. Davis and Stephen dove for the pistol. The rope around my neck pulled taut. I reached for the noose, shoving my hands inside the loop, trying to keep the knot from sliding tighter.

The sound of a gunshot paralyzed me. I saw Stephen stagger and I screamed. I thought he would fall, but he wrenched around toward me. Mr. Davis lay on the ground, unmoving, his hand on the pistol.

Fingers shaking, Stephen loosened the rope and slid it from my neck. His gaze, filled with concern and love, branded my heart.

"Dear God, woman, if you ever do that again, I'll die."

He pulled me into his arms and I clung to him, thankful to be alive, as Captain Jennison walked toward us with my father's rifle in his hand.

❧ *18* ❧

Over Stephen's shoulder, I saw Captain Jennison check Mr. Davis's pulse, then shake his head, and I realized for certain who had killed Mr. Davis.

"We owe you our lives," I said, easing back from Stephen's embrace. "How did you know to come help?"

"Hearing you shout, 'Reputation be damned, Stephen, tell me right now! Who killed Monsieur Goodson and Mademoiselle Vengle?' caught my attention. When I saw him"—Jennison nodded Mr. Davis's way—"holding a gun on you, I exited the front of the house and cut through the park. Looks like I was almost too late. That's a nasty cut on your arm."

"Nothing compared to what almost happened," Stephen said, as he pressed a handkerchief to his wound. "I owe you my life."

"Count us even," Jennison replied. "You telegraphed

me. Ginette said that she only asked you to post a letter to me."

"Ginette!" I interrupted, pushing to my feet. "She's awake?"

"She woke just minutes after you left the room."

"I must go to her." I took a step, then remembered Stephen's knife injury and turned back. "Your arm," I said, bending to him.

He motioned me away. "I'm fine. Go see Ginette. I'll be right behind you." I hesitated, but he urged me on with a nudge.

"Two minutes," I said. "If you're not there, I'll come looking for you." He nodded and I hurried to the house.

"Juliet, what has happened?" Ginette exclaimed the moment I entered the room. She reclined in bed, propped up by a mound of pillows. Though still deathly pale, there was a glow shining in her eyes and a soft smile on her lips.

"So much blood!" the nurse said, jumping up.

Looking down, I saw that I had as much blood on me as Stephen had on him.

"Stephen's arm is cut," I told the nurse.

"I'll get some bandages ready," she replied. Just before she left the room, she sent Ginette a firm look. "Miss DePerri, please don't try and get up again. You are still weak and you need to give your body time to recuperate from the poison."

The nurse left, and Ginette immediately tried to

rise. "James?" she asked, then fell back against the pillows.

I hurried over to the bed and took her hand in mine. "Captain Jennison is fine. He and Stephen should be here momentarily. The killer was Monsieur Davis, Ginette."

Ginette's eyes widened. "Monsieur Davis! But he's been—"

"Poisoning you and trying to kill me so that he could marry Mignon and have *La Belle*. He thinks Jean Claude hid the gold here." I shuddered at how close the man had come to destroying my family.

"The police are searching for Mr. Phelps," Captain Jennison said from behind me.

Giving Ginette's fingers a loving squeeze, I rose and moved away from the bed.

"I still can't believe you came," Ginette said softly, reaching her hand out to him.

"How could you doubt that I would?" Captain Jennison folded her hand in his and sat on the bed next to her.

Seeing the love for each other shining in their eyes, I eased toward the door.

"Forgive me for the pain, for the lost years," she said.

"There's nothing to forgive, my heart. What I couldn't have abided was losing you. As long as I knew you lived, I could face each day."

I slipped from the room to give them more privacy. Once in the corridor, I heard a commotion from the direction of the bath. Moving that way, I found Stephen under the crisp care of the nurse and her medical supply bag, which apparently contained a bottle of whiskey. The nurse was trying to get Stephen to drink some before she cleaned the cut on his arm and sewed it up. Stephen sat in a chair with his shirtsleeve in tatters, refusing her help and the whiskey.

"I've a good mind to let you bleed until Dr. Goodson gets here," the nurse said, pressing a towel to the wound on his arm.

Stephen grimaced. "Mark would not be so stubborn—"

"Doctor Goodson?" I repeated as a wave of shock hit me.

Stephen jerked his head toward me, and the nurse gasped as if she'd committed a grave mistake. "Dr. Mark Goodson," Stephen said quietly.

"He's related to the investigator I hired?"

"You hired his brother, John Goodson, to find Jean Claude." The shadows underlying his blue eyes had never been so stark.

"And you knew him. What Monsieur Davis said is all true. You have been in New Orleans for a while. You knew Monsieur Goodson. You lied to me."

"He was my best friend, Juliet."

"You knew *everything* before you came here. You knew about Jean Claude, the gold, everything!" I backed away as his betrayal sliced me open. Turning away, I ignored his call to me, glad that the nurse forced him to stay. I wanted to hide in my room, but realized that his scent would still be on my sheets, that the memory of his kiss and his touch would be too strong there. I ran down the stairs and went into my father's office. Sinking down into the desk chair, I gave in to my brokenhearted tears.

The door flung open. "I wasn't finished talking to you," Stephen said. "You will hear the truth at last, and then we can be done with this."

I swung around in the chair, dashing at my tears. "You are supposed to be getting sewn up." The thick bandage on his arm was already bloodstained; the fool was going to bleed to death on my carpet.

"Nothing can stitch up my heart. After everything we shared, I cannot believe you would even question that I love you." He looked at me as if he couldn't decide what manner of beast I had become.

"You cannot believe *me!*" I stood and planted my hands on my father's desk, thankful for the barrier between us. "I cannot believe, after everything we shared, that you *lied* to me. I was nothing more than a pawn in a game to you."

He raked both his hands though his hair and paced across the room. "All I knew about the situation was that John had a lunch appointment at Antoine's. He'd just arrived back in town from New York, and we were to get together that night. The next thing I knew, John was being carried into Mark's office, dying, and nothing Mark or I could do saved him. His last words were all I knew of you. He said, 'Juliet Boucheron . . . danger . . . gold missing . . . must save . . . promise me.' I promised him as he died that I would save you. And I promised myself I'd find the man who'd killed him. That this time, I wouldn't let someone's death occur without doing everything in my power to find out who did it. I made that mistake when Cesca died, and I wasn't going to make it again."

"Why all the secrets? Why didn't you tell me the truth?" New tears filled my eyes.

"Juliet, I didn't know whom to trust. In the beginning, I didn't even know if you were involved in John's death. But once I realized that you weren't, I couldn't afford to tell you. What if you had confided in the wrong person? What if you told Ginette or Mignon why I was here, and they told the wrong person? Then we all would have been in greater jeopardy."

"I could believe that to start with, but what about later, after we . . . we . . . Surely there was some point you could have trusted me?"

"I didn't think it best," he said. "Nothing about us, my love, or my past—none of that was a lie. You have to believe me."

"How, Stephen? How will I ever know? I thought there was only truth between us. I trusted you. I loved you as I had never loved another man before." I turned from him, tears blinding me.

"So everything between us is over because I tried to do what is right? Do you condemn me for trying to protect you, just as you tried to protect your son and family?"

"That is different," I cried, turning back to him. "I am a grown woman, not a child. You cannot have love without trust."

"And if a man makes a mistake, should it cost him everything?"

"I don't know," I said, crying. I couldn't think.

"If you don't know, then there is nothing I can say or do to convince you. I gave you my heart."

"You aren't the man I thought you were."

He stared at me, his eyes bleak. "You aren't the woman I thought you to be." He turned from me and walked away. The hurt that I thought could get no worse doubled.

I ran to the stairs, seeing his broad back disappearing around the landing.

"*Mère!*" Andre cried. "You're hurt!"

Whirling around, I found my son and Mignon standing in the center hall, their mouths agape. "*Non,* I am fine. This is Stephen's blood," I said, then burst into tears and ran up the stairs, knowing I'd never get him out of my soul.

The day waned and the dinner hour passed. I grew more miserable with every chime of the grandfather clock. It wasn't until I heard the knock on my door that I realized what I was waiting for—Stephen to come to me. Pulling the cold cloth from my tear-swollen eyes, I sat up. "Come in."

Mignon opened the door and disappointment pinched my sore heart.

"*Pardon,* Juliet. Sheriff Carr needs to speak with you in the parlor." Mignon spoke as if exasperated. "You look awful."

"I feel awful."

"Then why are you hiding in your room, rather than doing something about the problem? It seems rather simple to me. Either you love Monsieur Trevelyan or you don't."

"It is considerably more complicated than that."

"*Non.* You are making it so, but it truly is not. Because if you love someone, then you forgive them."

"If you love someone, you trust them."

"You didn't," Mignon said, with needle sharp accusation. "You didn't trust me, but I know how dearly you love me." I sat a moment blinking as she hurried from the room. Was I being obtuse about my standoff with Stephen? Surely not. But I went down the stairs to meet Sheriff Carr with less pain in my heart.

"Mrs. Boucheron," Sheriff Carr said, taking the seat I had offered to him, "I know you have had a harrowing day, so I will only take a moment of your time. I've just finished speaking to Mr. Trevelyan and feel as if I have a complete account of the crimes Mr. Davis has committed against you and your family.

"I want to assure you we have already begun a thorough investigation into Mr. Davis's activities here in New Orleans. He kept meticulous records. First he tried to obtain your home by sending Mr. Latour a letter, promising a considerable sum of money should he convince you and your sisters to sell. Also amongst Mr. Davis's papers was a signed will from Mr. Maison, naming Mr. Davis as beneficiary. Mr. Maison was murdered so Mr. Davis could inherit Mr. Maison's money and his law practice. When you refused to sell your home, he decided to attack you directly."

"By murdering me and poisoning Ginette . . . and he hoped to marry Mignon."

"Exactly. He was a menace to society and never should have been let out of prison. But considering his youthfulness, the authorities felt he'd paid for his crime."

"He was in prison?"

"It seems at fourteen he was caught being a double spy during the war. We also found a number of your husband's belongings at Mr. Davis's apartment. I brought these along with me—a journal of sorts your husband kept during the war, and some of his letters. And strangely enough, a letter from you to a Mr. Goodson, who I understand was murdered by Mr. Davis several weeks ago." He pulled the items from a bag he had next to his chair.

I nodded as I stared at the letter, shivering. A murderer had prowled through my house as my family and I slept. He'd worn a mask of civility and had terrorized my family and nearly succeeded in murdering us.

Sheriff Carr continued to speak. "The rest we will send to you after our investigation is complete. For now, it seems the matter of the gold is still a mystery." He held out the journal and the letters to me. My fingers shook as I took them, focusing my attention on the faded blue book. So many years had passed since I last saw Jean Claude; it was almost numbing to be handed back a part of him. I set the letters on the floor, but held the journal.

"Are you sure you have no idea where your husband may have hidden the gold?" Sheriff Carr asked.

"*Non.* I have given the matter considerable thought, and I honestly do not know."

He cleared his throat. "Well, were it me and my family, I would keep the matter secret in order to protect them. We will do our best to keep Mr. Davis's motives quiet. Gold is as deadly as yellow fever. If other people took the notion that you had gold hidden in your home, there is no telling what danger you would have."

He excused himself and I sat there holding the journal unopened in my hands. I wasn't ready to read Jean Claude's thoughts. Not while so much of my heart was in turmoil. But I knew one thing: I needed to forge a way past my own hurt, or my future would be no different than my past.

"*Mère*," Andre said softly from the doorway.

"What is it?"

"There is word about Mr. Phelps. The doctor thinks that he will recover."

"*Bon*. I do not know if I could bear the death of another on my hands."

"Monsieur Trevelyan said the same thing when I spoke to him earlier. He's leaving. I saw him packing his things."

"He's leaving?" I didn't think the pain inside of me could twist any sharper. It did.

"I . . . well . . . is it really any different, *Mère*? What Monsieur Trevelyan did when trying to protect us, and what you did in trying to protect me?"

"No," I said, clenching the journal in my hands. "It isn't."

"Then are you going to forgive him? Please, so many things are better since he came. I . . . I . . . don't want him to leave."

It would seem that Andre's heart was just as involved with Stephen as mine. My son's observation hit me hard. Stephen *had* changed us all. And I wasn't about to let him disappear, taking our hearts with him.

"I need to speak to Monsieur Trevelyan," I said softly. I stood and held out the journal to Andre. "This was your father's. Sheriff Carr has just brought it to us. Would you like to read it first?"

Amazed wonder filled Andre's eyes. "It belonged to my father?"

"*Oui.* There are also some letters from him. I hope you will find among the pages the heart he never got the opportunity to share with you. After you read the journal, then I will. Maybe someday we will find the gold and give him his honor back."

"How, *Mère?* How can we do that?"

I hugged him tight. "To restore Jean Claude's honor, if we find the gold, we will put it into the bank and give money to people who need help surviving the aftermath of the war, just as your father intended."

Andre looked at the journal with tears in his eyes, then clutched it close to his heart.

I went up the stairs to Stephen's room and rapped sharply on the door. "Monsieur Trevelyan, might I have a word with you?"

Mr. Fitz, Mr. Gallier, and Mrs. Gallier all peeked out from their rooms.

"Are you all right, Mrs. Boucheron?" Mr. Fitz asked, his dark eyes shadowed with pain. "Mr. Trevelyan told us everything."

"Utterly horrendous. In all my life, I have never heard of such blatant, wicked, sinful goings on," Mr. Gallier said. "Why, when I was in London last, they had a—"

"Oh, for heavens sakes, Edmund, be quiet. Can you not see the dear child is wrung out? She doesn't need to hear your drivel right now. You have never been to London in your life, and it is about time you stopped calling other kettles black, when your pot is so tarnished that all the saints and their brothers wouldn't be able to put a shine to you. Now, you had best get back into bed and rest up, because tomorrow we are going to town to buy that dress I want. I am wearing it to Charlotte's funeral, and that is the end of it."

Mr. Fitz and Mr. Gallier looked at Mrs. Gallier in shock. Then Mr. Fitz gave Mrs. Gallier a genuine smile. "If Edmund finds himself overwrought with his bowel infirmity again, Lenora, I would consider it an honor to take you. Perhaps we will lunch at Antoine's in honor of Charlotte, as well?"

"Thank you, Horatio. Charlotte would love such a memorial to her."

"This . . . this . . . this is preposterous," Mr. Gallier bristled.

"Edmund, go take another Dover's powder and go back to bed. I will also need another new dress to attend the upcoming women's suffrage meeting." She winked at me. "Good night, Mrs. Boucheron."

Stephen had yet to answer his door. I knocked again. Nothing. My fingers trembled as I opened the door to see that his room was empty.

"Stephen," I whispered.

Pulling the door closed behind me, I entered and lit the small lamp on the dresser. He couldn't have left me. Please, God, please. Slowly, as if a mist was clearing from my eyes, I saw a stack of papers on his bed.

Hurrying over, I picked them up, my heart squeezing painfully as I read the words on the top page. *Saving Juliet.* By Stephen Trevelyan.

I could not stop myself from reading the play any more than I could have stopped myself from breathing. With each witty remark, with each endearment, my heart swelled. Then little pieces became more and more familiar to me.

Would that I could count every nuance that makes it so . . . How can I not love you? . . . I can love you because your wit hones mine, your smile softens mine, and your laughter restores mine . . . I have never been loved so deeply nor so well . . .

And the last line of the play.

Would that I always be a fool for you.

I'd thought I'd shed every tear possible. I hadn't. I didn't care how far I would have to travel or how long; I would find Stephen.

As I sat there, I heard the soft notes of music floating up to me. I jumped off the bed and fumbled with the French doors, my fingers so jittery that it took me twice as long to unlock them. I went to the railing and stood in the moonlight, searching for Stephen and his music of the night.

The courtyard was empty and the music had stopped. Had my heart imagined it? "Stephen," I called, anguished for him.

" 'Half light, half shade, She stood, a sight to make an old man young.' "

I turned, and Stephen stepped out from beneath the

gallery's shadows to stand next to me, looking deliciously dark and dangerous in the moonlight. My pulse raced with anticipation.

"I thought you'd gone," I said.

"I tried, but an odd thing happened."

I swallowed the lump in my throat, almost afraid to ask. "What?"

"You're the woman I want and I can't walk away. If that makes me a fool—"

I pressed my fingers to his lips. "That makes me a fool for you."

He closed his eyes and pressed a kiss to my fingers. "I am sorry I hurt you. Had I known you then as I know you now, I would have taken you into my confidences as well as my heart."

"I believe you. I love you."

"Then there is one secret left that I need to tell you," he said.

I was not sure that I wanted to hear another secret. "What?"

"Actually, it's two secrets. I telegraphed my brother about leasing the land and building a Trevelyan Trading Company port here in New Orleans. He telegraphed me back that he is coming to investigate my excellent idea. I also told him about you, that I'd found the woman for me."

"You are very sure of yourself." I wrapped my arms around his neck, pressing my breasts to the solid warmth of his chest.

"Marry me, Juliet."

I had no doubts. I was lost in his dark desire forever. "Yes. Kiss me."

He brought his lips to mine and whispered, "My dear, I thought you would never ask."

He kissed me then, sliding his fingers into my hair and loosening the pins, letting my curls fall free. I felt his hunger, his heart, his soul reaching for mine in that kiss, and I gave myself up to the magic of his passion. Pressing tightly to him, I breathed in the scent of sandalwood and spice.

"Love me, Stephen," I whispered.

"As long as God gives life to our souls."

"I mean right this minute." I slid my hands down to his hips and pulled him closer.

He laughed. "My impatient Juliet." Sweeping me into his arms, he carried me inside the house. "Tonight the pleasure is going to last till dawn."

"Dawn? But that's hours! No man could—"

"Just wait," he said, silencing me with a kiss. Then he proceeded to fulfill his promise.

❧ Epilogue ❧

The full moon hung low in the sky, and a starlit path to heaven dotted the blue black night. Jasmine and sweet honeysuckle scented the evening breeze, along with the aroma of lit torches. Shadows darkened the courtyard, but the hearts of those who had gathered there were filled with light and love.

I turned to look at my silver and lace dress in the mirror, but instead of wedding finery, I saw a man more mist than substance. Dressed in worn confederate gray, he stood between the mirror and me, yet I could still see myself. He was familiar and I was unafraid. It was Jean Claude's ghost.

A heavy chill still hit me, but I smiled at him, realizing he had been helping us find his murderer all along, possibly even protecting us. Some miracle had put out the fire in the attic, I was certain. I heard a flutter and looked to my left.

The pages of his journal lying on my bed flew open

as if by magic, and the man of mists placed his hand over his heart, gestured good-bye, and disappeared. Tears stung my eyes, but at last I felt peace about the past.

Standing near the French doors, where I could hear the laughter from below, I read the passage from Jean Claude's diary again.

"Finally, my youthful wife, who has brought so much to me when I thought I'd have no joy to fill these years, I must ask you to forgive me. For if you are reading these words, which I pen in a lonely camp amidst a war that has become a folly of death and destruction, then I have failed my mission. My attempt to get the supplies needed for our dying cause must have ended in dishonor. Forgive me. For you must understand, I see ahead and the fields are barren. The South has murdered her sons, her husbands, and fathers, and there are none to plow the field and feed the hungry. I thought by this deed, that I might save us all. So I have commended my heart and the future of my son, Andre, whom I hold ever close to my heart, into St. Catherine's hands and lay all that has been dearly bought at her feet."

I shut the journal. Soon Stephen would be waiting for me in the courtyard below, and I would go to him.

"I must say, this is the most unusual wedding I have

ever attended," said Ann Trevelyan, Stephen's sister-in-law, as she slipped into the room. "It is absolutely perfect for you and Stephen. I am so happy for you, and now that I have met you, I am happy for him." She smiled, transforming her face to one of quiet beauty as she adjusted the deep red roses of my bouquet. "Are you nervous?"

"*Non*, I am anxious to be with Stephen. He is my heart, and I am blessed that he comes with such a large and warm family."

"I daresay the nine of us are a bit much to take all at one time."

I smiled. "You are all *très* wonderful."

"We are an overly lively and chaotic group, but it is nice of you not to say it."

"A wonderful lively, then," I said.

Two weeks ago, Stephen's family had arrived from San Francisco and filled *La Belle* to overflowing. In that short time, I felt surrounded by a bounty of love and laughter. Ann's practical nature seemed to keep everyone sane. No matter what havoc or disaster arose, her no-nonsense manner ruled, and Stephen's brother Benedict helped keep Justin and Robert, his sons, from getting too out of line with their exuberance. Already, Andre, Justin, and Robert had started building a tree house, the planning of which had required the expert advice of all of the men. Stephen and Benedict seemed to be enjoying the adventure just as much as the children.

The ethereal sounds of Ginette playing the harp drifted up from the courtyard. This time no sadness lay in the beautiful melody, and her voice rang with strength and happiness. In the morning, when the dew was fresh upon the earth, renewing all of life, she would marry the captain of her heart. But tonight, the moonlight was mine.

"It's time," Ann said.

Taking the bouquet she held out, I stepped onto the gallery and walked to the railing as planned. Stephen stood by St. Catherine's fountain, looking toward me, and I thought again how beautiful he was in the moonlight and the shadows. My cue to come to him was to be a rose he would hold it out for me. I expected for him to lift the bloom immediately; he didn't. Instead, he nodded his head to the side.

Turning to look, I saw Andre with his violin. He stood in the moonlight and played a softly, exquisitely beautiful song. Mignon stood by him, in silent support. My heart overflowed with love for both of them.

When Andre finished, Stephen held up the rose. Then Papa John helped me down the steps, where Mama Louisa stood with tears streaming down her face. "God's blessing," she said simply.

I nodded as Ginette and Mignon joined me.

"Juliet, you are breathtaking," Ginette said.

"Just until the dawn. Then it will be you who will outshine the sun."

My sisters' dresses flowed about them like beautiful

pastel ghosts in the moonlight as they followed me. Waiting in the courtyard was a sea of people I was just beginning to take into my heart. Stephen's sister, Katherine Simons, her husband, Anthony, and their daughter, baby Titania, Benedict, Justin, Robert, baby Elizabeth Ann, and Stephen's mother, Rosalind Trevelyan.

I walked to Stephen in the moonlight as he stood at the fountain. Benedict stood at his side, and next to him was Captain Jennison, the man to whom Stephen and I owed our lives. I gave Ginette my bouquet, placing my hand over Stephen's as he held the single rose out to me.

"I love you," he said, softly.

"And I love you." With our hands joined over the rose, we knelt at St. Catherine's feet to be married.

The minister began the service, and as I knelt before the statue, I remembered the words from Jean Claude's journal—that he'd laid all that had been dearly bought at St. Catherine's feet. And then I knew, with certainty, what he'd meant.

"Stephen, I know where the gold is," I whispered, then primly looked back at the minister, who was speaking about the duties of husband and wife.

"Where?" he whispered back.

"We are kneeling on it. The gold is at St. Catherine's feet."

"Good lord!" he exclaimed, causing a stir of movement among everyone. I laughed.

Stephen's brother bent down next to him. "Is there a problem, Stephen?"

Merriment danced in Stephen's eyes as he shook his head, then looked at the priest, who was frowning at us both. "Have you gotten to the kissing part yet?"

"No," the priest admonished.

Undaunted, Stephen smiled. "Then there will be two of them, for I cannot wait." He leaned over and kissed me, making my heart sing.

When the ceremony ended and Stephen swept me into his arms, I realized a new era was beginning. *La Belle du Temps*, the house of my heart, would now become the house of Stephen's and my hearts. Our fondest memories would live within her, times of laughter and joy as our children grew. She would hold our lives with gentle arms, and the strength and understanding of our ancestors would wrap around us as we walked from the shadows of the past to a bright new future.

Pocket Books
proudly presents
the next novel from

Jennifer St. Giles

Coming soon in paperback
from Pocket Books

Turn the page for a preview
of her next novel. . . .

CHAPTER ONE

The mist filling the Tennessee mountain pass was either fate's middle finger telling Erin Morgan she was screwed, or a beckoning finger from the grave letting her know that sooner or later she was a dead woman. Sooner, if Dr. Cinatas traced her escape from Manhattan into no man's land, realizing she'd discovered his evil secret.

She never dreamed—make that nightmared—that Dr. Cinatas was a blood-sucking murderer. She'd worked for the devil for three years and hadn't had a clue.

A sudden cold sweat made her shiver. How many people had she unknowingly helped kill during that time? From what she'd seen, four people had horrifyingly been killed to bring one back from the edge of death. And she helped treat dozens and dozens. Multiply that by four, and the death toll was . . .

Oh, God. She gripped the stirring wheel tighter.

Don't think about it!

But she couldn't stop.

She could still smell the antiseptic and the scent of the blood lab at the Manhattan clinic. She could still see the bodies: of a man, a woman, and two teenaged girls. Their dark hair, small stature, olive skin, and colorful clothes had shouted "over the border" to her.

Even before she'd walked across the off-limits, icy lab, she'd known they were dead. Her panicked breaths had frosted in the air and her gut had wrenched with dread as she'd touched them, checking for signs of life—first the young girls, then the middle-aged couple. They'd been strapped to stretchers and drained of their blood. The bags still hung on the hooks above them, tagged for the future recipient: the king of Kassim, Ashodan ben Shashur. Shashur, a close friend of the President's, would arrive tomorrow, and over the July Fourth holiday, Erin would administer the first round of transfusions in his treatment.

Kassim was the smallest but most oil-rich country in the Middle East. Shashur's security team, a force equal to the Secret Service, had arrived early this morning. They'd required the skeleton staff at the clinic—her, an aide, and a lab tech—to take a scary oath of secrecy. "Cross my heart and hope to die" didn't even scratch the surface of what they'd said would happen to her if she told anyone about the king. If word of his cancer reached the wrong ears, it would start a war nobody wanted.

But why *murder* for the blood? Surely there were plenty of donors willing to support Dr. Cinatas' investigative treatment for cancer. She herself gave blood for the cause on a regular basis.

She'd been hired by Dr. Cinatas to care for his "special patients," and all of the clients she'd transfused had been ultra rich. Now she wondered if the diseased rich were feeding off the poor.

How many other illegals had been lured to their death?

Don't think about it.

She shut her eyes, her body rigid as she barreled into the fog. She wished she could press the gas to the floor and meet her death at the bottom of a rocky ravine. It was no less than she deserved, but she'd see Dr. Cinatas in hell first.

Thwack. Something hard slammed into her windshield and she ripped her eyes open, swerving on the road. Good Lord! What had she hit? A person?

Pulse hammering with fear, she saw a rock wall dead ahead and slammed on the brakes. The seat belt cut into her neck and her pounding chest. Her chin smacked into the steering wheel, ramming her teeth into her tongue. Pain slashed through her, dimming her vision and cutting off her breath.

The center of her windshield morphed into a spider web of cracked glass, through which she saw a big, black thing on her hood. A bear?

Not a person. She sucked in relieved air. Fog whirled so thickly, she couldn't tell if the thing was moving or if it even breathed.

She prayed she hadn't seriously harmed the animal. She didn't have a weapon to protect herself so she beeped the horn several times, with no result.

Leaning closer to the glass, she hunched over the steering wheel; maybe she could drive to the nearest town with the animal on the hood and get help. Swiping her hand over the uncracked portion of the glass, she tried to see through the quickly fogging windshield.

The black form rose up and snarled at her. She screamed, as a pair of blood-red eyes with yellow centers stared at her from a jet-black face that seemed human, but for the color. Black hands and red, dagger-sharp nails splayed menacingly against the glass. She rammed back in her seat, pressing the door lock button.

"What the hell?"

The creature smiled, its lips snarling back to reveal an even row of teeth shaped like ice picks. Evil, as palpable and throbbing as her pulse, hit her, and another scream rose up deep inside her.

She couldn't look away. She couldn't move. It was as if icy death had frozen everything but her mind. The creature's eyes flamed like an ocean of fire but its gaze centered a cold burn inside her, making her feel as if she'd never be warm again.

Thunk. Something flattened the creature against the windshield. A silver claw, wrapped over the creature's face, snapping its head to the side.

Suddenly she could move, as if released from a spell. Every fiber of her being screamed at her to get the hell out of there, even as she watched a silver wolf combat the black creature on the hood of her car. Blood splatters on the windshield pumped adrenaline through her, and she stomped the gas. The creature and the wolf slammed against the glass so hard, Erin thought they would break through into the car.

The wolf had the black creature by the throat and turned to her. His gaze, a bright, clear blue like the hottest part of a flame, met hers, burning itself into her mind. Warmth and an other-worldly comfort seeped deep inside her, as if a greater spirit resided within the animal. She almost reached out to touch what she knew just couldn't be real.

The black creature reared up and sank its teeth into the wolf's chest. The wolf shuddered and howled, its scream chilling her soul. Unbearable agony echoed even as the wolf tore the creature from him.

Looking her way again, the wolf opened its fanged mouth. "LEAVE NOW!"

Erin heard the deep words as clearly as if a man had shouted them in her ear. She reversed, pressed the gas pedal to the floor and went flying backward, bouncing the tangle of black and silver from her car hood. She didn't want to leave the wolf since it appeared to be helping her, and it was badly wounded—she'd heard its pain.

How could she run like a coward?

Yet how could she fight the black creature? She didn't have a gun, and she had no doubt the evil creature would rip her apart before her pepper spray could render any help.

It's not real. It's not real. Yet her hands and body shook so violently, she had to fight to drive. She careened wildly across the road, barely able to see through the fog and the cracked windshield.

Suddenly an oncoming semi blared its horn. Blinded by the truck's lights, she veered to the right, skidded on the loose shale on the side of the road, and went flying into a black void.

Erin awoke from a drugging sleep; every muscle of her body ached and her head pounded like a sledgehammer.

Awareness came slowly for a moment, then roared into her mind. Her eyes sprang open, surprised to see daylight streaming in through her cracked windshield, a grassy field, a rushing creek . . . and a naked man on the hood of her car.

She promptly shut her eyes. She'd not only knocked herself out in the crash last night, but her nightmare had morphed into pure fantasy. She'd gone from "silver werewolf meets an obsidian Freddy" to a dark haired Adonis.

"Mmmnn." The groan, deeply male and filled with pain, did not come from her.

Erin's eyes shot open again. Hell. The man was still

there, still naked, still groaning, and now moving restlessly.

The man groaned again.

Good Lord! Had she hit something last night? Had
she hit *him*? Even if she were delusional now, she
couldn't just sit there. Snapping her seat belt loose, she
reached for the door handle. As best as she could tell,
she'd landed in some sort of pasture with several cows
in the distance.

Sliding out of the car, she paused, startled to see
dried blood on the front of her nurse's whites.
Tentatively, she touched her face, feeling dried blood
on her left cheek and a crusted gash on her left temple.

Behind her, ten feet up an embankment and past
barbed-wire fencing, sat the road she'd been on last
night. She had a vague recollection of bouncing over
rough terrain and the engine stalling, before she shut
her eyes against the pounding pain in her head. She'd
thought that she'd only rest a moment, not hours. As
she stood up now, she felt a wave of dizziness and had
to hold on to the car door.

The man groaned yet again, prompting her to move
cautiously to the hood of her Tahoe, her gaze scanning
his body for trauma. She saw no apparent injuries. No
blood. No bruising. No limbs twisted at an unnatural
angle. He appeared almost too perfect.

Was he real or not? Either way, it wasn't good. If he
wasn't real, then her mind had gone off the deep end.
If he was real, then she'd hit him with her car last

night—which meant he'd been walking naked in the dark, something only a person in trouble or mentally ill would do.

He lay on his stomach, one arm cradling his head, the other at his side. Longish coal black hair, with a shocking streak of silver at the crown, moved in the breeze.

She'd give her imagination a lot of credit, but was it really this good? She needed a Starbucks IV, stat.

Broad shouldered and perfectly sculpted, his body tapered to trim hips, muscular thighs, and long legs that hung off the edge of her car. The only oddity was the paleness of his skin. He didn't look as if he'd ever been out in the sun, which meant he had to be feeling the UV rays bombarding his backside.

She touched his shoulder and felt burning hot skin. She wasn't imagining this, and the man was ill. Fevered. Concern griped her hard. "Mister. Can you hear me?"

He groaned, but didn't answer. Moving closer, Erin slid her hands to his head, feeling the silk of his hair, searching his scalp for injury. Finding none, she moved her palm to assess his burning brow again. She'd never felt anyone so hot. "Hey, can you hear me? You're ill."

Still no response. Hiking up her dress, she climbed onto the hood, and grasped his shoulder and his hip to roll him over, trying not to think about what she'd see next. When she pulled on him, he reared up, groaning sharply with pain and knocking her backward. She tumbled to the ground, smacking her knee on the bumper.

Rolling to her feet, she stood and froze, looking at impressive male anatomy that was starkly enhanced by black hair, hard muscled thighs, and washboard abs. He'd crossed his thick arms over a chest that rivaled Atlas for broadness and strength. She lifted her gaze higher and poised herself to run.

He sat with his heels propped on her bumper and knees bent, with his legs spread—not extra wide, but he sure wasn't trying to hide anything. Seeming thoroughly comfortable with his nakedness, he stared at her with bloodshot eyes the color of iridescent blue topaz. They were familiar, but she couldn't say from where. Sweat beaded his flushed face, and she now noticed he held his left arm protectively against his chest. Dark stubble covered his chin, framing lips that had to have been fashioned by Eros—or Satan. It was the most erotically seductive mouth she'd ever seen, and the only soft spot amid his warriorlike features— chiseled nose, sharp cheeks, and brooding brow. His dark hair flowed past his shoulders, layered back from his face like the wings of a predator. He looked like a deadly warrior.

If she had hit him with her car, he hadn't suffered injury. She shook her head. No. If she'd hit him, there would be evidence of it on him and on her car, besides the windshield. This just wasn't real. This was a dream.

Erin grinned. "Hell-lo, Attila the Hunk." Except for

the provocative silver streak in his hair, the man could double for the star actor of a TV miniseries she and her college roommates had been glued to. *Sex and the City* just couldn't hold a candle to the Roman bath scene in Attila, or any of his kissing scenes, for that matter.

"You can see me?" the man asked in a deep voice.
"You are mistaken. Attila the Hun died well over a millennia ago, and I bear no resemblance to that Scourge of God. I am Jared."

Last night never happened. Yesterday's hell didn't exist. In just a moment, she would wake to her alarm clock in her Manhattan apartment after the wildest dream-nightmare of her life. All she had to do was open her eyes, flip on her Victorian feather lamp, and throw back her leopard print spread. Better yet, why not tuck her new hood ornament into bed with her?

"Jared, what?" she asked, hoping the man would speak in a Scottish accent, so completing her fantasy.

He stared at her another moment, then looked around him.

"If you won't tell me who you are, can you at least tell me how in the hell you ended up on my car? And where are your clothes?"

He flexed the fingers of his left hand, as if to see how it worked. When he moved his left arm, he groaned and pulled it tighter against himself.

"You're hurt and you have a fever," she said, reaching her hand out to touch him lightly on his arm.

"I'm damned," he said harshly. His eyes were so stark, they burned.

"Let me see your wound. I'm a nurse—I can help."

"Nothing can cure a Tsara infection." Still, he unfolded his arm and shifted it to the side.

Erin sucked in a sharp breath at the deep burn slashing his chest just above his left breast. Charred and angry, his wound oozed. It looked as if someone had branded him.

"How in God's name did that happen?"

"You say much, to know so little." He didn't seemed frightened. He slid off the hood, tentatively gaining his balance.

Erin stepped back, shocked. He towered over her five-foot-nine height. Without glancing at her, he moved closer to the creek, staring up at the sky.

"ARAGON!" he screamed. "WHY?"

His voice reverberated like thunder and the marrow of her bones shook at the agony in his voice. Maybe *she* wasn't the one having a hallucination. Who was Aragon?

"Mister, uh, Jared. I think we need to get you some help."

"There is no help." His head bowed as if shamed.

She almost said "bullshit" to his doomed nonsense, but instinct told her she wouldn't be able to convince him he wasn't damned. Rather than get lost in a quagmire of verbal hopelessness, she grabbed her professional wits back into line.

"Ridiculous. There is help. First, you're going to sit in the car before you fall down. I hate to tell you, but if you faint, you'll lie where you fall, since I can't move you alone. And the cows will graze on whatever is exposed— which is everything, in case you haven't noticed."

He didn't move or react to her warning. He just stood there, staring up at the sky, pain etched deeply on his face.

Grumbling, she marched to him and slid her hand over his right wrist, feeling again the burning heat of his skin. She pressed her fingers over his radial pulse, feeling the pace of his racing heart. She needed to get his fever down and dress his wound.

He startled at her touch, looking at her. The pain in his eyes appeared to ease a little.

"Please," she said softly, "let me help you." She put her other hand on his arm.

His gaze moved to her hand, as if her touch bewildered him. "This weakness of the flesh, this pain, is unknown to me. Why does it ease with your touch?"

"Nurses always make things better," she said, puzzling over his odd phrasing. He sounded as if he wasn't quite in tune with the world.

"Come with me." She tugged on his wrist, and after a moment, he followed her to the car. Opening the back door, she patted the seat. "Sit here and I'll get my first aid kit." *And something to cover him with.*

Going to the rear door, she retrieved the first aid kit and a towel from her gym bag. Then she thought of his fever and the creek, and drew out her water bottle and her cotton sports bra.

Hawkeye and Hotlips weren't the only ones who could improvise.

She didn't see Jared in the seat when she glanced up, and her pulse and stomach did an odd flip at the thought that he'd disappeared—ridiculous! Hurrying around the car, she found Jared lying on his back in the seat, which would make it difficult to tend to his wound.

She laid the yellow towel over his groin, gathered water from the creek, and joined him in the backseat, kneeling on the floor at his side. Dousing her sports bra in the cold creek water, she placed the cloth on his forehead.

"Jared?"

He opened his eyes.

"I'm going to put some medicine on your burn, then bathe you off."

"There is no reason to care for me. The path to the Fallen cannot be changed. I'd just as soon face it now, than to wait for the worst to come."

"I must," she said, refusing to respond to his delirious words of doom.

He gazed into her eyes as if looking for her soul.

"I see you must," he said. "This ill is not of your doing, but do as you will for now."

For the first time in years, Erin's hands trembled as she worked.

Jared reached down to the yellow towel across his groin, and frowned. She had covered him for some reason, though he'd not expressed the desire to be. He'd forgotten much of what he'd been told about the flesh and being mortal. He'd known little but war as he'd searched for and guarded the lost Chosen.

This mortal body was so different than his spirit form, and the pain of his flesh, though great, didn't compare to the torment in his soul. The Tsara's poison ate at him, screaming through his spirit like a raging storm. His body burned as the good within him fought against its inevitable death.

The woman shook as she touched him; bravely doing what her heart knew was right, even though she didn't understand how the Tsara poison affected her, made her weak. Something about her drew him in a way he didn't understand. He'd always protected and defended the Chosen, but had never given any thought to their spirits—only their purpose for Shaddai. But he could read her soul's beauty in her golden eyes, see her strength and her vulnerability.

Her touch soothed him, easing the pain inside him, and he closed his eyes. She was safe for the moment, but he would have to leave—before he killed her.

She was a Chosen one, and the Fallen fed upon the blood of the Chosen.

He would soon walk with the Fallen.

A *love* like you've never known
is closer than you think...

Historical Romances
from Pocket Books

Can three sisters tame three wild Highlanders? Find out
in three sensual stories from bestselling author
Jen Holling

My Wicked Highlander
Her magic is no match for a rugged Scotsman's desire....

My Devilish Scotsman
She doesn't know the strength of her own powers...
or the depth of his desires.

My Shadow Warrior
She desperately needs his help....
He desperately needs her love.

◦◦◦◦◦

One Night with a Prince
The Royal Brotherhood Series
Sabrina Jeffries
One night of passion....One night of intrigue....
One night with a prince.

Highlander in Love
Julia London
The only thing that separates love and hate...is desire.

12829